I0614893

RACKHAM

By
George Almond

Copyright © G.Almond 2025. All rights reserved.

The rights of G.Almond to be identified as the author of this work have been asserted by him in accordance with the Copyright, Designs and Patents Act of 1988.

All rights reserved; no part of this publication may be reproduced, stored in a retrieval system, or transmitted in any form or by any means, electronic, mechanical, photocopying, recording or otherwise without the prior written consent of the publisher or a licence permitting copying in the UK issued by the Copyright Licensing Agency Ltd. www.cla.co.uk

ISBN 978-1-78792-102-3

Cover Design. By Starfishcreative.co.uk

Book design, layout and production management by Into Print
www.intoprint.net
01604 832149

Principal Characters

FBI	MISS HARUMI TANAKA	Japanese FBI Agent. DNA expert
POLICE	FBI Director JENKINS	Commander of operations
ROYAL NAVY	SUTTON BRADLEY	FBI Undercover agent
	Captain BARNET- RN	Commander of RN Vessel
	Police Officers Providenciales	Various

RACKHAM	JOHN RACKHAM. (JR)	Family Head and overall Capitano
AND	ANN RACKHAM.	His wife / Principal planner
HIS CREW	SWANN RACKHAM	Their 19 year old daughter
	KLUDO	Their savvy dog
	MARY	Live-in lover to the Rackhams
	HELMS	Their jet and helicopter pilot - Australian
	CHAD	Wizard hacker and cyber expert - Ukrainian

LOCALS	JAVEL.	Jamaican Boat Driver/ Rasta
	CEEJAY	Trinidadian heavy
	JASMIN	Ceejay's girl who looks like Sarahanna
	LE SAGE	Haitian. who guards the money
	HAITIAN VOODOO WOMAN	Mother of Le Sage. Works at Conch Bar
	OLD MAN	Former Slave - A ghost?
	BOXMAN	Digger Driver
	ABLE	Bodyguard to Swann
	NANA	Seamstress
	TROY	Barman at the Resort hotel

GIG	SARAHANNA	Superstar Rapper singer
	WALTER SHULZ	Concert Manager
	RON	Sarahanna's Manager

Against Dr Felix Roblado and his Columbian henchmen on superyacht *Amazon Lady.*

RACKHAM – Chapter Headings

Chapter	Titles / Action	Pages

READERS – BEWARE
Our gang's DNA is dangerous!
Some of what you read is true and
is told by different members of our crew.
So bear that in mind as you begin each chapter.
Welcome aboard our latest venture in the Caribbean!

1

Thirteen Ears – Agent Tanaka of the FBI

THE BIDDING HAD been fast and lively until the pace faltered. In the auction-eer's hand the gavel hovered in vain hoping for improved offers but gaining no ground, the sale was made.

On her chair at the rear of the auction hall Miss Harumi Tanaka heard a sharp crack as the gavel fell. She opened the auction catalog to check that Lot #322 was next on the list. She had tracked it down on the Internet and had flown up that morning from Miami. If the price was right, she'd be taking it back home.

A crowd of several hundred dealers and collectors had also turned up at the Convention Centre in New Jersey. They had come for the Spring Sale of Miscellaneous Collectibles, a rather tame description for the exotic and unusual item now being displayed by the auction porter. Miss Tanaka noticed the auctioneer wince distastefully as he glanced at Lot 322. She saw how he took a sip of water before, with a burst of professional enthu-siasm, he resumed the auction.

'Ladies and gentlemen. Those of delicate disposition should be warned. You may choose to look elsewhere, as we offer for auction Lot 322, described in our catalog as a totally unique collection of thirteen human ears.'

Squawks of distaste came from sensitive individuals when the porter raised a leather necklace from which hung, like desiccated figs, a bunch of human ears.

The auctioneer pressed on. 'The vendor believes this is the very neck-lace worn by the famous pirate Calico Jack Rackham at his execution on Gallows Point, Jamaica. Reputedly the thirteenth ear belongs to Rackham himself. The hangman sliced it off and attached it to the necklace after taking down the corpse. We believe this was how Rackham kept tally of his victims.'

Another murmur of revulsion slithered through the crowd. On her chair

Miss Tanaka recrossed her shapely legs and raised her eyebrows as the auctioneer concluded his preamble.

'We cannot be totally confident of the provenance, however the necklace has been carbon-dated to be about three hundred years old around 1720, the year of Rackham's trial and execution. So, let's hear some offers? A singular item for an imaginative collector? I'll start the bidding at one thousand three hundred dollars.'

A hand shot up, but it was not Miss Tanaka's. She had inherited Japanese prudence from her mother and would not be the first to start the bidding. She had hoped demand would be minimal for this grisly record of historical violence but she noted that a public interest did exist with bids rising as the auctioneer pressured the pace. Only at five thousand dollars did the offers die away, and still Miss Tanaka was no bidder. The price for thirteen gnarled ear lobes had long surpassed her budget.

'Five thousand. Any advance on five? Online at five thousand and I'm selling these ears. In the hall now? Final offers? Sold to the web bidder!'

When the gavel fell, Miss Tanaka's shrug was imperceptible. She had a fallback plan so she waited until the porter had removed the item to the warehouse. Having gone to an Internet bidder, Lot 322 would not be leaving the premises immediately. Miss Tanaka pushed the auction catalogue deep into her shoulder bag, tucking it beside her Glock .23 pistol. Rising discreetly from her seat, she left unnoticed by the crowd. Young Asian women in laser cut business suits were a regular sight in many of the world's cities.

In the office adjoining the entrance lobby the auction clerks were busy. Miss Tanaka paused until a staffer looked up from her screen. 'If you wanna pay for your purchase, you need to…'

'No, ma'am. I made no purchase.' Miss Tanaka smiled.

'So how can I help?' The young woman asked brusquely.

'I want to know about Lot 322, the pirate necklace?'

The clerk straightened. 'I'm sorry, ma'am, but we don't release details of web bidders. Did you want to make a higher offer?'

'No, no.' Miss Tanaka's oriental features held steady. A persuasive smile was the best way to proceed with reluctant folk. 'I need to examine the lot briefly. The buyer isn't a problem.'

The auction continued in the background while the clerk considered the request. 'Listen, I can't figure why you need to look at body parts. We don't have time for inspections right now.'

'I appreciate that. But the item may provide clues to a case we're pursuing.' Miss Tanaka dropped her smile and produced her official ID card with its distinctive insignia of the Federal Bureau of Investigation.

The clerk stared for a moment. 'Oh! FBI? Well, now, that does make a difference.'

'Makes it easy or difficult. I just need a quick look,' Miss Tanaka repeated. 'Call my Director Mr. Jenkins if you prefer. You choose.'

The clerk lifted her fingers from her keyboard as she thought about the request. The young woman with FBI authorisation looked slick in her black suit and she had a beguiling smile. The clerk leaned toward her screen. 'The buyer for Lot 322 is John Barnet from Devon in the United Kingdom. I have his details.'

'Those won't be necessary,' Miss Tanaka's teeth showed perfect dentistry when she smiled. 'The FBI only requires examination of the necklace for DNA analysis. It won't take a moment.'

The clerk was startled. 'But I can't have you chopping up ears, officer. I'm sure the owner wants them all in one piece.'

'That's understood,' Miss Tanaka reopened her bag to extract a small case holding sterilised bottles, swabs, scalpels and needles. 'DNA can be extracted by various means. I only need a tiny shaving.'

'Just a shaving?' The clerk giggled. 'So that's a CSI kit? And I love those CSI programs on TV. Okay, I'll get a porter to help you, officer, but I reckon five thousand bucks is a weird price to pay for something so utterly gross. I wouldn't even use them as dog chews.'

2

Mr John Rackham is inbound to the Caribbean

IT'S EASIER THAN some folks think to liberate a private jet. In this case, liberation merely involved removing the aircraft without the owner's permission and yes I'll agree the deed required creative planning but realistically it was like helping oneself to a very expensive car. Just open the door, start the engines and vanish!

So we'll begin here as our sweet and recently emancipated jet cruises 2000 feet above the aquamarine quilt of the Caribbean. At this altitude, the Brazilian built jet is flying well below its usual ceiling, but that's for a reason. Come to think of it, my crew will do almost anything for good reason. It's up to me to provide the reason.

I can smell the full-grain calfskin on my headrest as I look down through the porthole onto the glistening turquoise seas. I see where the waves burst white where they ride over reefs only to turn to darkest blue where the drop-offs dive deep into the ocean. It's an impressive view because I can't see the filth and plastic that you, my friends, have so thoughtlessly deposited on Neptune's doormat. From up here, it's looks like a beautiful clean world down below.

You don't need to know about the previous owner of this jet, but be assured, I'm not feeling bad about his loss. The man was an unprincipled jerk who loved watching his morons mow down the rain forest with screaming chainsaws. As each trunk crashed to the soil, the jerk was clocking up more dollars than you can imagine. Destroying the Amazon, enslaving the jungle tribes or just killing them, he did all that so that you, my brethren, might enjoy fancy hardwood for your floors and furniture. Over the years the jerk made enough money to acquire several jet aircraft, so I figured the loss of just one set of wings would not screw up his grubby lifestyle. Meanwhile the river Indians, with all their birds and animals, were searching in vain for new habitats in denuded forests and soulless pastures where grazing cattle belch into a depleted atmosphere before morphing into hamburgers for the mewing children of city people.

So, my friends, don't rush to frown upon my way of life since many of you may have played your own small part in it.

The jet pulses forward on twin Pratt & Whitney engines as we head north from Venezuela. On my wrist, a Swiss gold watch indicates that in 90 minutes we'll be touching down and my gaze turns inwards to the cabin. Now I look down the carpeted aisle, past my sleeping sweethearts – bless all three – to the cockpit where my pilot, Harry Helms, scans the avionic signals on his dashboard.

Helms has been our sky jockey for the past five years. He's pure bred Australian. His leathered features, sharp blue-eyes, crewcut greying hair and lazy humour sit like rough silk with his ability to command any machine with aerofoils attached. Formerly Helms flew with special forces in Afghanistan, but later he opted for the rare pleasure of working with our company. When at the controls, Helms is drier than the Great Victoria Desert, but at play he can drink more than a thousand footballers. You get the picture. Pure Aussie as I said. Nevertheless I trust Helms big time. It's an honour to have him steal my transport and then fly it for me.

Beside Helms sits another essential expert. This is our Ukrainian weasel who comes with an unpronounceable name, so we just call him Chad. He joined us two years ago after I paid his prison guards in Manaus to take time off while Helms hoisted him from the prison's exercise yard using a borrowed helicopter. I was happy to pay for all that because I saw it as a crucial investment.

Prior to his prison sentence, Chad had been hacking into the State Governor's private bank accounts, a clever skill we may all agree. But then Chad unloaded his profits with a spate of bitcoin juggling before spending the proceeds ostentatiously, a silly move you may concede. When a skin-head geek purchases a Ferrari and a Mercedes sportster in the same week, alarm bells ring! Chad was seized by the Federales and forced to surrender the remaining cash and the car keys before going to jail. There's a time and place for ostentation, I always say. Often it implies a character flaw and inevitably attracts questions from nosey or envious folk. And don't we all know just how inquisitive the world has become these days?

Nevertheless Chad's digital skills are rated so highly that we really need him on our crew. In a world run by computers, goddammit, such talent is sorely needed and there's no point in asking how he does it. Our Ukrainian cyber wizard growls and grunts like a dog with a sore throat. We cannot understand how Chad obtains supposedly secure data. He's a very talented digital locksmith who knows about satellites, encryption, phones, radar, bank codes and surveillance systems better than most crunchers in Silicon Valley and currently he's helping with the navigation.

Below us I can see dark fingers of land. Off to one side is Puerto Rico, America's add-on territory. Through the other porthole I can make out the coastline of the Dominican Republic, an island where wild and gorgeous women jig to manic music and where the men polish guns and knives when they get caught in traffic jams.

Helms is driving our jet down the centreline of the strait that separates these two nations so I leave my seat and head to the cockpit to admire the view. On the way, I pass my girls who are asleep in their reclining chairs, all lulled by the soporific rumble of the engines. Only our mongrel dog Kludo notices me, opening one dark eye, as I pass between the seats, proving as always that he's the best of watchdogs for my little family.

Up behind the cockpit, I see Helms and Chad are immersed in the special mastery of their trades. Both are wearing crisp white shirts with blue and gold epaulets and both are wearing gold-rimmed pilot shades. Classic sky kit, you will appreciate, is needed for this operation and both men are clean-shaven and outwardly respectable. They turn as I squat behind their seats.

'Ok, guys? Is that Mona Island down there on the nose?'

Chad nods. He's navigating by dead-reckoning because Helms has turned off the transponder and GPS systems to reduce our electronic presence in the skies. To reduce I say, but not eliminate. The air traffic and coast guard stations around these islands are bound to register our presence eventually and though we're flying low and slow, hoping not to register too early we'll arrive in radar dominated skies soon enough.

'Yep. That's Mona.' Helms replies in his rich, twangy drawl. 'See the airstrip? A thousand yards. Just long enough to land if we need it.'

That's what I admire about Helms. He's always appraising emergency and alternative landing grounds. I can see the airstrip clearly, a grey scar cutting across the scrubby interior of Mona Island. 'But is it long enough for take-off?' I ask.

Helms grins, one gold tooth showing in his pearly whites. 'If we lose some weight we could lift off. Perhaps ditch Chad and the dog.'

'Hell no! That's not going to happen. We boys gotta hang together.' Laughing I place a hand on each man's shoulder, reinforcing my point with a squeeze. 'This is going to be our GOAT deal. Our Greatest Of All Time deal! To pull it off, we need to stick together like mating dogs. D'ya hear me now?'

Helms nods with his dusty outback smile and from Chad comes a grunt of approval. As I said, this Ukrainian understands canine communication but his eyes mystify me. They look like raw eggs.

'Now guys,' I continue. 'Remember we trickle in slow and easy. Nothing to declare, so Customs are welcome to inspect us. We're carrying amplifiers for the show and Customs won't object when we tell 'em who's singing.'

The two amplifiers, packing 500 watts of mega-sound, are in the jet's hold, all neatly packaged in shrink-wrap. In fact these are Chad's accessories. Inside each amp he has concealed the base boards and chips for the genius equipment he needs for his computer hooey. Only a highly skilled officer could identify the circuitry involved, and we're betting the Customs won't be up to that. So there's nothing to fret about. With not a single weapon between us we're as clean as the skies around us.

I turn back from the cockpit after a final glance at the horizon beyond the windshield. Pillars of cumulus cloud show in the west, rising like shaving foam in the brightest of blue skies. Somewhere below those clouds lies our destination where we'll be staging our operation. I'm getting excited at the thought of it. I won't share my buzz with the cockpit boys now, so I head back down the cabin, past my sleeping girls and again the dog lifts his head to stare at me. When I lean down to pat him, Kludo bares his lips in a snarl of fangs. That's the thanks I get for rescuing him from the drunk Brazilian scumbag who previously owned him. I can pat my boys, but not my dog!

Back in my seat, I pour a tumbler of Mount Gay rum, add a limed cola and lean back to admire the passing seascape. I know we're heading for a major play with no guarantee of success. So will it work, I wonder? Will we succeed or will we fail? Fuck it. Who cares? I relish the rum as I search in vain for an answer because no one, I remind myself, can foresee the future.

Either way, we're a big happy family travelling in style. And that's what I love about private jets.

3

Arrival in Providenciales as witnessed by Agent Bradley FBI

THE PANELS ON the pickup truck broadcast a clear message – *Sutton Bradley – Pools Installed & Maintained.*

The tools for these trades were kept inside a steel cabinet welded to the truck bed alongside drums of pool cleaner and filtration additives. A tall CB aerial reached skywards from the roof of the pickup which was sufficiently faded and battered to match similar service vehicles in the islands. If all this amounted to any deception it was entirely intentional.

For the truck's owner, Sutton Bradley, the pool work was easy and profitable, even though he confined himself to simple contracts at competitive rates. These odd jobs, coupled with Bradley's ultra laid-back style, provided more than adequate cover for his principal role as a Special Agent with the FBI. His job in that respect was to read the pulse of the Turks and Caicos Islands, the British Overseas Territory which had been governed by the Foreign and Commonwealth Office in London for nearly fifty years.

Bradley's chain of command was however different. He acted exclusively for FBI Miami whose headquarters lay 600 miles to the northeast. His role as a covert operative was to monitor any potential threats and nascent problems in the string of islands that rose randomly from the Atlantic between the Bahamas and the Dominican Republic.

When regarded as sufficiently serious, relevant information was shared between Miami HQ and the British authorities, often bypassing Bradley who resided beside a tidal canal off the Leeward Channel. Outside his timbered shack, two dogs lurked seeking shade below the discarded boats and maintenance equipment spread around the yard. Bradley felt his life as a young bachelor was close to idyllic.

Occasionally however a call to his cell phone would direct Bradley to a situation requiring discreet attention. This afternoon Miami HQ had called while he was drinking beer with some local tradesmen. He was instructed to proceed immediately to the private jet terminal at Providenciales airport where he was to assess an incoming aircraft detected by the defensive radar systems of the US Coastguard. The aircraft was inbound from the southern Caribbean but Air Traffic Control had scant details of its origin and flight plan. Bradley was ordered to monitor the arrival and report.

Probably little to it, thought Bradley, as he parked his truck near the private air terminal. It might be nothing more than a paper-shy pilot or a communications failure since both excuses occurred regularly. From the steel cabinet in the back of his pickup, Bradley extracted a camera with a 400 mm lens. While checking it over, he tuned the truck's radio to the local Air Traffic channel and then sat, with a chilled *Presidente* beer in his hand, waiting until he saw landing lights in the distance as a jet followed the ILS locator beam. He listened to the pilot communicating with ATC who had cleared the jet to runway 28. Bradley watched the aircraft descend below his sight line but soon it came skimming down the runway to exit into the private parking zone.

Remaining in his cab Bradley used the camera to record the aircraft type and registration which he noted was from Aruba, a Dutch island near Venezuela. After stopping in front of the parking marshal, the shrill whine of its twin jets soon faded into silence. First to appear on the extended air stair was a black rag-eared dog which came down on a leash attached to an attractive teenage girl with streaked brown hair. He noted pink trainers, pink shorts and a loose white T-shirt. Then came two high rolling women Bradley judged to be in their late thirties. One was a spike- haired blonde in a blue crew suit, the other a brunette in designer jeans and denim jacket. Next to show was a middle-aged caucasian male decked out in khaki shorts, a floral shirt with wrap-around shades and a black baseball cap. He came down the steps followed by two aircrew in white shirts and navy slacks. Nothing unusual so far, Bradley decided, as he clicked away on his camera. Just wealthy folk preparing for a dream vacation.

The arrivals disappeared into the private terminal while Bradley briefly edited the images before forwarding them to Miami where specialists would run them through a database. The FBI could obtain passport details from Immigration, but wealthy vacationers were common enough in the Turks & Caicos Islands whose economy depended on tourists chasing Caribbean dreams. Bradley put the camera aside and drove to another location from where he could monitor the arrivals when they emerged.

As he anticipated, ten minutes later, the arrivals left the terminal to board a black-windowed SUV supplied by a rental firm known to Bradley. He recorded the vehicle's registration and noted the stacked baggage trolley. As he was about to forward these images a text came from Miami, ordering him to stay with the case and to report again soon.

He texted back *OK Understood* and started the engine.

Trailing a specific vehicle in the islands required some skill. With few roads and low density traffic, it was easy to be noticed so Bradley waited half a minute before pulling out after the SUV. At the airport roundabout the SUV took the exit to the Blue Hills highway, a coastal road that led to several prestigious resorts. Doubtless the newcomers would be staying in one of these, thought Bradley, as he followed four hundred yards behind, one arm hanging in the breeze and listening to an island radio station as did most pool engineers.

After ten minutes on the road, the SUV turned into the parking lot of a famous watering hole known as Conch Bar. Again this was no surprise to Bradley. He continued on, bypassing the beachside bar which was a frequent priority stop for visitors craving a slug of rum with conch fritters.

Bradley swung the pickup off the road several hundred yards past the bar and parked in a grove of palm trees next to a local graveyard. Here head-stones of grainy marble covered the final resting places of the *Belongers*, those island families who had been resident for centuries. Beyond the solemn masonry Bradley found a sandy mound in the shade and here he checked his cellphone. No further orders had come from Miami, so he popped another can of *Presidente* and wondered how long the group might linger. One rum punch generally led to another and another. He had time enough.

But time for agent Bradley was rarely a pressing matter. He was the youngest son of an American mining engineer from Philadelphia who had married a joyful Bahamian woman. Of mixed-race, and slim in build, Bradley merged easily and related to most ethnic groups. After serving with the police in Philadelphia, he had joined the FBI for a three year stint in Atlanta before being selected for outpost duties in the Turks and Caicos. For a young man with his background it was no hardship destination.

Looking along the beach, Bradley could almost see the Conch Bar but there was no sign of his quarry. He drank some beer waiting patiently. Then the black dog appeared, bounding onto the white sands of the beach to leap and splash around in the shallows. The girl followed, loping down from the Conch Bar on slender tanned legs. Again Bradley noted the pink hot-pants and the loose T-shirt with a logo he couldn't decipher. He lay back on the warm sand, pulled a straw hat over his eyes and pretended to doze. Labourers and fishermen often took a nap along this shore, a natural snooze spot for many tradesmen.

From beneath his hat, Bradley watched the dog at play. The girl was using a tablet to photograph her pet as it boogied in waters which glittered in the gold reflection of approaching sunset. The youngster had a good eye for photography, he decided, as she continued along the beach until, only thirty yards from Bradley's position, she paused to photograph a fisherman working inside the conch pens. These lay close inshore in waist deep water holding fresh conch before they were cleaned and delivered to the restaurant kitchen. The detritus of disembowelled conch lingered around the pens providing morsels for rays and reef sharks that cruised nearby.

The dog and girl were enjoying their fun when she picked up a coconut husk and threw it into the shallows. The dog charged in, paddling with head held high towards the bobbing husk. Below it, a dark shadow noted an opportunity and moved in to attack. A sharp yelp came from the dog with turmoil on the surface. The girl yelled, dropped her tablet and waded in to rescue her dog while the shadow sped to deeper waters. It had to be a barracuda trying its luck, thought Bradley as the girl scooped up her dog and waded to the shore.

Bradley wondered if he should assist her but doing so might compromise his task. To ignore the event was the easiest option and the girl was wasting no time. Hugging the dog, she ran back towards the Conch Bar but leaving her tablet on the beach.

For Bradley here was an opportunity. He hurried down to retrieve the tablet. The girl was still running and did not look back as he recovered the tablet and returned to his shoreline cover. The tablet had not yet returned to sleep mode so by keeping it active he could make a data transfer to a hard drive he kept in his pickup. With professional skill Bradley downloaded the tablet while he noted gaudy stickers on its case advertising beach bars in Rio de Janeiro. The girl evidently had South American connections.

Bradley continued to feel lucky. Though his colleagues in Miami might not be impressed by images of dogs and sunsets, social media data with family photos and texts could yield useful material and Miami HQ considered these particular visitors merited surveillance. When Bradley next looked up, the girl was returning down the beach with a man whom he now assumed was her father. This time there was no sign of the dog so they were coming to retrieve the tablet. Time to go, he decided.

Bradley started the truck and returned to the coast road. He wasn't going to keep the tablet. The kid with long legs didn't deserve such a rough start to her vacation. Bradley knew how to return it, thanks to the help of a third party.

4

John Rackham at the Conch Bar

A MAN CAN know a lot of women, but I'll tell you this. Few women mean more to a man than his own daughter. A daughter is one half of him and by a click of her fingers, a clever girl can persuade her dad to do almost anything. Men are pure saps to most daughters and I'm no different.

Just as soon as Swann came running to our table holding Kludo in her arms, I knew she was in trouble. But Swann's no drama queen. Far from it. She can see through any games the older women play when utilising their deliciously evil minds and sinewy bodies. Swann can handle all of that with superb indifference.

However an attack on her dog, the scruffy mutt, was something that touched my young girl's heart. She came to me, eyes open but holding back tears. 'Something bit Kludo, Pa. A ray or a shark. I think he's okay, but I left my tablet on the beach.'

And so, like any sap, I left the table, asking Annie to care for the dog. I could see blood on one paw, but nothing worse. I told Mary to watch my briefcase and the white bag under the table. Then I took Swann by the hand and together we retraced the line of her footsteps that lay in dimples on the sand.

'Where d'you leave it?' I ask. I can see no sign of the darned tablet and usually a lump of glass and plastic is easy enough to spot on an empty beach. 'I don't see it.'

Swann, you'll appreciate, is like any kid with a tablet. It's an extension to her mind, a link to everyone, everything, everywhere. Personally I rarely use one because Chad handles all my communications using his clever proxies and backdoor methods.

'I dropped it here,' says Swann. Her dark brown eyes are glistening as her streaked hair catches the warm evening breeze. 'Just five minutes ago. Right here, Pa. When I ran to save Kludo.'

I cast around. There are too many dimples in the sand to follow and I don't have much time for a search. 'Perhaps a wave took it?'

'No chance, Pa. I was here. Ten foot from the water.'

So I wander into the scrub and rustling palms along the shore. There's no sign of an tablet in the high tide rubbish. No sign of anything. Apart from some light traffic rumbling along the road, the beach is deserted and the seawater is clear as a diamond. Seems to me the tablet is a goner. 'Well, we can't do more than that. I'm sorry, Swann. Let's get back.'

'This is so shitty,' Swann grumbles as we walk back along the beach. 'I was only gone a few minutes.'

'That's all it takes. An opportunity is all a thief needs,' I give Swann a comforting hug. 'I'll find you a new one tomorrow.'

'Thanks, Pa,' she smiles. 'But should we take Kludo to a vet?'

'Maybe so, but he looks okay to me.' I pat her shoulder. 'First I've got some business. We'll see about a vet later.'

Back at the table, Mary and Annie also try to comfort Swann. She settles between them, a cub between two lionesses, holding her dog and roaming into a teenage world of sulky worries. Too bad about the tablet, that's what Swann must be thinking.

Now I spot the two guys I came to meet. They've arrived at a neighbouring table, hunched over bottles of beer and throwing the odd, casual glance in our direction. These are the agents. I'm sure of it. I can smell villains faster than a drug-sniffing hound can hit on skunk. One wears a gold chain, a happy clapping church minister in black suit and white shirt. But I know different. His companion wears a faded T-shirt with blue shorts and he has the leg muscles of a prize boxer. I have $25,000 in my white bag and they're here to claim each and every dollar.

I pick up my drink, a Conch Bar special with a three rum mix before I stroll across to their table. 'Hi guys. Sure is a beauty of an island, you have here.'

The prize boxer rolls his head. 'Has been said. I might agree.'

'Well, it beats Barranquilla, that's for sure.'

'Never mind Barranquilla,' says the suit. 'Let's talk 'bout the goods you ordered.'

The password has been exchanged so we get down to business. I'm still admiring the view as I speak, giving the details quietly, to reduce random eavesdropping. 'I'm John Rackham, the concert promoter. Who are you guys?'

The horse hunk shakes his head. 'You don't need names. We just provide a service.'

'And I don't pay nameless folk.' I won't reveal I already know their names from the agent who supplied these two scumbags. I look them in the eyes. 'You could be anybody.'

Accepting my reasons, the prize boxer glares at me. 'I's Mekissu. He be Tamos.'

'Mekissu and Tamos.' I repeat their names. 'That fits. And I have the bucks – assuming the goods are set to go?'

'No problems man,' The church minister nods showing stained teeth. 'All you asked for. Ready for pick-up tomorrow at noon, as agreed. Look for a grey fishing boat one mile from West Caicos marina entrance. We will fix a grey surface marker, a diver's buoy, to the goods when you approach.'

Around us the chatter of Conch Bar rumbles on, mixing with the beat, beat, beat of the sound system. Reggae in the rum, reggae in the wind and reggae in my loins. I've got better things to do than hanging around with these two choirboys.

'That's good. We'll be there at midday for sure.' I'm pleased with their news. 'Now, guys, you see that blonde lady at my table?'

Both men glance at Mary. She has a drink in one hand and a cellphone in the other, like any tourist on vacation. It would be difficult to miss Mary. She's a knockout blonde with a figure that would cause an ogling Italian to crash a new Ferrari. In a white bikini she's a snap double for Honey when Bond sees her come wet and dripping from the sea, knife in belt and singing a weird little song. That scene still gives me a kick I will admit.

Mekissu nods. 'Yeah, I sees her.'

I lower my voice. 'When we go, she'll leave a white shopping bag by her chair. You'll find its contents useful.'

Mekissu and Tamos nod. They understand.

Leaving the pair of devil worshippers, I stroll back through the dining area. They must show up with the goods as agreed. Should they renege, that would go down badly with my people. Very badly indeed! And for that reason, I've asked Annie to take mugshots of both agents. I can see her now, aiming her iPhone at young Swann and her dog but in reality she's getting shots of the two skunks.

I should tell you that Annie, my legal wife and Swann's mother, is a brunette with a mass of curling corkscrew hair that tumbles to her shoulders. She's an eyeful to be sure. The red frames of her designer sunglasses contrast with her white denim jacket. Look more closely and you'll note she's wearing two wedding rings, one for me and one for Mary. We all agreed it was a neat idea, so now the three of us each wear two wedding rings.

At the bar, I get my drink reloaded. It takes a minute while the barman stirs up slugs of Mount Gay, fresh lime, orange juice and grenadine. I take a sip. Perfect! Swilling it on my tongue and with business done, I wander back to our table, pausing to say hello to other strangers en route. I'm a social type. I learn they are tourists on their first visit to the Turks. Just like me, I tell them.

My girls have now decided any harm to the dog was minimal. Kludo is licking a cut on his paw. His wounded pride may have diminished but not Swann's. It's clear the loss of the tablet is worrying her. She's not pleased.

'It's just an tablet,' I tell her. 'We'll get another.' I sit down beside Swann. 'We've got Kludo, and he's what counts.'

Annie agrees, leaning over to give Swann a hug. 'I won't let him get eaten by sharks, so cheer up. We're here for some fun.'

Mary doesn't appreciate Swann's petulance. 'All set then?'

'Yep,' I reply. 'Leave the bag under your chair when we go. They say it's all ready for tomorrow.'

But Mary is not smiling. The pupils of her blue eyes are just visible through her shades. 'I don't like 'em. Can we trust them?'

'We have to. If we don't get what we paid for, they'll regret it.'

We finish our drinks and get up to leave the Conch Bar. The sinking sun has layered a pink hue on seas stirred by the trade wind. Mekissu and Tamos take no notice of such natural beauty and sit like dummy mobsters while we pay up leaving the white bag under Mary's chair. She left a beach towel hanging there to partially conceal it and I see streaks of the dog's blood on the towel. Maybe that will serve as a warning when they retrieve the bag.

At the exit we find a souvenir stall where an elderly black woman sits hunched behind a wooden table. She's beckoning to Annie and Mary as I follow with Swann and the limping dog.

'Missy. Me tinks you's after something,' the old woman is saying. 'T-shirts, conch shell for twenty dollar. Good price for you.'

My big gals are compulsive shoppers, Swann less so, thank God. We pause to see what's for sale. It's all predictable and designed for milky tourists like us.

But this old woman is not selling to dumb tourists. 'Hey Missy,' she hisses in her singalong style. 'Somebody say you lose your tingemy-ting – the compooter ting?'

Annie frowns and Swann takes my arm. 'What's she talking about, Pa?'

'I don't know,' I tell her. 'She can't see the beach from here.'

Annie has switched to her alert mode. Her back straightens with a sharp glance at Mary. 'That's odd. What d'you think?'

'As I said. I don't like this.' Mary removes her shades to focus on the saleswomen. She points to a small doll, stuffed full of pins, sitting on the shelf behind the stall. 'You sell stuff from Haiti? That's a voodoo doll. Maybe you come from Port au Prince?'

The old woman grins, her chipped teeth rooted in dark crinkled gums. Her eyes roll like bloodshot marbles as she picks up the voodoo doll. 'Yes, missy. Dis from Haiti. You want de doll or de 'puter ting?'

My three girls are uncertain. At my feet, I hear a deep sound, a growl of warning from guess-who? Kludo has a wondrous sense, an ability to detect danger on land, but evidently not at sea. Kludo is growling loud and proud, even showing his fangs.

'For God's sake,' Annie says. 'What's this about a computer?'

The stall-holder is fixated by the dog. Her eyes narrow as she glares. 'You want de 'puter? Gimme two hundred dollar.'

'Let me see it,' says Mary. She's with Annie on this and they're taking no nonsense from this Haitian saleswoman and it sounds like a scam to me.

'First, we need to see it.'

'Two hundred on de table!' The game swings back to the stall-holder. 'Or I puts pins in de doll – one for each of yo!'

A guaranteed way to annoy my ladies is to confront them with a threat. And this pin deal sounds serious. I've had enough for one day, so I reach for my wallet and tweak out two 100 dollar bills. I slam them on the stall desk, keeping my hand on them while the dog growls on like a tractor trying to start a dead engine. 'Show us the tablet,' I say.

From below her stall, the woman brings out Swann's tablet. It can't belong to anyone else because of the Rio stickers on the cover. 'This your's, Missy?'

Swann nods. Annie grabs the tablet as I push the money over.

'How did you get it?' I insist.

'Someone find it on de beach. Dat's all I know.'

Kludo stops growling. Swann is smiling again but Mary, my hot blonde, is far from convinced. 'She's lying. Let's get out of here,' says Mary. 'Before I stick a blade in her.'

5

FBI HQ – Miami

FROM THE FOURTH floor, Harumi Tanaka could look down onto the courtyard that separated the two wings of the building. Now ten years old, it had been designed for Florida's FBI whose staff admired their glass barracks with its girdle of lawns, palm trees and lakes. Here the custodians of federal law strived to monitor the criminal ambitions of the local population and there was no shortage of either as far as Miss Tanaka was concerned.

Turning away from the view, she heard the alert ping and a face appeared in the top right-hand frame on her computer screen. It belonged to her Executive Director Oliver Jenkins, her section commander, who had a simple question. 'Hi Miss Tanaka. How's your DNA analysis progressing?'

Miss Tanaka knew she would be visible on his screen, creating a prettier sight she hoped, since Jenkins' face bore the wrinkled look of tired Camembert cheese. 'Sir, I'm working on fifteen cases. To which case are you referring?'

'Your trip to New York,' replied Jenkins. 'For those ears?'

Recalling the prevarication at executive level before Jenkins had finally authorised her to attend the auction, Miss Tanaka brightened. 'On track, sir. Most of the ears have sufficient DNA for analysis.'

Jenkins lifted his spectacles to rub his weary eyes. 'Sufficient? Can you do any better?'

'We've run them through age analysis in carbon 14. They all appear to originate in a time frame some 300 years ago.'

Jenkins replaced his glasses with a smile. 'Then we can be fairly sure they're not fakes.'

'Definitely not fake, sir. They're all human. Five from African tribal origins. Eight from Caucasian donors.'

'Donors!' Jenkins made a derogatory snort. 'That's a neat way to describe mutilation, Miss Tanaka. Not many folk willingly slice off their own ears.'

'I agree, sir.' Miss Tanaka tried to humour her boss. 'You may recall that the Dutch artist Van Gogh cut off his own ear after arguing with a fellow artist.'

'Incredibly stupid, wasn't he? But artists can be temperamental.' Jenkins sniggered.'And what about the analysis on the ear from the pirate Rackham?'

'That's ongoing, sir. It's with the DNA lab for a full examination, as you suggested,' she added.

'So I did. Okay. You can't do more than that.' Jenkins sniffed and began reading from a printout in his hand. 'You may want to know about this possible lead. A caucasian male, named John Rackham, has just shown up in the Turks and Caicos. We were alerted by the Coastguard when he arrived on a private jet. We have checked with Immigration there. Among the aircrew is a Ukrainian, possibly a fugitive who fled by helicopter from a Brazilian prison. Our agent has provided photographic details.'

'John Rackham?' Miss Tanaka was instantly curious. 'On Providenciales? That's amazing.'

'So it might be,' Jenkins agreed. 'Bear in mind, there are over 500 men with that same family name in the USA alone.'

'But in the Turks? Surely that's a coincidence?'

'Hard to say. But maybe you'll want to secure DNA from this John Rackham? Could help with your thesis.'

Miss Tanaka certainly agreed with this last point. She had been working for months on an internal thesis about the hereditary nature of criminality. 'Yes sir, I'd be happy to volunteer.'

Jenkins shrugged. 'Not yet. Miss Tanaka. Not yet. We've spent enough on this skylark already and I'll need better reasons before I send you out there to hunt for pirates. Just thought you should know. I'll keep you posted.'

The face of Executive Director Jenkins faded from the screen leaving Miss Tanaka staring at the empty space. She leaned forward on her elbows, frowning in surprise.

'John Rackham in Providenciales? Mmm… Extraordinary.'

6

John Rackham at Rum Cay

I'LL SHARE NO details about our first night at Rum Cay Resort. After a long flight and all that nonsense at the Conch Bar, we drove to our new base and turned in. No time for hanky-panky as the saying goes. My two gals seize that option only when they feel like it and that's not necessarily when I want to romp and roll. Anyway these are personal matters that I may mention later.

It's a fine new day and the early sun is pumping golden heat over the ocean to the rhythmic thump of surf on the reef. All the beauty comes for free so it's just the human element that costs a fortune, well into five figures if you must know. We've taken two villas on the coastal side of this five-star colony at Rum Cay. Snuck between palms and hibiscus bushes, they provide an ideal base, offering high levels of privacy inside a gated compound.

The scents of frangipani and other plants surround me as I stroll back from the villa where my two men are quartered. Helms just told me he slept badly, but that's normal. He puts it down to nightmares caused by military service in Iraq. Ambushes, body parts and terror were daily events that led to the nightmares in his sleep. But Helms gets enough shut-eye and now he has ordered a taxi to seek out our third man Javel, the Jamaican Rasta, who will be acting as our boat-master. Javel has been on the island for three months conducting basic research and soon I'll be joining him on the private beach just below our villa. Today is dedicated to preparation, weapon supply and a visit to the show ground.

As for the Ukrainian, Chad didn't sleep much either. That's because I told him to set up the communications centre before going to bed. That's all done now, says Chad. So I took a look at the various screens, keyboards and devices in his room but did I believe him? His eyes were dark with lack of sleep. In fact his head is just a scull, a bald, boney helmet protecting his wizard brain. All Chad's screens were running live, but heck, what do I know? Circuit boards and digital sorcery leave me cold.

So here I am, back outside our family villa where a humming bird is probing for nectar in the flowering bush by our door. The whirring of its wings remind me of bullets bypassing my ear. Such a beautiful bird. Thank the lord for beauty!

Inside the villa I see my girls are out by the pool. Swann, deep into her tablet, doesn't look up as I detour past her lounger. She's wearing a teeny weeny bikini minus the polka dots, and she's ravishing. Very proud of her, I am.

Annie and Mary are poised on the marbled edge of the pool dabbling their legs in the water. Both are naked since they only do all-over tans. Beads of water ripple down their spines towards their butts. Goddammit, the symmetry is so damned appealing. I'd love to linger but right now we have a business to plan.

'How are the boys?' Annie asks, as I kiss her forehead. Naturally Mary gets the same treatment before I reply, speaking quietly.

'Chad's operation is up and running. Helms has gone to find Javel. No problems anticipated. Chad will sweep our quarters when he gets a chance. We don't need hidden mikes or cameras, do we?'

Mary turns to me, a hard glint in her eyes. 'No, JR. We do not.'

This is the thing about Mary. There's a soft heart underneath but sometimes we must dig hard to find it. A consummate professional Mary is very much at the core of our enterprise. What Mary wants, she always gets by one method or another. Stay on her side and you'll be ok. At least, that's the way Annie and I play it.

'After we have recovered our stuff, I'll text you. Be at the beach thirty minutes after you receive my text.'

'And what must Swann do?' Mary asks pointedly.

'She stays here with Kludo to hold the fort, won't you Swannie?'

Swann doesn't answer, so I try again. 'Won't you Swann?'

My daughter isn't listening. She's hunched over the blessed tablet on her lap. 'Oh my God,' she finally splutters, turning to us in distress. 'Ma, come here and look at this.'

Calling for Mother is rare these days. In many ways Swann acts much older than her age, ten years older sometimes, but not this morning so it seems. 'Come on, Ma. You won't believe this.'

Annie swings her legs from the pool and ambles to a chair. She picks up her towel, wrapping it around herself to cover her breasts. They are bigger and more boisterous than Mary's slimline boobs but so what? I adore all four of them. I turn to look at Swann. 'So what's the problem, honey?'

'My tablet is playing silly. It keeps running a video I never chose.'

'I'll take a look.' I give Mary's shoulder a squeeze before she slides into the turquoise water, flips onto her back, paddling away with hardly a ripple. Mary's a brilliant swimmer. Her naked body flows like a bronzed seal teasing the surface. Now her head disappears, then her shoulders, breasts, stomach and pelvis. Below the water Mary sculls hard with both hands as she lifts both legs into a scissor pose. When at school, Mary became a synchronised swimming champion and she's as supple with her body as she is with her villainous mind. Slowly she splits those well-honed legs wide apart before subsiding below the surface. Nothing is left to the imagination as I hear Annie calling for me. 'Over here JR. Swann's tablet is all fucked up.'

So now I join Annie and lean over Swann's shoulders to study her tablet. The screen appears slightly out of focus. The image shows a black & white video as a ship's boat is rowed by a gang of ruffians away from a narrow strip of sand surrounded by sea. On the sand stands a woman in a long dress, bonnet and shawl. She is screaming abuse as she waves a fist at the departing crew. Her other hand holds the hand of a young child who stands by her side.

'She's being marooned,' says Annie. 'It looks like that.'

'What's marooning, Ma?' asks Swann.

'Leaving unwanted baggage,' says Annie. 'Not a nice thing to do, especially to a woman and child.'

'So why watch it?' I ask. 'Find something more interesting.'

Swann is irritated by my suggestion. 'Pa, I didn't want this video. It bumped all my other stuff. It's all I can get now.'

'So turn off the power,' I say. 'Then fire it up again. The glitch may go.'

Swann shuts down the tablet. The screen goes blank. Annie glances at me with raised eyebrows before sauntering to the poolside bar where a pot of coffee is brewing. I check my watch because my rendezvous with Helms and Javel is approaching. Now Swann powers up the tablet, enters her code and groans. 'Oh shit…it's still there.'

Annie brings me a mug of coffee and then goes to her lounger while Mary continues doing laps in the pool. In the shade, the dog is licking his paw and I'm growing impatient with Swann's problem. 'Your tablet's a bloody nuisance. First you lose it. Then we get it from a demented witch from Haiti, and now it's acting up again.'

I can see its screen as the monochrome drama continues. Now at sea, it's night-time and in the boat the oarsmen are dressed in rough shirts and raggedy shorts. In the boat's stern, the commander checks a pistol in his belt. The camera comes astern of the boat to reveal their objective. Silhouetted in their path of glistening moonlight is an old sailing ship.

'I get it,' I tell her. 'A raiding party wants to seize that ship.'

'What's on board?' Swann asks as the video shows the boat reaching the stern of the sailing ship where men sling grappling irons over the ship's taffrail. The leader swiftly climbs to the deck and aims his pistol at the startled helmsman.

'He looks just like Helms!' Swann exclaims. 'Just like him.'

I have to agree. It also occurs to me that the leader of the boarding party bears a remarkable similarity to myself. 'Listen hon, your tablet's running crazy. You best come with me on the boat today. I know you'll enjoy it, so go get your sunhat, sun oil and some bottled water.'

The suggestion cheers her. 'Can I bring Kludo?' she asks.

'Sure. Now turn this little sucker off and get ready.'

Swann flips the lid passes the tablet to me and stands up. 'Pa. I don't understand how that old video got into it?'

'Forget it. Chad will fix it when he's done sweeping the villa.' I smile at her, 'If he fails, we'll buy you a new one.'

'That's a deal, Pa.' Swann gets up, leaving the tablet with me. After she's gone, I re-open the tablet out of curiosity and the video resumes its compelling action as the boarding party takes control of the sailing vessel with no loss of life. Some of the pirates go below holding lanterns to plunder and pillage. But they're disappointed. Instead of gold and precious treasure, they find only ranks of chained and desperate slaves squatting in the lower decks.

To be honest, the sight of so many helpless souls in the dark interior of that ship is very upsetting. I'm glad Swann didn't see the sequence, or the one that follows. The boarding party takes vengeance on the ship's captain, a snivelling wretch who begs in vain for his life. The pirate chief pulls a knife and slices off one of the captain's ears. The pirate wipes the bloodied item around the victim's forehead and then heaves him overboard. Blood in the water only means one result in Caribbean seas. The video ends in a swirling turmoil of feasting sharks.

Which reminds me. We have work to do, most of it in shark busy waters. Meanwhile I can find no reason why this video has invaded Swann's tablet. Could it be a warning, I wonder? By nature I'm intensely superstitious. Distractions are the last thing we need and I'm somewhat shaken by the scenes I've just witnessed. A frisson of dread runs down my spine. I find it inexplicable.

I walk over to Annie who's drinking coffee under a shade of fronds. I put the tablet down beside her glossy magazines. 'Get Chad to check this out. I can't figure what type of AI glitch can produce such images. I don't want Swann using it again.'

Annie looks at me incredulously. 'Teenage girls are totally in love with their gadgets, didn't you know?'

'Then buy her another. Soon as you can.'

Mary has finished her laps. She springs from the pool glistening and towels her tattooed arms. An odd way to start drying off, you might think, but Mary has huge affection for those tats, her works of art, she calls them. She pats them dry before lying down on a lounger and closing her eyes in the bright sun.

7

A Concert is Imminent – FBI Agent Bradley

SUTTON BRADLEY WOKE that morning to the frantic barking of the two dogs guarding his home. Many islanders kept dogs of dubious pedigree to discourage unsavoury individuals from visiting. His dogs also responded vigorously to packs of feral dogs that roamed the coast rummaging for leftovers. In a perfect world, Bradley told himself, there'd be no need for any guard dogs.

From his window Bradley saw a pickup truck arriving. The vehicle, similar to his own, belonged to an electrician who often helped him to install pool lighting and pump equipment. He went to his window and called out. 'Hey mon. What yo doin' out so early?'

The driver grinned. 'Hi, Brad. I's hunting three-phase cable, the heavy-duty stuff. You know it, 'cos I lent you a drum last year.'

Bradley recalled the occasion. In fact the cable drum still lay intact in his workshop, alongside other equipment of the pool trade. 'Yeah, mon. I'll come down and get it. It's all your's.'

Bradley put on his flip-flops and went down to meet his friend. The dogs fell silent as he came into the yard. He unlocked the workshop, located the drum and wheeled it out. 'Hope you have good use for it?'

'Good or not? I dunno. A big job come up all of a sudden.'

Bradley knew big jobs in most trades were rarely spontaneous. 'This job, mon? You think they have a pool?'

The electrician heaved the drum of cable into his pickup. 'I dunno, mon. All I knows is someone is making a big party down by Grace Bay. Near the Fish Fry. You knows where.'

'So they won't be needing a pool.' Bradley understood. 'And when's this party, man? Mebbe we can go to it?'

'You's asking plenty. Saturday I think. I dunno.'

'Okay. I see you, mon.' Bradley's fist pumped the air as the electrician climbed into his cab, returning the gesture.

Instinctively Bradley felt he had squeezed enough. Cloudy information was often better than none at all, but in any event he should investigate because last night's unexpected arrival of fat cats at the airport had evidently triggered interest in Miami. Bradley opened his cellphone but no further instructions had come from HQ overnight. He would brew some coffee, feed the dogs and prepare for a day's work in the sleuthing business which was possibly more fun than sluicing down pools.

An hour later Bradley was rolling along Leeward Highway in his pickup. He had tuned the radio to a local station where The Mighty Sparrow was singing the classic, *Ah Fraid Pussy Bite Me*. Its stirring calypso beat made Bradley tap his left foot as he turned down Allegro Road towards Grace Bay whose sweeping panorama of soft pale sand was rated by travel writers as one of the world's best beaches. In the morning sunshine, the sea cast a dazzling blue translucence as far as the white beard of surf on the coral barrier which protected the island from the power of the Atlantic. Beyond the reef, on the darker blue waters, Bradley saw several white vessels were trawling for fish.

He too was ready to trawl. The electrician's comments had triggered his professional interest and as he turned onto the coast road, his hunch was fortified by a text which pinged on his cellphone. He pulled off the road to read the instruction from HQ in Miami to maintain discreet surveillance on the recent arrivals. Bradley smiled as he drove on. He enjoyed the hunt.

Ten minutes later, he slowed at a junction where the Lower Bight Road overlooked a broad piece of land known to islanders as the Fish Fry. Here barbecues and musical events were regular features for local entertainment. It was immediately evident that someone was planning an extravaganza.

Bradley remained in the cab, parked on the verge where he could survey the scene without alerting the workforce. Scaffold lighting towers rose on either side of a stage and through his tactical binoculars Bradley identified his friend's truck and the three-phase cable drum resting in its bed. The electrician was somewhere among the workmen moving around the site. Using his binoculars, he focused on a sight which caught his attention. A crowd of spectators had gathered near a group of local girls preparing for dance practice. Among them he recognised two women who were leading the choreography. Bradley sharpened the focus to confirm his identification and then reached for his cellphone. He keyed the number for his HQ director in Miami and tapped out a message. *I believe the new arrivals are here to organise a concert.*

8

Now Annie has her say

AND NOW IT'S my turn. You've heard enough from my darling husband so let me tell you what we're doing today.

Mary and I came here to the Fish Fry concert venue in our SUV, leaving Swann to go fishing with JR (my husband) and Helms. Chad remained to guard our base while he tunes our digital systems. He also promised to check that damned tablet whose erratic behaviour caused so much trouble yesterday. But that's behind us now. I certainly hope so because we have plenty to keep us busy.

First we must liaise with the show's director, a seasoned music insider from Florida named Walter Schulz. He claimed he could provide all the kit needed so we sent him a sizeable deposit without meeting him. A risky move you might agree, but you have no idea how Mary and I treat people who double-cross us.

We find Walter strutting around the stage with a clipboard and it appears he has delivered in full. We inspect the stage, the Portakabins, lighting towers, crowd control facilities and toilets. They're all okay as far we can tell, some being permanent features of the Fish Fry. Schulz is an attentive professional, very keen to please, though I soon notice he can't take his eyes off Mary's butt.

Mary and I are both wearing track suits, pink for her, lime green for me with expensive sneakers. Plenty of women look like us in the Americas but that of course is our intention. Having finished with inspection we move over to our hopefuls, a bevy of local girls recruited by Walter. They will be dancing as warm-up performers to kick-off the show.

I count fifteen dark-skinned lovelies, some more cute than others, but they're all young and eager, smiling and happy. Who wouldn't be? Reggae's been pumping through their veins since birth and they'll each get paid $1000 for the week's work.

Not so happy are the handful of local men loafing in the wings near the stage. They're clearly wondering what all this amounts to, and why their women been chosen to come and dance? Very well, we'll show them.

Mary opens her shoulder bag and finds a memory stick which she tosses to Walter. 'Put that in the sound system and give it some throttle.'

'You bet, ma'm,' Walter says. Mary thanks him with a beguiling, smile. She uses eyes and lips to cajole others to do almost anything. She tries it on JR when he's feeling stroppy, and generally gets her way but it doesn't work for me though. I'm the one who found her, gave her a meaningful role in life, and to be fair, she's never forgotten it.

'Okay, ladies,' I say, stopping in front of the line up. 'I'm Annie Rackham and we're promoting a big concert on Saturday next. We have a big star coming to headline, but we need you to wind up the mood. Give it all you've got. I can see you've got plenty to give!'

Walter's sound man goes to work. The memory stick is loaded with music that would get cardinals rocking in the Vatican. We've loaded King Marley, Nicki Minaj, Tosh and some new artistes from Rio and San Paulo. The air suddenly comes alive to the compulsive beat of steel drums.

'Now, gals. In a straight line and follow the leader!'

Mary's a natural mover. In her pink track suit she sways in time to the rhythmic boom-boom-boom. I join in too, reaching out to touch her outstretched hands. As usual an electric ripple whips down my spine. Nothing new there.

I don't dance for long as I need to shoot a video, something to show JR and our star performer prior to her arrival. As I jump down from the stage, one of the men, a surly, suspicious son-of-a bitch as big as an Angus bull, comes hoofing over. 'What you doin' with my woman?' he asks.

I look up at him as he stands above me. 'The same as for all. They get a thousand bucks for a week including rehearsals.'

'Dat ain't 'nuff,' he says staring down at me. I can see his eyes have a yellow tinge. He smells too. Sweat and cigarette smoke.

'What's your name, Mister? And which of these lovely gals is your woman, as you put it?'

'I'm Ceejay.'

He points to one of the dancers. Her face seems strangely familiar. Even her body rings a bell so I beckon Mary over and whisper in her ear. 'Doesn't she remind you of someone?'

Mary floats over to the girl for a closer look. Then she nods in agreement. 'Could be ideal,' she calls back.

'Ideal fo' what?' says the charming Ceejay.

'Does your woman have a name?' I ask. 'She looks pretty enough to deserve one.'

Ceejay only just manages to restrain his temper. 'She's my woman and she be Jasmin. But that ain't nothing to do with you.'

I wish I had Mary's versatility in false smiles. But I have the ice when I need it. 'And you need plenty more manners, sir. Where you from?' I ask.

I notice other men are coming over to watch. Meanwhile Mary is gliding up and down between the dancing gals, giving them hints on how to move and shimmy. I can see she's watching me as the gang of dudes crowd in. Walter hurries over with worry all over his face. 'Everything okay?'

'We're fine,' I tell him. 'I'm just asking where this gentleman comes from? Nothing wrong with that.'

Ceejay's brutish face leans closer and he's so much taller than me. I could do without his intrusion into my personal space. I can also smell beer on his breath. Ugh!

Walter attempts to defuse the situation but the big feller waves him away as easy as squishing a fly.

'It's okay,' I say to Walter. 'This feller's a huge piece of shit. He can't help that he's got no manners.'

My comment triggers his attack. Ceejay lunges at my throat with a hand like a dinner plate. I was anticipating the move and before his fingers so much as tickle my nose, I've floored Ceejay in a perfect drop and armlock. 'You should know that I enjoy Kung Fu, and also Krav Maga, so do you have a preference, amigo? Or shall I snap your arm while I'm at it? Believe me, I'd love to.'

His chums weren't expecting that. To a man they've pulled back while I push the bruiser's arm harder. I can hear him grunting in pain above the music, and bless her, Mary's still dancing to and fro like a pink marionette. I catch the wink in her eye meaning she's ready to launch if I need her.

That's what I love about Mary. She'll fight like a honey badger to protect me. And I'd do the same for her.

I ease the pressure on Ceejay's arm. 'Now my friend, it occurs to me you have a genuine issue. We will employ Jasmin, but I need some brothers for other jobs on this concert. If you want a dollar or two, maybe you'd like to consider the opportunity?'

The big man grunts again. He's been humiliated, so I need to rebuild his dignity. 'A dollar or two?' I hear him whisper.

'Sure, man. Crowd control and other duties. We're willing to employ you along with the best of your brothers.'

Another grunt as I apply more pressure. 'So none of that appeals?'

'Yeah,' Ceejay finally stutters. 'How much dollar?'

'We'll talk about that. More than we'll be paying your woman.'

I can see him working it out. Finally he figures it means more than a thousand dollars. 'Yeah, ma'm.'

'So no more nonsense?'

'If you say so,' he whispers.

'No.' I apply pressure. 'Wrong. It's *you* who must say so.'

'I say so.' That's his final surrender and I release him. 'Where you come from? I was asking you very nicely.'

'Ceejay Cambell from Trinidad.'

I smile at Ceejay as I release his arm. His nose wrinkles and I turn to his colleagues. 'Ceejay here just hooked you a good deal. Those of you who want some bonus dollars, leave your contact numbers with Ceejay or Mr. Schulz. We'll get back to you.'

I climb the steps back to the stage and rejoin the chorus line. Mary blows me a kiss as I take Jasmin's hand and move into a new number. She's a pretty young woman with a gorgeous smile and wondrous teeth. 'Don't worry about Ceejay,' I tell her. 'Soon, Jasmin, you're going to be a star.'

9

FBI Headquarters. Miami

MISS HARUMI TANAKA, in regular black suit and high heels, was sitting outside the office of Director Jenkins as she waited for his door to open. What, she wondered, was she about to learn?

While she waited, Miss Tanaka recalled that most of southern Florida had been little more than an inhospitable swamp when Jack Rackham went to the gallows in 1720. The state had remained that way until 1896 when the city of Miami was officially inaugurated with no more than 300 inhabitants.

How times had changed, she thought. Since then the initial population had expanded into 9 million inhabitants over the southern half of the state. My God, she thought, where would it all end? Florida was among the most successful states in the business of incarcerating criminals and Miss Tanaka felt proud to be part of the system.

Then Jenkins opened his office door. 'Come in Miss Tanaka. Some coffee?'

Miss Tanaka took a seat and then attempted to enjoy a cup of coffee, the tasteless black fluid dispensed in many American organisations. 'What's new, sir?' she asked brightly.

Jenkins sat down, lifted his spectacles and squeezed his eyes. 'It's more a question of what's not happening,' he replied. 'I asked you to come by as I felt we should discuss this in person.'

Miss Tanaka drank some coffee. 'I'm listening.'

Jenkins could have been a career executive in any corporation. Slightly balding, harassed and pressured, he looked the part. In this case the directorate dealt in criminal enterprise and there was plenty of that in Florida.

'You've been working your DNA program for some time, producing excellent work and this Rackham case with the thirteen ears is proof of your persistence in the analysis business.'

'I hope so,' said Miss Tanaka. 'And you're about to say you're discontinuing the program?'

Jenkins stared at her. 'How could I put it better? Yes, I'm sorry about this but the case falls into one of those we classify as borderline, with no imminent threat to American interests. No clear or present danger. No good reason to waste tax payer money. Basically Miss Tanaka, it's as simple as that. I guess this may be a disappointment, a set-back to your thesis, but the Director recommends we curtail further investigation. If any of Rackham's crew are refugees from justice in another South American country, we'll tag the aircraft when it flies home and inform the authorities about its movements.'

Director Jenkins smiled professionally as he prepared to wind up the meeting. He liked Miss Tanaka and her work was exemplary but FBI budgets were running to new federal guidelines and that was about all he could say. 'Mr. Rackham and his people are on the islands to promote a pop concert and such events in the Turks and Caicos are for the local authorities to manage. Not us.' Jenkins shrugged his shoulders. 'I'm real sorry.'

The Japanese ability to remain inscrutable under pressure served Harumi Tanaka well. Jenkins had no idea of how she really felt after he had effectively belittled her research of DNA relevance in criminal bloodlines. 'It's too bad, I agree. But we can't argue with the Director, can we?'

'No sir.' Miss Tanaka stood up. 'So it means I don't get to visit the Turks.'

'Not on our time and money. No.'

'But may I choose to go independently?'

Jenkins pondered the question. 'What you do in your time is for you to decide. But don't go creating any problems. That's all I ask.'

10

John Rackham on the water

ANNIE AND MARY have left to supervise preparations for the concert and I doubt if they'll find any problems. Everyone loves music, fun, colour and drama and we'll be offering loads of that.

I'm fairly sure we can deliver but inevitably any plan carries a potential for risk so we must install safeguards, alternatives and improvisation where possible. These are major components in our line of business where higher risk merits more reward. I'll get back to that later, after I complete this morning's main duty.

Swann's coming with me today. She can bring the pooch along but she'll leave her tablet for Chad to test. He'll also be hunting for any bugs or clandestine cameras that might be installed in our rooms. We know of hotels whose management earn tidy sums from explicit videos they secretly hide in guest rooms, especially bridal suites, but here at Rum Cay I doubt they would dare go that far. Big stars of screen and sport, business maestros from New York and Europe visit Rum Cay for their R&R. To them that means Rest and Recuperation. For others it may mean Rock and Roll but to us, I guess, it stands for Rob and Run.

Swann and I walk down to the private beach below our villa. The beach is clean, shaped like an elephant's tusk with thick foliage along its landward border. It's a beautiful day with sun, tiny clouds and a sweet trade wind. Timing is important today and, sure enough, our chartered fishing boat is approaching the shore as we reach the beach. Helms sits in the bows and standing firm at the wheel, is our trusted boatman and longtime colleague Mr. Javel.

Born in Trenchtown a neighbourhood of Kingston, Jamaica, Javel travelled at the age of ten to London where his father, a legendary Yardie ran a thriving drug supply enterprise until he died in a shootout with a rival Brixton gang. Young Javel then returned to Jamaica where a local posse took him under their wing, trained him in multiple skills including boatmanship which is a neat way of transporting illicit goods from one region to another. I met Javel on a visit to Columbia several years back. Couldn't miss him. He wore enough bling to sink a boat, let alone drive it. This morning thankfully, he's cut back on the dazzle. Today he's only wearing a huge ear bangle and a slim gold chain around his neck.

The boat slows as we wade out to meet it. I'm in swim trunks, a T-shirt and a straw hat. Swann also in shorts climbs aboard while I carry Kludo. He'll not be swimming today, not after his tussle with a barracuda, so I put the dog aboard and pump fists with the skipper.

'Mawnin,' I say to Javel.

'Whaap 'm,' Javel replies in his mellow tone. 'Where to, boss?'

'Through the reef, then west towards Molasses Reef. Helms, you and I will get some rods ready.'

Javel pushes forward on the throttles and both outboards thunder into life. Swann nearly falls as the boat leaps forward, but I catch her and push her to a seat. 'It looks lumpy out there, so best you sit down and keep Kludo off the fish deck.'

'Yeah Pa.'

I hadn't planned to bring Swann along, but she was spooked by that video last night and I don't blame her. It rattled my head for a while. Meanwhile Javel drives our boat through a narrow break in Rum Cay's guardian reef. On either side, the Atlantic tips breakers into frenzied surf as we power through into the moody ocean waters beyond. Instantly the wave motion changes, the swells running like corrugated hills below our hull. Javel adjusts the whining outboards and we settle to a moderate speed, leaping from crest to crest, graceful as a flying fish. It should take nearly thirty minutes to reach Molasses Reef, but with the sea running against us our progress is slowed. There's another problem too.

'Pa.' I hear Swann murmur.

'Yeah, honey?'

'I think I'm going to be sick.'

'Oh for chrissake!' I hear myself saying to my lovely daughter. 'We got serious fishin' to do. Tip it over the side.'

'Pa, I really don't like this.'

Standing beside Javel, I look at Swann who's not joking. She's looking pale and tight lipped so I have an idea. 'How 'bout we put you ashore on West Caicos near Yankee Town? You've got a phone. You'll be safe. It's uninhabited and we won't be fishing for long. An hour or two at most.'

Swann is trying not to puke, so I make the decision for her. 'Javel, find somewhere to put her ashore.'

Javel swings the craft towards the long coast of West Caicos island. There's no reef here where the ocean floor sweeps up through clear waters to meet the coastal shelf whose cliffs rise ten feet or so above sea level. Javel sees a small cove where he can run the boat onto the sand. I see no submarine hazards while Javel makes the approach. Swann scoops up her sunhat, shades and lotion as we scrape onto the beach.

'You'll be fine, honey. There's nobody here so there's nothing to worry you. Take this map and some water for you and Kludo.' I pass her a bottle of mineral water with a brochure about the island before she climbs down and puts her feet on dry land. Kludo prefers to leap for the shore. 'We'll be back very soon, I promise. In about an hour and a half. So be here.'

Javel reverses from the shore, spins the boat around and heads back to sea, travelling faster. Somewhere in the back of my busy mind I recall Annie telling Swann about the practice of marooning. It's a thought that niggles me, I must admit. I wave to her with a rare feeling of guilt in my heart.

Ten minutes later sharp-eye Helms spots our target, a grey fishing vessel. It is very similar to ours, lying ahead just where it's supposed to be, several hundred yards off the coast. Using binoculars I scan the shoreline but see nothing to alarm me. This is a largely deserted marine park off the coast of West Caicos, which is why we chose it. All the same we are playing it safe. Very safe.

Javel stands like a Grenadier guardsman at the wheel, his hair rising in the rasta style known as *thirsty roots*. We reduce speed and put out two fishing lines. Neither is armed with hook or bait because the last thing we need is a lively fish on the line.

'Time for a beer?' I look at my shipmates who shake their heads, so I pull a can from the Esky, tear off the tag and take a long draught. It's hot out here under the boat's awning and we have serious work to do. Helms and I squat on the gunwale while Javel works the boat, zigzagging along the edge of the drop off. The differing shades of sea floor show where the sea floor tips away, heading down several thousand feet. We don't want to position ourselves over that chasm.

Some three hundred yards from the grey fishing boat, we see its crew reel in their lines and head off at a moderate pace. Javel continues to zigzag until we reach the area where the departing boat was positioned. Somewhere here we should see a grey surface marker buoy that might indicate the presence of a diver below.

'There mon!' Javel has seen the flag so we sidle over, keeping it to the seaward side of our vessel hiding it from any land based snoopers. We close on it slowly and Helms leans over and hooks it with a gaff, lifting flag and buoy aboard as we come to a stop. Immediately Helms starts hauling in the rope which is attached to its load forty feet below. It should take only a minute, but suddenly the rope snaps, throwing Helms backwards into the boat. The rope's end comes aboard broken and frayed.

'Fuck it,' I say with the deepest sincerity. 'Fuck, fuck!'

Helms and Javel stare at me, both short of words. So much planning, cash and effort has been invested in this marine pick-up and now we must assume our expensive merchandise is sinking back to the sea floor.

I look at my Aussie friend. 'You like swimming, Helms?'

'No way,' Helms replies with a dark look. 'I just do flying.'

'How 'bout you, Jav?'

'No boss. I's no diver. And sharks ain't my brothers.'

Again I recall Swann's video. That feeding frenzy on the wounded skipper from the old galleon comes to mind. And yet here I am, in one of the most shark busy spots in the Caribbean, searching for any reason why I should not be going over the side. The depth is not a problem. Nor is the equipment since scuba gear and bang-sticks are stacked in our boat's cabin but let's face it, I need those supplies down there. Our entire plan depends on them so I have no choice but to dive and try to raise the load to the surface.

'Take a bearing, Helms,' I say. 'Keep Javel on this precise location while

I investigate. Prepare another line, and make sure it won't break.'

In the distance the delivery vessel is vanishing into the haze. 'Wait till I get my hands on those bastards,' I tell Helms as he passes the scuba harness. 'Our goods better be down there – or else.'

Javel juggles the throttles as I prepare my diving gear. I confess this is the very last thing I'd ever choose to do, especially in these waters. But needs must, as the saying goes, and without more delay, I check the tank valves and air flow, and then tip backwards over the side, taking the recovery line with me.

Firstly I feel the water is warm, 80 Fahrenheit according to my marine thermometer, but this is the only advantage on my side. I see no sign of the load but in the bowl of clear water where I'm now paddling like a juicy frog, I can see half a dozen sharks. Four are blacktips but two have those weird head-wings with nasty scrutinising eyes. Hammerheads! I remind myself that sharks are at their most unpredictable at dawn and dusk when they are attracted to shiny objects. According to a marine photographer I know, sharks don't bother you unless they can't help it. Since I'm not bleeding, these fellers are simply cruising in their natural habitat.

I still see no sign of the merchandise, so I head towards the drop-off, wondering if the current might have carried it that way. As I swim along the edge of this giant submarine cliff whose depths lie far below my view, my heart begins to pound. I'm experiencing vertigo and I hate sharks, so what am I doing here? I should have stayed in South America with my three girls and the blessed dog. Why was I persuaded to fly here, investing a fortune in seed money, just to attempt one of the greatest heists of my career? Greed, says the Bible, is a cardinal sin and sharks get greedy when they scent easy targets. More and more I feel like a slab of steak towing a rope tied to a boat whose crew can do little to protect me. Who wants to do this for a living?

Suddenly I spot the merchandise. Four dark scuba tanks, all strapped together, are lying on the very edge of the submarine precipice. Far above I see the hull of the boat as I swim down to the tanks, reaching them as one hammerhead, a large bastard, comes sweeping over my shoulder. The proximity of its outlandish appearance and spooky eyes almost stops my ticker but I must ignore it, finally grabbing the tanks to which I tie the line. I give it a tug and begin my swim back to a world I was born to inhabit.

When I break the surface, I see the sprouting thirsty roots of Javel's dreads leaning down to haul both me and the load aboard. 'Whaap 'm?' he says. 'Why's you wastin' time down there?'

As soon as we've secured the four scuba tanks, I peel off my kit and get back in the Esky again. 'Fuck you, man! Half a dozen sharks down there and I hate 'em!' I open a beer, trying to grin at Javel. 'Time to get back to Swann. So let's hurry.'

11

Swann relates her island adventure

OH MY GOD. Am I pleased to get off that boat! Bumping along on the waves, I was feeling horribly seasick, which is something my parents regard as a weakness. Why, I can't imagine? Many people suffer when pounded in a wild ride but you should know by now that my parents are not typical. They're weird misfits in any world.

After Pa leaves me on the island I immediately feel better. I'm pleased Kludo is with me since wandering around on my own isn't much fun. West Caicos may not be inhabited so I do feel rather marooned. Pa says it won't be for long and I must trust him. Girls, as Mary often tells me, must learn to stand on their own feet.

Clearly Mary learned how to do just that but I know so little about her life before she joined our family. She was born somewhere in northern Europe and was thrown out of school for disruptive behaviour even though she was a champion athlete. That's when Ma first met Mary. They both loved martial arts and I too have learned basic self defence for life on the streets of Rio de Janeiro, so I'm not nervous as I set off to explore the island. Kludo trots on ahead in the hot morning air, stopping to sniff at scrubby bushes and rocks along the way. He's happy to be off the boat and running free. Occasionally he stops to lick the paw where he was bitten. Luckily it didn't suffer much damage, even though it made an odd start to our holiday.

Holiday? Well, this isn't what most people would describe as a vacation. Just because we're staying in an exclusive resort doesn't mean we're goofing around all day because I know we're up to something, though I haven't a clue what it is. My parents and the crew say very little about any plans until after the event. This, as Ma often tells me, is the best way to protect me from authorities who might come visiting with questions galore or from members of the public who can be hostile to my parents' unconventional habits.

I mean, who do you know whose father sleeps with two women on a full time basis? It's a private matter, they've told me and I've learned to accept it as such. It's easier that way. Maybe that's why I'm not so easily spooked when I'm marooned on my own. I can look after myself and others can do as they must.

Now I stop as the path opens up to show a long stretch of concrete, some kind of airstrip. But it's certainly not operational, as Helms would say, because large concrete blocks have been dumped across the midway point on the runway.

I take a few shots with my iPhone before following Kludo onto the concrete. The surface is too hot for his paws so he hops quickly onto the sandy border and we walk several hundred metres to reach the first block. It's about the same height as me and there's a metal ring on its top. It must have been dropped there with a hoist.

That's what Ma has taught me, to use my eyes to see what others may miss. In Nature she says those animals and birds who develop such skills are the best survivors. I'm sure Ma's right and I want to be a survivor. Do I have a choice, living with my family?

I continue exploring and head on towards a long stretch of water nearby. According to my guidebook it's Lake Catherine. Odd to find a land-locked lagoon here with pink objects on the surface and as we approach Kludo races ahead barking and the pink objects get airborne. Flamingoes! Wow, that's so cool. I wasn't expecting that.

Calling Kludo to my side, I turn back into the scrub. I don't want to lose him here as I walk towards Yankee Town which is also not what I was expecting. The stone huts have collapsed into ruins since they were occupied by sisal farmers. I've no idea what sisal is, or why they needed a narrow-gauge railway to transport it to the beach to be loaded onto ships. Who cares where they took it? I don't.

While I'm poking around in the ruins of Yankee Town I'm suddenly surprised to see an old black man. He's sitting on a flat rock near the rusting remains of a steam engine. It's quite a shock but strangely Kludo doesn't seem to notice him, even when the old feller smiles at me. Pa has always warned me to be wary of strangers, but this man has a friendly twinkle when he beckons me with his finger. He looks safe enough so I walk over and sit down on a rock. He's wearing a straw hat, an old cotton vest and a faded sarong. Then it occurs to me that slaves used to wear clothes like that. Kludo continues nosing around taking no notice of the black guy meaning he's safe enough. When Kludo smells danger, he's always right.

'Do you live here all the time?' I ask. 'Or are you here just for the day, like me?'

He nods with a sweet and gentle smile, but says not a word. He just waves his fingers this way and that, like he was pleating an invisible rope. Perhaps it's how they bound the sisal?

Now I wish I had my tablet because it takes such clear pictures so I pull my iPhone from my bag and show it to the old man.

'Do you mind?' I ask. 'So I can show my Ma later.'

He smiles again and swings his foot to and fro, using his hand to rub his ankle where the skin looks red and raw. Then I wonder if he might be dumb. Or perhaps he's from Haiti which Mary says lies over the southern horizon? Many illegal immigrants come from there, she reckons. Maybe this elderly gentleman is one of them?

I take several pictures of him and then a few shots of the old steam engine which has been rusting here for over a hundred years. It has the manufacturer's plate on the side, *Fenton, Murray and Jackson of Leeds*. I take a close up. Helms will like this as he's crazy about machines. But when I turn back to the old man, I have another surprise. He's gone! Just like that! Without a sound.

'Well, that's fucking weird,' I tell Kludo. 'Where did he go? You'll have to excuse my language because it's all I hear from Pa, Ma and Mary. I often had trouble at school for using foul language and that was before I was expelled for fighting boys in the school yard. I never fought with girls. Only the boys. When I was insulted by the son of the headmistress, I socked him in the eye and was expelled that same day. Ma and Pa weren't too pleased but Mary felt I did the right thing.

Anyway, my watch tells me I've been on the island for ninety minutes meaning Pa will be back shortly. Kludo and I head back to the coast and I must find the same beach where we shall sit and wait. I wonder if they got lucky with their fishing?

But when I reach the beach there's a surprise. In the shallows where my father left me, is a white boat. The painted letters along its hull spell it out. *POLICE. TCI GOVERNMENT.* Seeing me come from the scrub with Kludo, one of the two policemen on board waves. Then he jumps into the water and wades ashore as Kludo starts to growl.

'Hello Missy. What you be doin' here today?'

'Visiting Yankee Town while my father goes fishing.' I tell him the truth and he nods.

'So your father just dumps you here for the day?'

'My idea. I don't like rough water. Nor does the dog.'

'Okay, Missy. We get plenty of illegals here. Our job is to watch out for them and to guard our flamingos. Your dog was alarming the birds so we noticed. Don't let that happen again, Missy, or there'll be a fine for you and your father.'

I blink with a smile. 'I'm real sorry.'

'And you should be. Them birds don't like disturbance.'

I can now see Pa's boat coming down the coast. Its bow-wave thrusts the blue seas aside before they merge with the white scar of its wake. I can see Pa stand up as Javel approaches the shore. The policeman fingers his belt and I can see he's armed.

'Is this your father?' the policeman asks.

I nod and keep smiling as Pa jumps into the shallows and wades ashore. Helms and Javel stay aboard, drinking beer while they can. Both look relaxed and even my father is smiling.

'Hello, officer,' Pa says. 'Thanks for looking after my girl. She's not so fond of fishing so I put her ashore to explore the island.'

'And let the dog chase flamingos? That's something we don't encourage, sir. I already warned her 'bout that.'

'Thanks for doing so,' says Pa, remaining extraordinarily cool.

'Where you folks staying?' The policeman enquires.

'At Rum Cay resort for a week's vacation,' says my father.

'Rum Cay? I knows it. Real fancy place… And do you have a licence to go fishing? That's a requirement for all our visitors.'

'Well, we didn't catch any fish. Do I need a licence for failure?'

The policeman laughs. 'Catch a fish or lose it, you still need a licence. I want to look in your boat, sir. Now.'

'Please do so,' says Pa. 'All your's.' Pa nods to Javel and seconds later the policeman climbs aboard to inspect the tiny cabin and stern deck. 'You been diving?' he asks when he spots the scuba tanks. 'We have big fines for taking coral here, ya know.'

'I can imagine.' Pa agrees. 'I'm big on eco stuff, I assure you, officer. Wouldn't dream of taking a single twig.'

The police officer appears to be satisfied when he turns to my Pa. 'Also we don't approve of folk who abandon young women on these islands, but seein' as she came to no harm, we can forget that. I want you to bring ID papers to the police headquarters tomorrow. It's near the airport so be there at ten or we'll come looking for you at Rum Cay. Is that clear, sir?'

'Yes, officer, of course.'

Pa remains relaxed. 'We'll be there.'

The policeman has a closer look at Helms. 'Bring him too.'

'Very good. Is that all, officer?'

'That's it,' the officer says. 'See you tomorrow.'

Minutes later, the police boat lifts off to speed away down the coastline. We watch it until silence returns.

'Madre de Dios!' Pa snaps. 'This is no place to linger. Let's get home for something to drink and before I fucking lose my nerve!'

12

John Rackham reviews the situation

BACK AT BASE, I head straight for the shower. Just a quick one, because the day's work is not yet done. When I return to the living room my daughter and Mary are sitting together on a sofa. Annie is still at our other villa having a chat with Helms and Chad.

Mary starts with a question. 'So the cops nabbed Swann for disturbing flamingos? That's a new one.'

'She did well, real well. But the bastards who sold us the kit forgot to use a new rope. I hope that's all they forgot.'

'We'll soon find out,' says Mary. 'Swann says she found an airstrip there. That might be useful?'

'Yeah. Helms mentioned it too, but it has concrete blockers on the runway. To stop smugglers, I guess.'

Swann holds up her iPhone. 'Take a look Pa.'

I take a good look. Just as she says, there are five large obstacles to prevent unauthorised landings. 'See the hooks on top? Means that someone must have dropped them there.'

Mary chews her lip, thinking aloud. 'Maybe they left a digger at the abandoned development on the east side?'

'Good thinking, M,' I reply. 'Javel can make enquiries.'

Javel, our scout for this operation, has been on the island for several months and, thanks to his ethnicity, now knows many of the brothers. I gave him enough cash to buy a house in Jamaica and my generosity wins credit aplenty with Javel. He owes me big time is another way of putting it.

If you're wondering how I find the funds for all this enterprise, I reckon you're entitled to know. Simply put, I invest in high risk operations and by surviving for another round with Lady Luck.

'I also met an old black guy,' Swann pipes up. 'I found him in the ruins of Yankee Town.'

Mary frowns. 'What? That island's supposed to be uninhabited. No shops. No churches. Nothing. What was he doing there?'

'I don't know,' Swann replies. 'The policeman said they watch out for illegals coming up from the south. Maybe he was one of them.' Swann scrolls her iPhone but her face freezes. 'Oh! I don't get it. I took a photo of him but he's not in it. That is super weird.'

Mary is very fond of Swann and never had a child of her own. She puts a hand around Swann's shoulder. 'Let me see.' She frowns again and passes the iPhone to me.

'There's nothing to see,' I agree. 'Just an old rock with a lump of iron in the background.'

'That's a steam engine, Pa,' says Swann. 'But he was there, I promise.'

I scroll forward to see a second image which features more of the rusting steam locomotive. 'Well, I guess he slipped out of frame. I'll ask Chad to take a look.'

Mary is scowling now. 'Hasn't Chad got enough to do? There are scores of old black guys around if all you want is a photo.'

But Swann remains upset, confusion etched all over her face.

'Listen, Swannie,' I say. 'You gotta shape up. We're here for serious business that you know nothing about. Absolutely nothing. Just remember. It's very important. Meantime, I'm sick of your assin' around with these gadgets, 'specially when they don't function correctly. So please, no more nonsense, do you hear me?'

'It's not her fault,' Mary points out.

'I took a picture of him.' Swann continues. 'He was in a sarong and a straw hat. And he was scratching his ankle which looked very sore to me.'

'At least your memory's working.' I leave Swann on the sofa staring at her damned iPhone. 'Fancy a rum punch, Mary?'

Mary shakes her head and crosses those fabulous legs of hers. 'We have work to do.'

'And I've been dodging hammerheads longer than that sofa, so I need one.' Then my Annie arrives while I'm mixing my drink. I see that she's holding Swann's tablet. 'Everything okay?' I ask.

'Sure. They're both fine. Helms is going to take a nap and Chad has sent the tablet back. He checked it over and swears there's nothing wrong with it.'

Annie hands the tablet to Swann who brightens now she has her gadget again. God knows when I was a boy in South Carolina, we never had toys like tablets to amuse us. We had bikes, basketball and sports. Only when I was drafted into the marine corps was I exposed to computers and dangerous weapons. Now of course I couldn't operate without them.

'So that's all settled. Everyone's happy,' I declare. 'Swann, please feed Kludo. Then leave him here and go over to the hotel restaurant. Reserve a table for four and we'll join you in half an hour. Is that clear?'

Swann nods as Mary rises from the sofa. I down my drink before walking to the main door. 'Let's go admire the beach, ladies.'

Soon the three of us are heading down to our beach. I have some basic tools with us and, as I've already explained, this secluded bay is supposedly private, a bonus feature of our exclusive deal in this absurdly expensive resort. We kick off our footwear when we reach the beach. Underfoot the sand is soft and warm after the day's sunlight. A flock of wading sand-pipers scurry along the shore, dodging the wavelets while further out a pelican flaps to its roost as the sun stoops towards a sharp horizon. I'm fairly confident no one can observe us because the surrounding shrubs are impenetrable.

Javel put us ashore here when we returned from that challenging parley with the local police. That was a close one! After sending Swann and her flamingo-chasing hound to the villa, I helped Helms to conceal the four tanks that I rescued from the seafloor. We hid them behind a thick hibiscus bush and now, one hour later, I push the flowering branches aside to find the tanks are still there. Annie will keep guard as we start scooping out a trench in the sand.

After making a decent sized hole, Mary and I get to work on the tanks. Using an adjustable wrench I unscrew the stainless steel regulator valve to release an internal locking bolt. Then, after a sharp tap from the wrench, each tank splits in half to reveal water-proofed packages inside.

Mary opens one package with a kitchen knife while I work on the three remaining tanks. We paid a small fortune for this delivery arranged by those unsavoury gentlemen Mekissu and Tamos we met in the Conch Bar. They specialise in offshore deliveries of most blacklisted goods and after

Mary has checked the contents, it seems they have fulfilled our expectations. Airports these days are risky places for moving contraband. X-ray machines and the nostrils of sniffer dogs are far too effective, so we opt for this bypass service.

The rays from the setting sun sink across the bay as we bury the weapons, ammunition and miscellaneous materials in the sand. Annie, who normally hates housework, takes special care to drop discarded grapefruit and orange skins on our kit as she fills the hole with sand, sweeping and brushing it flat. Skins, I hear you ask? The smell of citrus is one that most canines, including foraging beach dogs, tend to dislike. Like their airport cousins their nostrils are equally sensitive and we don't want any old hound digging up these particular goods, do we now?

13

Agent Bradley of the FBI meets the Royal Navy

DURING THE AFTERNOON Bradley heard from his handler in Miami that FBI interest in the case had evaporated. If the visitors had dropped in to promote a concert, then it was of no further concern to the federal agency.

Bradley felt disappointed after experiencing some professional excitement caused by the original directive. Life in the Turks was often repetitive and the prospect of a fresh hunt had been invigorating. Nevertheless he'd still be a concertgoer whenever the event occurred even though the details remained sketchy.

While driving around the island that morning, Bradley had noticed a dark silhouette far out to sea. Now as he returned along the Leeward Highway he glanced again in the same direction. The silhouette had enlarged considerably and bore the indisputable profile of a warship. Since it was in the territorial waters of the Turks and Caicos, he assumed it was most likely to be British.

Bradley knew that the Royal Navy assigned ships to duties in the West Indies whose waters they had patrolled for many years, in fact for centuries. At regular intervals these warships would visit the Turks and Caicos, anchoring offshore so that officers could pay their respects to the Governor and administrators. For the locals it was like having a visit from a school inspector.

Though US Naval Intelligence was fully informed of all warship movements around the Caribbean, Bradley felt he might make enquiries about the warship's presence. On occasion, a member of the Royal family or an Admiral could be involved with such visits. It was all standard practice, Bradley told himself, as he stopped and brought his binoculars to bear on the new arrival.

The warship had dropped anchor beyond the cut in the reef that led to Grace Bay. It made an impressive sight, with the grey flanks of its dark hull reflecting the rays of the falling sun. Lights and flags twinkled on a superstructure with multiple radar and communication units. A 30mm cannon stood poised for action on the foredeck and on its broad stern a powerful helicopter stood ready to sting like a huge wasp. He noted smaller launches transiting from the warship through the cut to a debarkation point at Turtle Cove. These local boats would be ferrying naval ratings ashore and taking fresh supplies back on the return journey. Naval crew implied that any bar in the vicinity of Turtle Bay would be doing great business.

After parking near a popular bar called Tommy's, Bradley changed into a clean shirt before sauntering along the sidewalk to the bar. As he anticipated, noisy British sailors were celebrating shore leave in the traditional manner and Bradley soon befriended three young ratings who welcomed his offer to buy them a round. 'You guys must be thirsty,' he said as he placed the order.

'Thanks mate.' A young sailor seized the beer to gaze lovingly at its frothing head while Bradley passed around the glasses. 'A sight for sore eyes.'

'Don't stare at it. Just pour it down your throat,' advised another.

The warm evening and lively conversation soon helped the rounds go down again, and again. Bradley knew how the Royal Navy issued the strictest orders that operational information should never be divulged on shore leave, so he did not foresee info of substance. The Brits were allies with Washington. The relationship was long standing and supposedly special having endured two world wars and many joint military ventures. Bradley was not fishing for information in that sense, but as the beer sank into the British Jack tars, he casually enquired how long the warship was likely to be visiting Providenciales?

'Just a day or so, but what do I know,' replied one rating. 'We just follow Captain Barnet's orders. You know, mate, what life's like on a warship. Rum, buggery and the lash!'

'Surely not.' Bradley recoiled. 'No more cat-o-nine tails?'

'No, no.' The young rating licked froth from his lips. 'These days punishment is less harsh, but we still patrol for the same reasons, maintaining peace, cleaning scum from the high seas and if a hurricane pops up we ferry the Governor to safety.'

'Sounds a great life to me,' said Bradley as he downed his beer. 'Now it's your shout at the bar.'

14

Annie reports how the damned tablet plays up again

WHAT MY FAMILY loves about Rum Cay Resort is the restaurant whose wide outdoor terrace overlooks an infinity pool focused on the ocean beyond, offering turquoise horizons near and far. The teak tables are arranged to provide discretion and we can talk without being overheard. Mind you, I never discuss business if there's any chance of being overheard by nosy types. The table staff, mostly Filipinos, have all the tact required by clients on the luxury circuit, and there are plenty of them here tonight.

To be truthful, we're feeling mightily relieved. Importing illegal arms is stressful, but now these are buried, we can relax for a few hours. Surely that's the whole idea in these islands, isn't it?

Swann found us a good table and she's tucking into crispy fried prawns when we arrive. Naturally she has the company of her tablet which I promptly remove and put in my bag since I'm one of those mothers who hates digital entertainment while dining.

After viewing the menu, we all order Shambhala salads, selecting one that appeals to Mary. She supports wellness and her choice of salad is called Stress Reliever. After that we'll each have a lobster as the islands have plentiful stocks of these succulent crustaceans. Divers go down on lung power to pluck them from the ocean floor so that folk like us on leisure power can enjoy them in Rum Cay. Strange world, isn't it?

We're interrupted by Walter Schulz who suddenly shows up at our table. Our concert organiser is keen to talk, maybe hoping to join us. I pretend that I'm really interested. 'Hi Walter. What is it?'

Walter places a brown paper parcel on the table. 'I've just come from the Fedex office. Here are the tickets you ordered.'

My husband JR is lapping up his third rum punch of the evening. He puts down his tumbler and uses a restaurant knife to prise open the package revealing a block of jazzy tickets with that fresh off-the-press smell. 'They're good. Just what we needed,' he says, nodding to Walter. 'Thanks for all that. I hear rehearsals went well this morning.'

'Ace. The girls danced as natural performers.' Walter Schulz leers at Mary and then me. 'Just like you both.'

'No need to flatter my ladies, Mr. Schulz,' says JR. 'It might make them big headed.'

Walter ignores JR's advice and presses on. 'There's one thing that's puzzling me.'

'And what's that?' I ask before JR has the chance. 'I bet you want to know who's headlining the show?'

Walter looks at me with trepidation, no doubt remembering how I dealt with Ceejay. 'Yeah. It generally helps if the show's organiser knows who's who in the line-up.'

'I get that, Walter. You're right about that.'

'So?' Walter pauses. 'Then, who's the star?'

'Tomorrow I'll know,' says JR. 'And you'll be the first to hear.'

Walter remains mystified, continuing to hover around our table. 'Are you saying you don't know if the artiste is coming, or not? Rather late for that, don't you think?'

'Listen, Mr. Schulz,' says JR in his firmest tone. 'At this hour of the evening, I don't think. I only want to eat and drink. Tomorrow I'll open up my brain and see what happens. You get paid either way. Is that okay?'

Walter does not understand. But he's smart enough to know he's not invited to join us, so he leaves. Just in time. The first course, the Stress Reliever, has arrived at our table.

One hour later and we're all feeling so much better. Delicious Shambhala, super lobbies, served cold with real mayonnaise and two bottles of chilled Chablis. I'm not objecting, I must admit.

On the other hand my daughter Swann is complaining. 'Listen Ma,' she says. 'I'm feeling real tired.'

'Of course you are, honey.' Swann is sitting beside me so I give her a hug. 'You've been wandering around that island all day. Why don't you run along and go to bed?'

'I'm sorry about the flamingoes, Pa.' Swann says to JR as she gets up pushing back her chair. 'Real sorry.'

'Forget it, Swann. These things happen,' says JR.

Swann goes to Mary and kisses her cheek. Mary smiles and picks up her wine glass. 'Sleep well, luv.'

My daughter comes around the table. 'See you tomorrow, Ma.'

I also get a kiss and then my young girl has gone, moving through the restaurant with the grace of a young cygnet. For a moment, I want to call off this whole venture for the sake of my sweet daughter, however we've spent months planning this operation and we can't go back. We've never done so. We're a committed team, glued by the adrenaline of action and possible gain and we're also glued together by our love for one another.

Mary is reading my mind. 'Can we do this to Swann?'

JR also has a view. 'We have to. No choice, is there? It depends if our man comes to the bait. Chad will know for sure tomorrow. So how about a night cap before we follow Swann?'

During our meal a full moon has been rising to spread a shimmering path across the dark ocean. Meanwhile our waiter is hovering to take our order.

I lead the orders. 'I'll have a Grand Marnier, please.'

Mary wants limoncello and JR orders another rum. When I reach for my shoulder bag, I find Swann's tablet is lodged where I left it. Now I put the tablet on the table beside my wine glass as I rummage for the insect repellant. In the subtle lighting on the terrace, I see swarms of eager insects hovering in the tropical air but then as I reach for my drink the tablet lights up. Mary's eyes pop open and even JR recoils visibly.

'What the hell is that?' JR asks. 'Chad assured me it's clean of any virus.'

'I swear to God I didn't touch it.' I say as I take a look.

The tablet screen is active and inexplicably it returns to the monochromatic story we witnessed yesterday. Now the location is a beach where the pirate captain is inspecting slaves taken from the hijacked ship. The slaves squat on the sand while the pirates roam between them and then to my surprise I hear a crackle as some sound filters through. I press the tablet's volume controls and a sputtering sound becomes audible.

'We must be assured of your allegiance. Or ye can join the skipper and play with the sharks. Ye may choose.'

'What's with the fucking *Ye*.' JR asks. He's not remotely amused by this latest aberration in our daughter's tablet. On top of that, he's had four strong rum punches and a bottle of wine.

Again I note the on-screen character bears a strong similarity to JR but seconds later I can hardly believe my eyes. The scene focuses on the group of seamen seated on the sand. I assume these must be the sailors from the captured vessel. One of them seems very nervous and suddenly jumps up to sprint into the scrub behind the beach. A pirate goes in pursuit and sequences follow the chase along the shoreline vegetation until the fugitive trips and falls. This allows the pirate to close the gap and leap on the unfortunate escapee. Drawing a dagger he threatens the victim by seizing and ripping open his shirt to reveal that the prisoner is a woman.

'Jesus!' says JR. 'What the hell is this? Chad checked this tablet and now it's gone fucking crazy. How can I trust him with our real business, that's what I'm wondering?'

'Watch your tongue,' Mary warns. 'We're in a family restaurant.'

So I add my own thoughts. 'Mary's right. We must talk to Chad tomorrow. I don't want Swann seeing this.'

However JR is not listening. His attention is riveted to the tablet's screen where the pirate smiles while fondling the captive's breasts. Then to our surprise the pirate raises a finger to touch both their lips. A vow of silence must be shared as the pirate removes a binding wrap to show that he too has breasts. The video fades as the scene suggests a rape or an act of a vivid consensual nature is about to occur.

'Two women!' JR hisses. 'This is very, very close to home.'

Mary grips my arm but, unlike my husband, she's smiling. 'And it describes how we felt about each other. I can never forget how you first took me.'

'And nor will I.' I place my hand on her's. 'It was, and will always remain, an electric memory.'

'Now, now girls,' says JR. His dark eyes flicker, wicked as ever, as he finishes his drink. 'We're in a family restaurant, so cool it!'

'Cool it? No, no. Not a chance,' grins Mary. 'Let's get back to our place. We're on heat right now. And when that kicks in, you know what we want!'

15

John Rackham makes a visit to the police

HELMS IS DRIVING our rented SUV and my head feels as if someone has twisted barbed wire around my temples. I'm not sure how much sleep I had. Maybe none at all. My two girls have sucked the last joule from my aching frame.

'A tough night, boss?' Helms shoots a questioning glance at me. 'Looks like you've done twelve rounds with Tyson.'

'Thanks, buddy. Feels more like twenty and that's all I'll say. How about you and Chad?' I finally ask, showing some concern for my crewmen. 'Got all you need in that villa?'

'I could use a Sheila – if you have a spare one.'

'Fuck off, Helms.' I try to laugh because he's jealous that I happen to have two on my hands.

'So what's the form boss? What do we tell the police?'

'Hell, I don't know. I'll think of something.'

'We were lucky yesterday,' says Helms. 'Very lucky,'

'That's the name of our game, Helms. Luck's the key feature.'

We drive for ten minutes in silence, taking Blue Hills road to the airport where Google Maps leads us to Police HQ. It's a typical admin block, roof antennae and security cameras pointing all over. We park in the yard and I turn to Helms. 'How do I look?'

'I already told you,' says Helms as he steps from the car.

I follow, taking my briefcase in one hand, to stroll with false nonchalance into the jaws of the law.

To my surprise the interview is not searching. Notes are taken by the same officer who cautioned us yesterday. He's doing his job, I tell him, and I'm real sorry about the dog molesting flamingoes and for not having a fishing licence.

The officer, like many policemen in the West Indies, wears a white shirt and blue pants bearing a scarlet seam stripe. Plus he has mirror polished boots and a gun belt. He hears my apologies, photocopies our passports and then orders us to stay in the interview room while he locates the duty sergeant.

'How are we doing?' I whisper to Helms.

'Keep the faith, boss,' Helms mutters. 'And stop your hands shaking.'

I take a look. Helms is right. My hands are trembling but that's due to the alcohol I pumped on board last night. 'Yeah, okay.'

The patrolman returns with the duty sergeant. I'm hoping they won't turn this into a drama just because Kludo chases flamingoes.

'You gentlemen are staying at Rum Cay?' the sergeant enquires.

'Yep. For a ten day trip.' I reply, hoping the police don't need to antagonise tourists who support the island's economy. Patrons of Rum Cay are among the biggest spenders.

The sergeant returns our passports but then pulls a finger-print kit from his desk drawer. Now this isn't what I need. We weren't dabbed on our arrival, and to refuse him might be difficult.

'No problem, officer. But is this really necessary because of a dog chasing pink birds? Where I come from, that might constitute a serious breach of human rights. In my line of business we wouldn't dream of dabbing a dog handler.'

The sergeant pauses. 'May I ask the nature of your business, sir?'

Now here's a question for which I have no truthful answer. I could tell him to fuck himself, but I'm not that stupid. 'I'm in entertainment. Stars and concerts. Promotion you might say.'

'Word on the street says a big concert is coming up.' This tells me the sergeant is well informed. 'At the Fish Fry.' he adds.

'Yeah. That's all true. It's one of my promotions.' I radiate confidence as the sergeant pushes aside the dab kit. Quickly I open my briefcase holding the tickets provided by Walter Schulz at dinner last night. 'See here, officer. Free tickets for the show. I'm happy to offer you these, for you and all your fellow officers.'

'Well, sir, I'm not so sure.' The sergeant hesitates.

'Hell yes. I'm sure.' And this is my killer line. 'And when I tell you who's the big star, I'll bet you'd pay plenty dollar to see her.'

The sergeant and patrolman exchange glances. I may be gaining control of this interview so I wait until natural curiosity comes into play. A big star on their patch? And cops are supposed to excel in the intelligence business? Yes, of course, they need to know.

'Who, sir, are yo' talkin' about?' the sergeant enquires.

'It's a little secret,' I reply. 'But I can whisper it in your ear.'

The sergeant, bless him, brings his ear into play and cups his hand around it. 'I's listening.'

I whisper the name and the ear nearly falls from his head. 'No! Man! She's huge! You mean she's coming here to Provo for to sing to our islanders?'

'Now you know why it's secret. We don't want to stir excitement too soon, do we? So, how many tickets do I give you? It's all for charity too. For the hurricane relief fund amongst others.'

I know that there are about 400 police officers in the islands, so I offer him a stack of tickets. 'These are free and we'll be starting the publicity shortly. Bring your wives and girl friends. It's going to be a great family show.'

Five minutes later, Helms and I are back in the SUV. I tell him to stop at the first bar we find. 'Hair of the dog, Helms. And fast.'

16

FBI Headquarters, Miami

IN MIAMI MISS Tanaka was juggling with indecision. Jenkins, her department chief, had told her to drop her investigation into the influence of criminal DNA and specifically in reference to Rackham and the thirteen ears. Spending funds on the case was regarded as unnecessary. Since thirteen was often thought to be an unlucky number why should she feel dismayed?

On the other hand Jenkins had indicated she might pursue the enquiry with her own resources and in her own time. That furthered the dilemma, her professional curiosity on one hand, a possible waste of her money on the other. So what should she do?

After some minutes, Miss Tanaka abandoned her problem. She checked her bank balance and then downloaded the timetable for flights to Providenciales. She could make a trip if she chose.

While her fingers hovered on the keyboard, she found the Wikipedia page in her bookmarks that reminded readers of Jack Rackham's two female consorts in 1700. Ann Bonney and Mary Read were both European women who met Rackham in the Bahamas. Having stolen a ship they vanished into the blue wilderness around the Turks and Caicos Islands where for years they dealt ruthlessly with unhelpful individuals and crews of passing ships. Not a pretty tale, concluded Miss Tanaka as she closed the file.

In addition she had still not compiled the report on Mr. John Rackham and his DNA. In her computer sat the data from the DNA lab, the initial analysis of the thirteenth ear on the necklace but why, she wondered, would anyone bid for the item at auction? Unless the buyer shared a similar interest to her own? But there again, she found no easy answer for this logical question.

Back on the keyboard, she pulled up the photos sent from the private jet terminal. The photographer had not delivered the best results. A tree, a person, some obstacle or even a shadow could often ruin what might have been a valuable shot. Paparazzi had an easier job. They could swagger around with their long lens kit hunting for a scoop to sell on the open market. FBI agents could not always adopt the same tactics. Or could they?

If a concert was the stated reason for Mr. Rackham's visit, then perhaps she might attend posing as a paparazzi? A Japanese photographer with an ID card around her neck bearing the name of a Japanese news organisation? Surely a perfect disguise?

Miss Tanaka took another look at the images of Rackham's party as they exited Immigration at Providenciales Airport. Though clearer than those taken when leaving their jet, the images had not registered significantly on the FBI's facial recognition database. The forensic experts had tried to find clues from the downloaded tablet but these mainly featured a shaggy black dog. No family pictures had been found in the tablet files and that Miss Tanaka decided was unusual. Teenage girls generally had an incessant desire for selfies and meaningless pictures of anything around them. Maybe this young woman had deliberately cleaned her tablet of all potential leads and links before landing at Providenciales? That suggested one of the teenager's parents had persuaded her to do so. In Miss Tanaka's opinion teenage girls rarely edited their photos, if at all. This was therefore unusual. Miss Tanaka felt she was grasping at straws. Anything odd, unexplained, out of the norm, or just plain weird, was meant to trigger disquiet in self-respecting agents and for Miss Tanaka such reactions really mattered.

The latest report indicated the Rackhams were in Providenciales to promote a pop concert. Nothing illegal in that. Nevertheless details of this so-called concert were non existent. This was unusual since promoters generally devised campaigns to drum up public awareness. So where was the campaign, she wondered?

Again on the keyboard Miss Tanaka's fingers soon found a Google page for Entertainment in the Turks. She was redirected to the local pages for such events and there across the headline was a name she immediately recognised. She read the announcement again and decided to contact Jenkins on the internal system with this new information regarding the Rackhams.

Jenkin's face showed up in the corner of her screen moments later. 'Yes,

Miss Tanaka? I'm listening.'

'You might like to know about this concert in Providenciales. Reportedly Saharanna, the American star, is headlining. Stars of her stature frequently attract a heap of potential customers for federal attention, you might agree?'

Jenkin's bland features did not register. 'Sarahanna?'

'Yes sir, a huge star on the reggae and soca circuit. Billing her would be a major deal for any concert.'

Jenkins blinked. 'Okay. That changes the assessment. I suggest you take the first flight to Providenciales where I'll notify our local man that you might need him. I'll send his contact details.'

Miss Tanaka smiled. Persistence had made her point. 'Thank you, sir. I'll let you know when I land.'

'And don't forget your DNA kit,' added Jenkins before he closed the screen. 'We can't forget the thirteen ears, can we?'

17

Mary reveals her background

WHILE JR AND Helms are at the police station, I'm staying here with Annie and Swann by the pool of our lovely villa. It's a good moment to tell you something about myself so here's a potted version for your enlightenment.

For the first ten years of my life, I lived in a conventional brick house in the suburbs of Utrecht, a pretty little town laced with canals in the Netherlands. Both my parents worked in local government administration until my mother died of monotony, or so I understood. Later I learned it was cancer that took her down, but my father had other ways of dealing with civic boredom. He began by coming into my bedroom at night and giving me lectures. Initially these talks were harmless enough but they became more explicit and intimate. My body was a tool, he explained, which could serve me well in so many ways. Being young and naive I believed him, even when he probed with his fingers between my thighs teaching me how to derive pleasure from the experience. My girl, use those assets wisely, he would say. They will take you far if you are clever.

Growing older, I became interested in competitive sports, especially in swimming. I was fast in the water and increasingly unbeatable in freestyle stroke and back crawl. One day in the municipal pool I was practicing lengths when a high diver landed on my back, putting me out of action for six months. During this period I took up pistol shooting and soon learned that I was a natural deadeye. When competing in Bulgaria I led the Nederland women's 9mm team to victory over the Bulgarian cham-pion who, though defeated, taught me how to shoot even better and how to expand the boundaries on my sexuality. She was a feisty woman who suffered from persistent genital arousal disorder. I became her eager partner, and soon I too had a nymphomaniacal appetite.

My father died when I was twenty and with little to keep me in Europe I flew to Curaçao, the Dutch colony in the Antilles. There I found employ-ment as a trainer in a sports centre. I met young men and women bursting with testosterone and attracted many new encounters for my hungry body. It was a reasonable job until I flew to Venezuela for a weekend in Caracas.

Here I ran into trouble on the first evening when a slick character hit on me in the hotel bar. Wearing a smart Italian suit he knew how to make a point as he praised my physique, my blonde hair and tight fitting black dress. In his opinion, I could make a fortune if I exploited my attributes in a professional capacity. High class prostitution was, he put it bluntly, the best way to buying my own home and securing my financial future. If I was interested, he would run me through his training programme and manage my introduction to major clients in South America.

So I quit teaching gymnastics and enrolled as one of his flock of lovelies offering *super-sex* as he called it. He took 50% of my earnings but I began making serious money, several thousand dollars a week by pleasuring both men and women who were wealthy enough to have anything they desired.

During this period I always carried a gun in my purse, Caracas being possibly the most dangerous city on Earth. I used to practice my shooting on public ranges and after discovering how often I encountered risk, I took courses in self defence. Karate and Tai Chi became my favourites and that's what I liked about Annie, my lovely, loyal Annie, when I discovered she too was also a highly-proficient martial artist and markswoman.

In fact we met in Rio, when I was working the fringes of a South American banking conference. One night some porky financier, pumped high on his own importance, summoned me to his penthouse suite in a fancy hotel. He snorted a bucketful of cocaine and chained me to the bed while he fulfilled his deviant fantasies. I had no means of defence while spread between the bed posts and he kept me like that for hours until eventually I had to pee. When I released on the bed sheets, he was so incensed that he punched and beat me before he unchained me. Telling me to gather the soiled linen before he summoned room service it gave me a chance and I took it. Don't ask me why, but I picked up a heavy bedside lamp and brought it down forcefully on his head. The bed linen became a pool of scarlet and I left him there with his tongue sticking out and his penis peering through the slit in his underpants.

I did not panic. I showered and put on my clothes before wiping everything I had handled in the room. Then, as I was doing my make-up, I noticed an attaché case lying under the bed. I took it along with his well stuffed wallet before using the fire escape to leave because I had noted the security cameras in the hotel lobby.

Once outside I strolled through the crowds to another hotel popular with other banking types and it was here I first met Annie and her husband, the handsome John Rackham. They were lolling in the lobby sofas like basking seals, and I remember Annie beckoning me over to ask if I had noticed the blood on my shoes?

'And how do you know it's blood?' I asked.

'Seen it often enough. Come and sit down. Have a drink.'

Our friendship began on that note. Within hours it had escalated to a bond of three, all like-minded souls bent on mischief. Five hours after killing a man and making my escape I was back in bed, sharing it with my two new friends. I remember thinking such behaviour was extreme even by my own standards, but Rio's a city where reckless behaviour is quite normal, almost fashionable.

Next morning, as we lay in bed watching TV, we learned the police were hunting for a blonde woman suspected of murdering a senior Columbian banker. So I was now a wanted woman. My new friends could have turned me in there and then. Instead they chose to protect me, whisking me out of Rio to safer territory up the coast. We drove all day and late in the evening we began wondering about the briefcase of the banker Fatso. Since we couldn't open its locks we prised it open with a tyre jack.

At first sight the contents were printed documents of no immediate significance. However my new friends were more knowledgeable than me and after close scrutiny John Rackham suggested I should take a strong drink. Then in so many words he told me that I had just taken possession of scrip, vouchers and bonds worth many millions of dollars. In addition, he said, there were details of transactions with many individuals and organisations in Columbia, Brazil and Venezuela. In short, this was a significant treasure and we agreed to share it in equal proportions.

For three years we successfully avoided detection while converting the banker's documents into hard cash. Few threats of complaint were made as much of the wealth had been won by dubious practice. Protest was a non-starter when so many government officials were themselves corrupt.

The problem with harvesting such wealth was that we always wanted more. Pleonexia, the Greek name for excessive greed, is a well known feature shared by millionaires, billionaires, corporations and national governments and don't forget churches. Inevitably they all demand more to strengthen their case.

Team Rackham, as we called ourselves, was not immune to the scourge of greed. With my partners' consent, I returned to the world of high-stakes prostitution, basing myself in Barranquilla, a busy city on the north coast of Columbia. We chose this location because, in the files of our treasure trove, we had discovered how a certain Dr. Felix Roblado played a significant role in laundering funds for the cartels and racketeers of South America.

I'll spare you the details of how I was invited to show off my charms to this individual. He spent most of his time on a super-yacht euphemistically called *Amazon Lady.* From the decks of his great floating home, Dr. Felix and his henchmen spied me sunbathing on the deck of a neighbouring yacht that we had chartered. With judicious use of my thong and body language it only took three days until one of the yacht's officers arrived with an invitation. Dr. Roblado would be so happy if I joined him for cocktails at six?

The victim, little Miss Mary, duly turned up wearing a simple white summer dress and white underwear. I asked for fruit juice and was given mango and orange. I smiled. I acted nervous. I told Dr. Felix Roblado that I was recovering after a messy divorce from a record producer in New York.

Dr. Felix with some of his officers and their women comprised something of a challenge, but I felt up to the task and, among other things, I discovered that Dr. Felix was a massive fan of the singer Sarahanna, a reggae rapper who was a chart giant in the USA. I had met her, I told Dr. Felix, while he guided me around his quarters on the luxurious yacht.

I knew how rich men and women love to show off their extravagances even while they feign modesty in doing so. What's the point of owning rare and expensive assets if you don't win the praise and acclaim of lesser mortals for the achievement?

As I toured his saloon and adjoining suites, I noticed his collection of paintings and rare artefacts. Wisely, I said nothing, not a word, apart from saying how I found them all so beautiful

Later JR told me that many of the world's stolen artworks often found their way to ocean going yachts. The reason for this was as simple as the flag on the vessel's stern. *The Amazon Lady* flew the flag of Liberia, a single white star on a blue square over a background of red and white horizontal stripes. In brief, the laws of Liberia prevented other authorities from boarding and inspecting.

Before I was escorted home by the yacht's first mate, I promised to return next day for lunch with Dr. Felix. Go softly to catch the monkey, JR advised later that evening as we discussed progress. With my sharp eye and memory we identified that Dr. Felix was safe-guarding highly-prized missing paintings, including several from Hitler's booty looted in the second world war. They might have been fakes and copies, but the size, style and security afforded by the *Amazon Lady* suggested this was unlikely. Once again, it seemed, we had stumbled on a treasure trove.

Next day little Miss Mary returned for lunch with Dr. Felix. This time there were no other guests and we sat in his saloon tasting his favourite cocktail, something he called The Stingray. I sipped away, enjoying a fruity flavour mixed with champagne and we listened to music by Sarahanna, a solid sound with a distinctive throbbing base track. Did I know if he could meet Sarahanna? That's all Dr. Felix wanted to talk about until the Rohypnol kicked in.

When I awoke I was still on board but I was naked, strapped face down on a bed in his personal suite. I knew I had been raped, and I could also feel intense pain on my right buttock. A smell of burning flesh flavoured the air. The bastard Roblado had planted a hot branding iron on my lovely backside.

I lost count of how many hours or days I was on board. The pain in my butt was eased by medication, but his bold effrontery was not so easily subdued. As soon as the opportunity arose, I escaped from the cabin by tossing two guards over my shoulder and then diving from the yacht straight into the murky waters of the Barranquilla wharf. I was, you'll remember, a highly competent swimmer and I soon made it back to safety without much effort.

So now you'll understand why, some fifteen months later, Team Rackham has laid plans for Dr. Felix and his *Amazon Lady*. These plans you may correctly assume are inspired by another human characteristic. It's called Revenge and it comes with a capital R!

18

Annie – Our Parasailing Venture

AFTER HIS RETURN from the police station, my husband JR was feeling unusually chipper. Not only had he defused the difficulties created by Swann and the dog, but he had also won the goodwill of the entire police force. He felt Sarahanna was guaranteed to attract most of the population including all the police to her show.

Our scheme therefore now hangs on two variables. First we have to assume that the *Amazon Lady,* with Dr. Felix aboard, will actually sail to the islands. Secondly, we have to believe Sarahanna will also arrive for her gig. We've made our plans on that basis so you'll be thinking there's plenty of scope for both individuals to divert to other priorities. We recognise those possibilities. It's like fishing for predators, just a question of spreading enough chum in the water.

Someone must remain at Rum Cay to guard our base since we're not welcoming uninvited guests. This morning JR will stay to monitor the CCTV systems installed by Chad around our quarters. I've asked the hotel to suspend room service so that my husband can rest. In fact, keeping watch will do JR no harm though I don't entirely trust him with the Filipino maids. I've noticed they're very willing to serve and most are very pretty.

The rest of us have driven to Turtle Cove, a local marina, where I've chartered a parasail boat with crew to entertain us. Helms has come along to help Chad with some experiments and Swann agreed to join us with Kludo, so long as we stay in calm water. Mary and I, both in bikinis, will go aloft together under the canopy.

The parasail tow boat is now cruising over shallow waters inside the reef. Here the sea floor is as clean as a new carpet. When the boat slows Mary and I slip into harness and transfer to a platform below the blooming parasail in the stern. I have brought with me a small camera and binoculars. Mary has a short-range radio for testing with Helms as he sits in the boat below. We stuff all this kit into a waterproof bag.

Once we are settled, the boat turns into the wind and we rise from the platform like angels into the sky. Some angels, you say, but it does feel as if we've grown wings to soar to 400 feet above the sea. Below our bare toes I see the towline reaching down to the tow boat as it pushes into the wind. We've been advised by Javel to watch out for the police launch which often returns from patrol about this time of day. Its officers like to get home for lunch.

'That must be it,' says Mary, pointing to a vessel beyond the reef where the sea shimmers in darkest blue.

I take a look with my binoculars, while familiarising myself with the local geography. From up here, we can see along the coast for miles. As our boat draws closer to the reef, the breeze carries us over the breaking surf. It's immensely spectacular to see the waves churning below our feet, but we're not here for sight-seeing in the true sense of the term. 'Yes,' I say. 'That's the police boat.'

I feel warmth in my ear. Mary is purring to me.' I want you, Annie,' she whispers. 'You mean everything. You know that.'

I turn to Mary, gripping her harness and pulling her body closer to mine. 'This is what you mean to me.'

I place my lips on hers and our tongues meet, silky, warm and altogether lascivious. The act needs no description. The lust and love we share rides like silver on the tips of our tongues. With my eyes shut, I do not see Chad's camera drone until I hear it, buzzing some ten feet in front of us.

Mary grabs her walkie-talkie radio. 'Chad, get that thing out of here!'

Down below Chad and Helms are laughing as the drone dips and soars away out over the swells of the Atlantic but we need the damned thing, so it's essential to test its efficiency. The men may be laughing because the drone intruded on our private moments of affection, but since we need their expertise to achieve our objectives we try to see some humour in it.

'Tell the driver to head for the police vessel,' says Mary into her radio. 'Let's test the suppression kit.'

'Roger,' Helms replies. 'It's all set to go.'

This piece of equipment is among our more sophisticated items. Chad imported it hidden in the electronic circuit boards of the loudspeakers. It is designed to suppress radio communications within a specific range and soon we'll see if it works.

'Try it on us, up here,' I suggest.

Seconds later the walkie-talkie crackles like hot bacon, effectively shutting off conversation. 'So how do we use our walkie-talkies if Chad is dousing the airwaves?' asks Mary.

'Chad will set our personal radios to a wave band outside the jammer.'

We ride on up the coast, watching the sea passing below as we approach the police launch. Mary keeps open the walkie-talkie channel while we pass near the police vessel.

We hear our boat driver calling to the police launch. 'Hey, there. You been outside the reef? Any humpies there today?'

He's referring to the humpback whales that migrate past the islands en route to their breeding grounds. The police vessel begins to reply but the exchange then dissolves in a crackle of suppression caused by the jammer in Chad's hands. Finally the static clears.

'...I's hearing you now,' says the police officer. 'Yeah, there's a few around off Leeward. A mother and calf for sure.'

'That's cool,' replies our boat driver. 'Thanks for that.'

I like the way these islanders can call up a police launch to enquire about the local whales. Makes a lot of sense. Whales are nicer than most people. At least that's what Swann tells me.

I can see my daughter sitting in the bow section of the tow boat. The rascal dog is peering over the gunwale as the waves flash past and I'm glad Swann is here with us. The thought of leaving her in South America gave all three of us the heebie-jeebies. We haven't decided on Swann's part in the action, but that's on our list once we've dealt with more immediate requirements.

'So tell me, Helms, did it work?' I ask.

'Yeh. Spitting very well. Great suppression. Over.'

'Turn around and let's get back to the marina,' I say to Helms. Chad is content with our three tests. Radio, drone and suppressors are all ready to do our bidding.

'Is your radio turned off?' I ask Mary. 'I've had an idea.'

Mary nods. 'Tell me.'

'You saw the police boat back there. It may be safer and easier to board than the *Amazon Lady*. What do you think?'

Mary bites her lip and considers the proposal. She's always quick with decisions. 'First the police boat? And then the *Amazon Lady*? Yes, I like that. It might work. In fact I like it a lot.'

'So that's all neat and dandy,' I say. 'Come here and give me another kiss before we drop down for landing.'

19

John Rackham makes time to recruit

WHILE MY GIRLS are out sight-seeing under their parasail I've been reviewing plans in the shade of our verandah. Before me on a glass-topped table are marine charts, lists of requirements, notes with multiple sketches and details. Few, I should add, have been photographed or digitised so hacking them is less likely.

Hacking is an enterprise of unauthorised nature says the dictionary. Yet over the years its devotees have infiltrated the CIA, the Pentagon, Wall Street banks and countless corporations. Hackers can find the backdoor in the most heavily protected systems. Think of it this way. If you design a castle to withstand attack, you can bet there'll be a weak point some-where. It could be a faulty hinge in the main gate, a hidden escape tunnel, a bribable guard, or simply bad foundations. Hackers are digital locksmiths. They find that weak point and in they go.

Our man Chad has done a fine job to date. Most superyachts, ships and aircraft can be traced by popping their names and registration details into the system and within seconds you'll know their exact position. If they turn off their transponders, accuracy becomes murky but via his computer Chad has already raided the *Amazon Lady,* infiltrating her navigation, satellite equipment and other systems so now we know exactly what the lady is doing night and day. Currently *Amazon Lady,* according to Chad, is sailing at ten knots on a northerly course, having departed Barranquilla in Columbia yesterday evening. She could arrive in these island waters within 48 hours.

Mary has already provided you with a description of her own role, revealing her personal vendetta with Dr Felix and we'll do our best to help her while also preparing to seize the yacht's prize possessions. Since Mary's recce on board the vessel some fifteen months ago, we have fully appraised his floating gallery. Due diligence is what bankers call it and it all leads to one conclusion.

No sane person would dream of raiding the *Amazon Lady*!

So it's just as well none of my crew are fully sane!

That realisation makes me reach for my best friend, Ron Zacapa Centenario, the smoothest of rums. After a few slugs of Zacapa, anyone can howl and reach for the stars.

But I guess you're wondering how we can be so sure that Dr. Felix will show up. His home may be riding on the high seas but it doesn't necessarily follow that he'll be aboard. He owns several fixed wing aircraft and keeps a helicopter on the stern of the yacht and these considerations are on my mind today. Luckily the rum kicks in and soon provides some answers.

On the glass table stands a monitor screen set up by Chad. The display is subdivided into four sections, each covering the routes to our villa and onto the beach where our kit is hidden. Chad fixed mini-cameras to various trees and these transmit direct to this monitor. Now in one quadrant, I see a figure approaching. It's my friend, the Rasta brother, Javel.

Javel comes onto the verandah, walking in the languid style of a Rasta, so cool and self-confident. We touch fists before he drops into a chair. He won't touch alcohol, but he's no stranger to ganja. As I top up my glass, he rolls a spliff and the herb smoke blends with the sweet scent of tropical plants around our home. Can you think of a nicer way of doing business?

For half an hour Javel passes opinion on the strategy and tactics we've been developing. He has his views on how the brothers should play their parts, an important element in the game plan.

Mary, Annie and Swann finally return from their parasailing. They head straight to the pool in their bikinis and dive in while Javel and I wind up our discussions. Javel learns that tests with Chad's technical kit all performed to order and when he's finished his spliff he unrolls from his seat, adjusts his mass of hair and returns to languid mode. 'Lata,' he says as he slides out of sight.

'See you, man.' I call after him as Annie comes dripping from the pool. She has the executive stride of a driven woman. Knows what she wants and comes straight over.

'Okay, JR, it's going to plan, and you best be heading off with Helms. When you get back Mary and I will have a new plan.'

My wife reminds me I have a date to keep so I tell Annie I'm looking forward to hearing her plan before I take one more whack from Zapaca's bottle of wisdom. Then I set off down the pathway to our hired car. Helms and Javel are there waiting and soon we're on our way, out through the Rum Cay's security gate and onto the public highway of Providenciales.

Helms drives us to an isolated region, out beyond the airport and the fishery sheds where fresh lobsters are brought and packed for export. Javel mentions that after a recent hurricane the lobster divers entered waters so clouded with sediment that the sharks, normally visible at a safe distance, suddenly appeared at their shoulders. This scared the divers witless so their labour was suspended until the sediment cleared. I call that sanity and now the water is clear the divers are back at work.

From such fishermen, Javel and Ceejay have recruited a spirited bunch of seafaring men for our inspection. There are ten in total and I'm told they have families in a shanty town near the airport. Knowing what life is like in shanty land, these volunteers should welcome the offer of a bonus for any extracurricular activities. They watch me cautiously as I wander over to them.

'Now guys,' I say, regarding each face in this gang with a brief but direct look. 'Pleased to meet you. Most of us make plans for our futures, but I want my moonbeam laced with plenty dollar. Are you guys on the same moonbeam as me?'

Heads bob up and down and seeing no detractors, I move to the first man in the line, looking him in the eye. 'What's your name? And what do you do?'

'I's Able.' The man stammers, pushing away a tape measure Javel is using to record his arm length. 'What's with the tape? What do I do, man? Hey, I's not saying.'

Able doesn't want us to record his measurements or to know about his trade. Can't say I blame him, but time's not on our side.

'The measurements are for clothing you may need. That's all I'll say, but, Mr. Able if you don't know what you do, then I have to assume you're good for nothing. Is that what you call an ability?'

Able looks upset. 'Hell, no. I do construction. I drive diggers.'

'Well that's perfect, Mr. Able. Can you fix 'em too?'

'Sure. I do that.'

'Even better. Javel here will take you to some diggers that may be operative. Fix a digger and you get a job. Easy as that.'

I go to the next man. He's a beefcake with no charm in his eyes. 'How 'bout you?' I ask. 'What's your game?'

'I'm Boxman. I do security at the casino.'

'That's perfect too. I like it.' I watch Javel with his tape. 'And I bet your pecker's a legend with your girl friends?'

My crude observation about Boxman's easily noticed undercarriage triggers a blast of laughter. These guys find humour in anything lewd and I laugh with them. It helps to break the ice with these hitherto suspicious characters.

Boxman grins. 'It's my secret weapon, man.'

'Ever heard of Sarahanna?' I ask him.

'Oh man! Sure.' Boxman grins. 'She be the black fox of reggae.'

'Well, I may ask you to guard her while she's here. Can you do that without using your secret weapon?'

'Unless she wants a viewing.' Another burst of laughter follows as I move to Ceejay, the big feller from Trinidad who was floored by Annie using her merciless karate. She has put me down once or twice, so I commiserate with Ceejay. 'And what's your game?'

Javel butts in with the answer. 'He be a tool specialist. My yard knows him for that.'

'Toolie meaning hit man? That could be handy.' I say. 'You the guy who goes with Jasmin?'

'She's my woman. That's so,' he confirms. 'My Jasmin.'

He's wearing a dirty T-shirt and shorts. Why such a lovely girl as Jasmin could fancy this sinful devil makes my skin curl. 'I don't use weapons for fun, man. It's ma business.'

I nod and move on to another recruit. He's a small feller, the only one not wearing shades but he's in a blue baseball hat. 'Hey, pal. So what's your name and game?'

He speaks in higher pitch. 'I be Le Sage. I do the philosophy.'

'Philosophy?' I wasn't expecting that. 'How does that help me?'

'I knows what people are thinking. That's what I do.'

I shall call his bluff. 'Okay, so try me.'

'You's thinking how de hell to get your show on de road with a bunch of black jacks like us?'

Goddammit. The man's correct. 'I guess it's because I'm offering five thousand bucks for each man if all goes to plan.'

'So how can we know for sure we get paid? You came in a private jet. Very easy to leave without paying.'

He's right again. I understand what he implies. 'Yeah man.'

Ceejay and Boxman add their opinions. 'True, man. True.'

'Then one amongst you must keep the money for all. Can I suggest this man Le Sage acts as your banker? Is that a fair deal?'

It should be evident I'm serious about this. Le Sage is clearly a lead player in this motley crowd so I must think fast. I repeat my offer. 'Surely that's a solid deal?'

Le Sage nods. 'I'm from Haiti and you met my mother at Conch Bar, so we know what is what.' He looks at his friends who seem to agree with him. 'I say we're all riding the same moonbeam. We'll t'ink on it, man.'

The other volunteers for my team create no problems. They seem less suspicious now that Le Sage and their deal with the money is sorted. They're the kind of characters you might find in the gentlemen's exercise yard at your local gaol, all of them likeable in no way whatsoever.

Armed with the measurements and a note of each man's skill we need to move the action forward. 'Don't tink on it too long, Le Sage. I'll be in that bar behind the lobster shed. Come and join me with an answer in ten minutes.'

20

Agent Bradley investigates

RUM CAY RETAINED its own staff to service all swimming pools and hot tubs within the complex. This created for agent Bradley a small problem. How could he gain entry using his regular subterfuge as a pool professional? The ruse was successful elsewhere but Rum Cay's security team were instructed to deter unauthorised tradesmen and non-residents since a high level of privacy was demanded by the guests.

Bradley was reviewing his options for surveillance on the Rackham family whose arrival had alerted Miami HQ. He had received no further instructions for two days while he kept an eye on the show ground activity. From his electrician colleague, he heard that Walter Schulz was in charge. Bradley ran a background check on Schulz, learning that the man ran a bonafide business with a clean record, but of the concert itself Bradley found few details. That he felt was rather odd.

Then this morning his cell phone beeped to broadcast an advertisement from Island News. A mega-event was imminent. Next weekend islanders would be welcome to non-stop reggae, soca and calypso at the Fish Fry leading to a finale of awesome excitement led by the world famous and award winning star Sarahanna!

Wow! Bradley re-read the text to make sure. Sarahanna was famous with hordes of fans across the Caribbean, the USA and the broader world. Known for raunchy gigs to the beat of heavy rock and reggae, Sarahanna could magnetise huge crowds simply by displaying her splendid figure. So why, Bradley asked himself, was this red hot star of the reggae circuit coming to Provo? It had to be a spontaneous engagement, avoiding the demands of the regular tour circuit and mega venues. Was there some other angle to it all?

Bradley was absorbed by these thoughts when a second text arrived, telling him to call base. Using WhatsApp encryption Bradley got through to Miami instantly only to be told what he already knew, that the superstar would be headlining. He was further advised that a fellow agent would also be coming to conduct ongoing research into DNA profiling. The agent had his contact details and would be in touch when she arrived.

She? This caught Bradley's attention as he finished the call. A female agent was on her way to join him? This was intriguing since Miami had never before sent him any assistants.

Bradley ambled to his coffee machine and poured a cup. Then he sat down to review all the news. The first job, he decided, was to tidy his home just in case this woman came to pay him a visit.

21

Mary has to pay our debts

I'VE BEEN THINKING about Swann's tablet and all the trouble it has caused with its errant behaviour. I've no idea about the technical aberrations but I've never seen JR pop his cool so much as when those videos showed up. In fact I too experienced inexplicable sensations when I saw that latest clip. Call it déjà vu, but I felt I was returning to events I had experienced. Totally creepy. Especially at this stage of our operation which in other respects is going to plan.

I've just left Annie and Swann in our villa while I stroll down the path to our other villa, the office as we now call it. Inside I find Helms spread across the sofa holding a beer while he toggles the TV remote to get the weather forecast. On his lap are flight manuals for the helicopter Dr. Felix keeps on the stern of the *Amazon Lady*.

'Doing your homework, Helms?'

Helms looks up. 'Yep. The data is useful when borrowing strange choppers. Give me a Black Hawk or Apache any day.'

'We can't always get what we want, can we?'

'You seem to.' Helms might be joking but I can't be sure. That's Helms for you, a mixed up sonofabitch whose head was scrambled by post-traumatic stress after battle action in Iraq and Afghanistan. I doubt if he expected to survive and when demobbed he was so surprised to be alive that it screwed up his Aussie brain. I felt much the same when I finally escaped from the *Amazon Lady* in the marina of Barranquilla.

'All I want is to fix Dr. Felix so he'll never slap hot iron on another butt. What's wrong with that?'

'Fair dinkum,' Helms pauses. 'Try stuffing his balls up his arse.'

'I'll do better. Let's drop him off at 1000 feet.'

'Easy now!' Rackham appears from the computer room. 'Enough of that, Mary. You'll get your chance once we've got our hands on the assets. First things first, and right now I want you and Helms to deliver some cash to Tamos and Mekissu.'

JR is referring to the money we've agreed to pay the suppliers of our illegal kit. To insure against them breaking their silence, we set a payment schedule, deposit, interim and final. JR passes me a thick envelope. 'Twenty five K,' he says. 'When you're done, come back home for dinner.'

Helms gets to his feet. 'Right'o, Boss. We'll pay the bastards.'

After taking the envelope I kiss JR on his bristly cheek. 'Please shave before dinner,' I tell him. 'I don't love stubble.'

JR nods. 'Yeah. I hear you.'

Helms and I make our way to the SUV. The security guards at the gate now recognise us. One of them steps out, hand held high, so I lower my window.

'Excuse me, ma'm,' he says. 'I heard it said that Sarahanna is flying in for a show? Is that true?'

'I hope so.' I give him a hot smile. 'And I'll get you a ticket.'

'Thank you ma'm,' the guard grins as we accelerate away.

Helms is feeling better now he's in action again. 'Easy to make friends with her name, isn't it?' he remarks. 'But what happens if Sarahanna is a no-show?'

'We lose money and she'll piss off her fans.'

'Mmm?' Helms wonders. 'And if Dr. Felix is a no-show?'

'He's already on his way says Chad. But if he fails to surface, I'll hunt him down.'

'And I'm happy to help with that.' Helms does his kookaburra laugh. 'Anyway, I'm betting they'll both show up.'

It takes us fifteen minutes to reach the Conch Bar while I'm thinking just how much I want to get even with Dr. Felix. It's not for my sense of revenge, because I failed to mention how Dr. Felix showed me photos of other victims. 'Mis potras especiales.' That's what he calls us. In English it means 'my special fillies'.

My guess is that Felix branded each and every filly on their buttocks just like a horse rancher. He enjoyed planting the hot iron while I lay strapped face down on the bed. He laughed hysterically while I screamed.

I haven't told you this but after recovering from the assault on my backside, JR persuaded Chad and Annie to make discreet enquiries and they succeeded in locating nine other girls who had been forcibly enlisted into the brand of *Amazon Lady.* So, whatever retribution I choose for Dr. Felix, I'll be doing it on behalf o these nine victims as well.

At the Conch Bar, we slip into the routine. Back at the bench table, we sit down and order. A beer for Helms and a fruit punch for me. We'll have some conch fritters to keep Helms happy.

Ten minutes pass before the slime balls arrive. They wander in with the charisma of hip-hop hyenas. I don't want to be seen talking to them so I wrap the envelope in a beach towel and ask Helms to take it over.

'No worries.' Helms ambles over and puts the towel down on their table. It's strange to recall he was a special forces delivery boy dropping hardcore ordinance on the Taliban. He asks them a few questions and then returns to my table.

'Good job, Helms. What did you say?'

'I quizzed them 'bout the weather. Any hurricanes around?'

'And?'

'Guy in the suit said the Lord giveth and taketh away.'

'JR thinks Tamos is a church minister in his spare time, so you can claim your salvation from him. I'm going to the rest room. Back in a few minutes.'

Actually I want to pay someone a visit. I'll give you one guess who's in my sights? Yep. It's that sweet woman on the souvenir stall. I saw her there on the way in, sitting behind the counter and pretending not to notice me, even though it was only a few days ago when we met. Believe me, women from Haiti have the vision of fish hawks. When three high rollers, a teenage girl and a growling hound come by to claim a lost tablet, you'd think she'd remember.

'Perhaps you can recall we paid you two hundred dollars?' I begin, noting the woman continues to show no sign of recognition. She's working her embroidery with busy hands. Her nails are long and curved, painted in rainbow hues and the Haitian doll still sits on the shelf stuffed full of pins. 'We paid you two hundred bucks.'

'Mebbe so,' the vendor finally admits. 'Mebbe.'

Her eyes flicker and she shrugs indifferently. But I never take No for answer. 'Maybe is not good enough. I want to know if you did anything to the tablet to make it unusual?'

'I dunno. These t'ings mean nothing to me. I just give it to you.'

'And yet you have the power?' I say quietly. 'From the *loa*.'

This comment stops her weaving fingers. Her features harden and the tungsten in her eyes comes into play. 'You spik of *loa*? T'is nothing to me.'

I know this Haitian vendor is lying so I produce a hundred dollar bill from my purse which she snatches it in a flash.

'The *loa* is not in my puissance. I cannot tell the *loa* what to do.'

'But voodoo can. So you help me. Okay? The young girl has seen many nasty stories. I'm asking you to beg the puissance to stop.'

'Ain't so easy,' She stares at me, a dark and dangerous spirit from another realm. 'But you, Missy, you have seen them too.'

'You asking or telling?'

'The *loa* will know what you know and the *loa* knows what to do. Dat's all I's saying.'

That seems to be her last word on the matter so I'm forced to return to the restaurant where I find Helms staring at an empty glass. The two hyenas have departed and I've done my business.

'Shall we go?' I suggest. 'I had a word with the Haitian lady from hell. Can't do more than that for young Swann so can we go, please?'

'You asking or telling?' Isn't it odd that Helms uses the same phrase as he gets to his feet. 'Either way, I'm ready for tucker. I could eat a whale.'

22

FBI agent Tanaka leaves Miami

THE DAY BEGAN early for Harumi Tanaka. Leaving her apartment in Pembroke Pines, she drove to the mall where she bought lotion, moisturiser, two pairs of jazzy sun glasses with other essentials for her visit to the Caribbean. As she paid, she felt a stirring excitement, a sense that her pace of life was changing. Instead of the daily commute to her office she'd soon be in the Turks and Caicos.

But was this hunt for the DNA of John Rackham a misguided notion? Would this fanciful pursuit lead to an outcome similar to the movie *The Minority Repor*t? A failure might be absorbed by taxpayers but a success might open new chapters in her career.

Running such thoughts through her mind Harumi returned to her apartment to finish packing. Her beach wear included swimwear, a floppy sun hat and flip-flops. On the flight she'd be wearing trainers, a cotton shirt, jeans and a Patagonia fleece. A copy of *Giza* magazine and a Japanese paperback would travel with her iPhone in a satchel bag. A pair of lightweight aluminium crutches were often helpful in attracting kindness from strangers so she added these to her kit while she considered her Glock 23 pistol and the DNA kit. The weapon could not be legally carried in the Turks unless local police approved, which was unlikely. She would leave it with the FBI armourer but the transport of liquids, swabs and sample containers might create difficulties at airport security. Doubtless the FBI's surveillance specialists would offer advice.

Towing her suitcase, she locked the door to her apartment and drove to the glass fortress of the FBI headquarters. Here an expert provided a skeleton DNA kit which, in his opinion, would generally pass through airport security with no problem. Miss Tanaka then went up to the fourth floor where her computer showed two overnight messages, the airline confirmation and an instruction to call Director Jenkins. This she did immediately, fearing a change of plan. But this was not the case.

Instead Jenkins urged her to stay on the case. He had received clearance to increase her operating budget so she should reserve a room at Rum Cay. Now this was a surprise. Then Jenkins gave her a cell number not to be entered in her phone. Memorise or hide, he advised. The number was that of agent Bradley, to be contacted if needed. 'Have fun, Miss Tanaka,' said Jenkins. 'Bring back some pirate DNA. Let's call it the fourteenth ear, shall we?'

An hour later Miss Tanaka parked at Miami airport. Taking her baggage, she walked into the terminal to the American Airlines desk. Providenciales here I come.

Once through security, she enjoyed some retail relaxation. Among the stores in the marbled mall, she came across a shop dedicated to merchandise for the music industry. There in the window stood a mannequin displaying a T-shirt printed with SARAHANNA in wild colours. Below in smaller print was a reminder of the star's exotic character *Voice of The Beast*.

The T-shirt was soon in her shoulder bag so, finding a Mexican restaurant, she ordered a margarita and chicken burrito to celebrate her fortuitous purchase.

An hour later, she was in her window seat on a 737 gazing at the seas below. White clouds huddled on the horizon while shadowy islands appeared and faded from sight below the wing. It was all a big improvement on life in Pembroke Pines. Soon the cabin attendants passed out Immigration forms asking passengers to enter their details before the 737 swooped down to a crosswind landing. Sharp brakes and reverse thrust helped to shift the overhead bags before the aircraft taxied sedately to the terminal.

Providenciales airport provided no jetways to incoming aircraft so passengers had to disembark into a blast of tropical heat rising from the tarmac. Harumi Tanaka was used to the humid conditions of Florida, but this heat brandished a vibrant bite. Small wonder, she thought, that the Rackhams of previous centuries had made it their base. Only the brave would venture here.

Inside the terminal Miss Tanaka waited in the Immigration line until she was beckoned forward by a young female officer wearing a navy blue tailored suit. The officer's hair was tied in a shining tangle of tiny braids. She wondered how long it took to create such a hairdo as she presented her passport.

'What's the reason for your visit, ma'am?' The officer asked.

'I'm here on vacation,' Miss Tanaka replied. 'And to see Sarahanna at her concert.'

The officer thumped a stamp on the passport page, her teeth shining white as she smiled. 'Isn't it great that Sarahanna's coming here? You're most welcome to Provo, ma'am.'

23

John Rackham and that damned tablet again!

I'M AT THE bar with Walter Schulz on Rum Cay. Troy the bar tender already knows what I like and has just poured me a punch with enough rum to blow my pants off. Meantime Walter and I are discussing outstanding details for the concert. He's a nervy guy and I'm not sold on his sense of humour which is non-existent. Maybe the prospect of working with a rapper sex bomb is unnerving him?

'I hope we can accommodate the crowd,' he's saying. 'Every islander I meet intends to come. It's a sell out!'

'That's the objective, Walter.' He's drinking mineral water while I relish my rum. 'Don't worry. Most of the local police will be there. Crowd control won't be a problem.'

'But what if Sarahanna fails to show?'

'Then you return the gate money. Your fee's guaranteed either way. But Sarahanna is coming. Affirmative. We had an email from her manager an hour ago. All going to plan.'

Schulz is a business man. He's running the figures like all these guys do. 'What I don't get is where you make your return?'

I'm looking around the bar as we talk. Other hotel residents, New Yorkers, Canadians and silver heads from Florida are chatting amiably. I notice a young Asian woman entering from the lobby. She's a classy type but I see she's using crutches, poor girl. I like the look of her as she pops her cute little butt down at a table and opens a magazine. I turn back to Walter Schulz.

'Walter. I can answer that. I'm a wealthy man, you understand, so I'm paying Sarahanna's fee. Think of it as a party for my wife and daughter who both adore Sarahanna, and we're real happy to share her talent with everyone.'

Schulz blinks, attempting to understand such magnanimity. 'You must have done well in business.'

'Sure. Real estate, insurance, mining and timber. Brazil's awash with potential.' The smile I give Schulz reflects the rum I've been drinking and I think he actually believes me. 'Tell you what, buddy. I'm going to wind up now. I'm dining with my girls shortly.'

I leave Walter to his water and his envy for a man who can afford to hire a chart-soaring rapper. On the way out I have another look at the Asian woman. She's busy reading and doesn't look up as I pass by, admiring the glossy sheen of her hair.

In the hotel's lobby I find my wife Annie at the concierge desk. To my surprise she's arranging for the hire of bicycles.

'Why do we need bikes?' I ask. 'Haven't we got enough to do?'

Annie's glance precludes further enquiry but as we stroll back to our villa I learn that Annie intends to go cycling next day. 'To keep Swann entertained,' she explains, giving me a wink. Saying one thing but meaning another, is part of our trade, I have to admit.

Swann has also learned the art. Back beside our private pool, she's watching as I mix another drink in our bar. 'Pa,' she says. 'I'm sick of watching you drink yourself silly. I'm going for a walk.'

'That means that you're bored.'

'Yeah,' Swann agrees. 'I guess so.'

'I understand, honey. But things will liven up soon enough. When Sarahanna arrives you won't be bored, I promise.'

Annie and Mary exchange glances. We've been careful to keep the master plan concealed from Swann. Innocence and naivety is likely to be her best excuse if things go wrong. I imagine most people wouldn't use their offspring in games of subterfuge and deceit. All I can say is that it runs in our genes.

'I have an idea,' says Annie raising her finger. 'You could take Kludo for a walk to that hill over there. I heard there's a stone hut on the top where pirates used to live in the old days.'

Swann raises her eyes skyward. 'Old huts are so-o cool.' Kludo, sharp as ever, has heard the word 'walk' and he's ready to go.

'Don't lose Kludo. On your way back stop at the hotel and order six pizzas, okay?' This idea comes from Annie and seems to work for our girl.

She's no different to most kids of her age and leaves without a word.

It's another beautiful evening with a soft trade wind as we sit around our table. I'm feeling rum mellow and the promise of pizza strikes a chord. While Swann's out, I shall mix the evening cocktails. Then I note that Mary and Annie are opening Swann's tablet which is lying on the table.

Mary's keen to make a point. 'I want to see if that bitch at the Conch Bar did what I paid her to do.'

'Don't mess with Haitian *loa*. I've warned you.' Annie wags a finger at Mary who enters Swann's pass code on the tablet.

You may wonder how we know Swann's code? The answer is Chad. He can find codes and much more with a few clicks on his mouse. What's the world coming to, I ask? I add a splash of Jonah's Curse Black Spiced Rum to my glass. No wonder it's cursed. This stuff will be the death of me.

'Well, now. Let's see if the *loa* is at home?' Mary peers at the tablet and does a double take. 'Bring me a drink, JR,' she calls out. 'This is something else!'

Mary moves the tablet into the shade for better viewing. Annie peers over her shoulder. 'And one for me, 'she says. 'And hurry.'

'What do you think I am? A fuckin' slave?'

'You are to Captain Morgan,' Annie snaps back. 'Hurry up JR. You're not going to believe this.'

Spurred by their intense interest in whatever the tablet is screening for its daily dose of nonsense, I fix the drinks and ferry them to my two gals. When I look over their shoulders, I can't believe my eyes!

On the tablet screen are three naked individuals who at first glance appear similar to us. Details may be vapid but the impression is strong. The man's back view is central to the shot. He's kneeling between the women who have balanced a dish of sliced fruit on his head while he clasps both hands behind his arse. The women, it seems, must now attempt to tickle, tease or distract him sufficiently so that he loses control and the dish falls from his head sending fruit and juice all over his body. Tongues appear to be the only means of clearing up the mess.

'What the hell is this?' I stammer. 'Chad checked it and found no faults. I pray to God he's not so careless about our main purpose.'

My girls don't comment. They're laughing but I can tell they're not entirely sure about this unexpected visual drama.

'This is porn. I don't want it on Swann's tablet,' Annie decides.

'Seems there's no choice. Does what it wants,' replies Mary. 'It's not really porn. We must try this one day'

'Oh, God. What have I married?' I ask, as the trio on screen change places. Now the woman, who looks so like Annie, places a tankard of mead on her head while the others set about teasing her. The other woman starts by seizing the victim's earrings and yanking them. Thankfully the scene ends in screams of laughter which fade to an exterior scene. Remember, all this is in black and white, plus it's fuzzy and unpolished by modern standards. I'm lost for words. 'Just tell me. What's this all about?'

Indistinct though it may be, there's no mistaking the next scene which features two rat-toothed pirates lolling in the shade of a tree outside a stone hut. The sea is visible in the background with a patch of white showing on the horizon. One wormy picaroon is about to smoke a clay pipe and while striking a flint, he raises his head and spots the sail. Standing up, he grabs a telescope, trains it on the distant ship to confirm the sighting before he shouts. Moments later, the trio emerge from the hut in various stages of undress, pulling on their clothes, as they seize the telescope to confirm the sighting. A final shot through the scope shows a square-rig ship sailing peacefully along the coast.

I'm speechless. I need a fresh blast of Jonah's Curse right now. Both my girls are giggling, comparing notes if you can believe! I don't follow their thinking. Somebody, somewhere is feeding this tablet with pure junk and it's making my nerves unwind.

24

Swann comments on her cycle ride

'SWANN! UP YOU get. You're coming with me today.' Those are the first words I hear on waking. 'So hurry along for breakfast.'

I guess most girls of my age don't rush to get out of bed. They generally prefer to enjoy some comfort while considering what to wear for any plans they have made for the day ahead.

From previous experience I get five minutes to wallow. After that, my mother's language heats up and breakfast may be denied. It's carrot and stick discipline, and since we can't choose our parents I must comply. Tough shit is what I get if I don't.

Luckily for him, Kludo ignores all control freakery, taking little or no notice of the adults in our party. He's been with me for three years since we found him in a garbage bin near my school on the outskirts of Buenos Aires. Having saved him, Kludo rewarded me with total devotion which is what my parents might desire from me. Instead they are engrossed with their own intimacies, and today they're busy preparing their concert. While I have my fruit juice, egg and toast, they're laying out schedules and plans like you cannot imagine. My father will spend the morning with Chad and Helms. Mary will be dealing with the seamstresses and other workers at the show venue while Mum and I will be riding bicycles.

'And why do I want to go cycling?' I ask.

'Because I do,' says my mother. 'We'll ride over to the other coast and visit your friend Javel.'

'And why is he my friend? Javel is cool, yeah, but I don't like his hairdo and he reeks of skunk.'

They all find that funny but my mother Annie is unmoved 'Well, ain't that too bad. We're going to see him whether you admire his dreads, or not.'

After breakfast we heave two rental bikes into the SUV and Ma takes the wheel leaving Mary at the show ground. When Mary gets out I take her place, putting Kludo on my lap, as Ma drives to Southside Marina. It's a quiet road that dips down between lakes of tidal sea water with rocky shores and sandy beaches. Then my mother parks in a lay-by where we extract the bikes and put them on the road.

'I don't get this, Ma. Why don't we just drive to Javel?'

'You need exercise, darlin'. We all need some each day.'

My mother settles on her bike. She's in white shorts with a tank-top vest revealing her midriff. 'Kludo can run beside us. It's a lovely day and there's plenty to look at.'

'But it's not Copocabana, is it?'

'I never said it would be. It's the Turks and Caicos, Swann, where time stood still.'

'Yes Ma,' I say as I push on the pedals. We're approaching a hill with Kludo loping alongside me. 'Where time went backwards might be better.'

'Yes, Swann. If you say so.'

At the top of a hill, we find a gradient leading down to a small marina where assorted vessels lie in the sunshine as the breeze rattles stays and halliards against their masts. My mother freewheels ahead, down to the dock and along its line of mooring bollards where at the far end, we can see Javel beckoning. Nearby is our boat that took us to West Caicos, moored alongside other craft.

'Hail ma princess,' Javel greets my mother.

'Hi,' she hops off the bike, props it against a wall and taps fists with Javel before turning to me. 'Swann, you and Kludo can take a stroll while I discuss arrangements with Javel. Ten minutes and we'll be finished. Okay?'

'Whatever you say, Ma.'

As ever, I'm obedient! Though I don't understand why Javel and his boat are involved with a reggae concert? Kludo and I wander along the jetty finding no answer. Somewhere above us an osprey calls as it approaches its nest on a telecom mast. Out in the cut leading to the sea, a flock of white terns beat their wings towards their destination. Ma's right. Time here is motionless and nature has a chance of sustainability. Like many girls of my age I take ecology very seriously.

Turning a corner I see a pile of conch shells stacked against the harbour wall. Silky white, cream and pink, they all have frilly edges and crusty surfaces. Kludo goes to sniff them but fails to notice the old black man who appears to be cleaning the shells. He's squatting on a crate beside the pile and then I realise he's the very same character I met on West Caicos. At least he appears to be identical. Same grey frizz of hair, age freckles on his cheeks, watery eyes and gnarled hands. Even the raw ankle looks the same.

'So you live here too?' I ask. 'I thought you came from Haiti.'

He nods and smiles, again a sweet and gentle smile, but says nothing. He just waves his fingers at the pile of shells. I guess he sells them to tourists. I show my iPhone to the old man.

'Do you mind?' I ask. 'So I can show my Ma.'

He smiles and now I think he's dumb or vocally impaired in some way. I take two pictures before finding twenty dollars to give him. Then I select one of the most beautiful conch shells.

I hear a shout from my mother and she's cycling down the jetty towards me. Kludo runs towards her but when I look back to the old man, he's vanished! No sign of him anywhere and that makes me feel strangely dizzy and confused.

'Are you okay?' Ma says as she brakes to a stop ' You look pale. What's the matter?'

I show her the conch shell. 'I got this from an old man. He was here, right here, only a moment ago and now he's gone.'

'That's a mystery. Maybe he's not allowed to sell the shells and he ran off when he saw me coming?'

'He couldn't run, Ma. With a bad ankle, just like the man in West Caicos.'

'Him again?' Ma is unconvinced and she frowns. 'Are you sure?'

'I took a photo of him. I offered him twenty bucks.'

'Yeah? I can see it lying there on the dock.'

I stoop to pick up the bill, staring at it. 'Why didn't he take it?'

'Because he didn't need it, Swann. He's not real. He's in your mind, girl. I bet Kludo didn't notice him and there'll be no picture on your camera roll.'

I thumb my iPhone and, just as she says, there's nothing in the Photos library, only images of shells and the harbour wall. Now I don't know what to think and I'm feeling really upset.

Seeing my concern Ma dismounts and gives me a hug. 'We'll sort this out, I promise, but now let's get on our bikes. I want to take a look around the harbour before we return to the car. Okay?'

'Yes Ma,' I say. 'But I swear I saw him.'

'Yes, you did.' Ma smiles before adding, 'in your mind.'

A minute later, we're cycling along the jetty where the larger vessels are moored. One seems familiar.

'Isn't that the police boat we saw yesterday, when you and Mary were parasailing?'

Ma nods. 'You're not imagining things now, are you? Yes, it's the same vessel. Same registration and aerials.'

So I'm seeing realities once more and I feel more confident. Twice that old black guy has sucked the wind out of me. Now we cycle slowly past the police vessel and Ma waves to an armed police guard who stands at the top of the gangway. He raises a thumb with a half smile in return.

'They're so sweet, these island fellers,' says Ma. 'I need to take a few photos. Stop here and pose with Kludo, will you?'

'Do I have to?' I ask.

'Please, Swann. Is it too much to ask?'

So again, I'm doing what I'm told. It's much easier to agree with Ma who in reality is a manipulating, scheming and self-serving woman of mixed principles. She may look sweet and feminine in her fancy clothes and make-up but underneath she's a sneaky, devious, dangerous and merce-nary beast.

Or perhaps all of that's only in my mind too?

I pose with a change of stance while Ma goes to work with her camera. Finally she's content and remounts her bike to pedal back, passing the police boat. Again we wave and the guard smiles. Daft white women with their cameras and kids. That's what he must be thinking as we pedal back up the hill towards our car.

At the top, we pause for breath and Ma takes out her camera again, taking several panoramic shots of the harbour and marina below. Now it dawns on me this bike adventure is just another phoney exercise.

'You weren't interested in a bike ride. You only wanted pictures of the harbour and that boat down there.'

'I was inspired by the view, darlin'. That's all.'

'You're lying,' I tell her. 'You didn't believe me when I saw that old man. And now I don't believe you. Simple as that!'

'I don't need an argument, Swann. I've got a lot to do today. You can apologise.'

When my mother gets angry, you really know it. She's capable of charging any atmosphere with toxicity. And I fear one of those moments is coming on. 'Okay. I'm sorry.'

She relents and climbs onto her bike. 'That's better. Now let's get back to join Mary at the show ground.'

'Whatever you say.' I push my feet against the peddles, wishing I could be free from this woman. Then I add one simple phrase that Ma always appreciates. 'And I love you too.'

25

John Rackham checks on the target

THE WOMEN HAVE left me alone this morning. Mary's at the show venue to finalise choreography with the backing group. In reality there's not much to it. When Sarahanna starts waving her assets to a tsunami of sound rolling from the loudspeakers, there'll be no need for the finer points of dance discipline. Forget shuffles, pivots and pirouettes, these local gals can hip-hop in their sleep. So for Mary, it's a question of fine tuning their act, running rehearsals and improving delivery before dealing with other jobs in hand.

We've decided that Jasmin is a near perfect lookalike for Sarahanna. Jasmin has a great ass, big tits and a sassy smile and from a distance she's a dead ringer. Up close the fit is less accurate. Jasmin's lips, eyes and neck are slightly different to the star's features, but my Annie is an expert make-up artist. She will disguise and recreate these superficialities.

Currently Annie has taken Swann and her dog on a bike ride to South Marina. She'll conduct a recce on the police launch based there, conveniently close to where Javel moors our boat. When she's finished, Annie will join Mary to finalise the hairdressing and wardrobe factors for which they've hired skilled ladies in the seamstress trade. Armed with the right materials and enough dollars these island women could outfit an army.

But I don't need an army.

I'll be happy with a few warriors to support our tried and tested team. Annie intends to meet Ceejay again to interview other ruffians he has recruited. We tell them it's to manage security at the show and that's true to a point. Maybe we'll have other ideas and Annie will be keeping those options in mind.

Throughout all this we'll keep Swann out of the loop. If the game goes against us, we don't want her falling in the mire. So does she need to know our plans at this or any stage? Absolutely not! She could unwittingly compromise all our stratagems so Annie will leave Swann in the Pepper

Mills shopping precinct while we go to work. Swann knows how to handle herself and Kludo is with her. I guess you've realised the mutt has a useful role in our crew. Kludo can smell sinners a mile off and he can warn against unwanted visitors when we're sleeping off our excesses. In fact, Kludo's better than any alarm our techie Chad can provide.

Speaking of Chad, I must get over to our office for updates. Both men are under a form of lockdown as I don't want them wandering around Rum Resort without good reason.

Freed of my feminine acolytes and their nagging comments, I've just popped into the hotel bar for another libation. Troy knows what I like. Easy on the lime, and steady with the brown sugar. I need energy and liquid courage for this little game I'm playing.

Sitting there, mulling over my priorities, I look through the bar window to the hotel forecourt. It's actually a paved turnaround for the electric carts used by resort clients and staff. There I see the Asian girl limping along on her crutches. Minutes later she comes into the bar and finds a chair, laying her aluminium sticks on the floor. Troy goes to take her order while I finish my rum. It's time for me to get over to Chad and Helms.

The Asian woman is rummaging through her shoulder bag as I leave. There's no eye contact, nevertheless I'm not entirely sure about this lady. Why does she show up when I'm in the bar? It feels odd to me or maybe it's paranoia? You can get that way if you spend too much time in my business.

Outside in the open air, I walk to our HQ, passing the many shrubs and trees that proliferate around this beautiful resort. It's an expensive way to pass a few days, but it's money well spent. I recognise the basic fact, namely that my business is about as dangerous as it gets. Relieving people of their property can be stressful and risky. Especially when the people concerned are bigger rascals than us with no qualms about using weapons to defend their property. And when the action is on the high seas, they are even less fussy about shooting to kill. Hence we want to spend a few days in luxury before we get started on the *Amazon Lady.* And her status will be my first question for Chad when I find him.

Five minutes later, Chad brings up the Caribbean chart on his computer screen. He points to a spot somewhere between Haiti and Cuba, just south of Devil's Point in Inagua. Here an orange marker glows bright, showing the exact position of the *Amazon Lady*.

'How far from here?' I ask.

Chad and Helms deliberate. 'A day's cruise is my guess,' says Helms. 'Sea conditions aren't perfect, so she won't be going fast.'

'Any proof that Dr. Felix is on board?'

Chad makes one of his deathly grunts but it comes with a smirk. 'Yeah, boss. I have some of his talk recorded.'

Chad touches his keyboard and I hear a criss-cross chatter between various parties. Chad chooses a Voice Recognition file for Dr. Felix and each time he speaks, the wave signal turns green.

'So he's on board and coming our way,' I say.

'Just as we hoped,' says Helms. 'We're gonna fry that fucker.'

'Easier said…Maybe it's time to send him an email?'

Let me explain. Knowing that Dr. Felix is absurdly bewitched by Sarahanna, Chad has managed to insert a covert listening system into *Amazon Lady's* computers. It's an advanced and illicit technology that I cannot explain. All I know is that the yacht's computer system appears to be none the wiser. Columbians don't care much about technology. Guns and bullets are more effective.

'Did we leave our Kevlar jackets on the jet?' I ask.

Helms nods. 'In the wardrobe locker.'

'Then fetch them back here today, Helms. And while you're at the airport get the bird fuelled up and ready. Take the SUV when the girls get back.'

Helms is willing enough. He can't wait to get back to the sky, his natural domain. 'Sure, boss.'

'And there's another job. Go by the Fedex office, as they have some parcels for collection. Take ID with you.'

'What are they?' asks Helms. 'I ought to know.'

'Wigs and materials for Annie's wardrobe. They're from a supplier in Florida and guess what?'

Chad and Helms cannot guess, so I tell them. 'Annie has a wig for you, Chad. I can't have you walking around in this hot Caribbean sun. Your scalp will look like a peeled tomato if we don't protect it.'

Helms does his kookaburra laugh, but Chad fails to see the humour. 'I like my head. What kind of wig?'

'Only one that suits you. It's blonde Rasta.'

The kookaburra howls again while Chad glares at me with disdain. 'You need what's in my head. It holds more than what you have in yours.'

This sounds like incipient mutiny so I seize our digital engineer by his ear lobe and squeeze it hard. Ukrainians have an odd sense of humour so maybe he'll understand this. 'I can drop you back in prison, if you prefer?'

Chad yields with a pale plea. 'Please no, boss. My life is in your hands.'

'Then wear a wig when I tell you!'

So we're all friends again. Helms grabs three cans of *Presidente* beer from the freezer and pulls the ring tabs. They froth for a moment as he passes them out. 'Here's to white Rastas! That'll give Javel and his friends something new to talk about.'

26

FBI Agents confer

MISS TANAKA CALLED Miami HQ from a taxi to report her success in locating the Rackhams. She then called Agent Bradley, the resident FBI rep, to propose a rendezvous. Bradley said he'd be at Tommy's in the Pepper Mills Plaza at 1 p.m. He'd be wearing a red shirt in the terrace bar bordering Grace Bay Road.

With time to spare, Miss Tanaka asked the taxi driver to take a swing past the show ground where Sarahanna would be performing. There she noted generator units, lighting gantries and Portakabins behind the stage. She took photos for reference purposes and then instructed the driver to head to the private air terminal. This, she felt, might be worth a visit if only to fix its location in her mind. Presumably the Rackham jet remained parked there while its owners were at Rum Cay. She didn't alight or take photos but asked her driver to go via police HQ to Pepper Mills. In one brief taxi ride she had familiarised herself with the key locations of island life.

At the Pepper Mills Plaza Miss Tanaka paid off the driver intending to meander in the shopping precinct with no crutches. She saw no point in using the facade when outside Rum Cay.

She came across a Cuban Cigar shop and went in to enjoy the rich atmosphere of tobacco leaf being crafted into cigars. She would buy some cigars of the type sold in aluminium tubes. They might be useful, she hoped, as she tapped her credit card on the reader.

Near the cigar shop, Miss Tanaka was intrigued by a premises named Potcake Party. This was a local charity that cared for homeless dogs seeking adoption. While reading the charity's appeal on the window, a young girl walked past her with a black potcake at her side. Instantly alert, Miss Tanaka felt sure this was the teenager in the initial photographs at the airport. Immediately her thoughts returned to DNA. While tasked to examine John Rackham's bloodline, surely the girl also deserved a place in her analysis, especially if she was Rackham's genetic daughter? Such questions required answers, though not immediately. She waited until the girl disappeared around a corner and then slipped into a store selling watches, jewellery, fashion clothing and souvenirs. She found little to entice her especially as the prices were higher than in Florida, so why waste money?

With no further sightings of girl or dog, Harumi Tanaka found her way to Tommy's where below a sunshade sat a young man in a red shirt. He rose to his feet as she reached his table.

'I'm Harumi Tanaka, so you must be...?' She left the sentence hanging, as there were two other men in red shirts on the terrace.

'Sutton Bradley,' the young man nodded. 'I'm your man. So what's your drink?'

'A beer. Like yours, please.'

Bradley beckoned to the waiter but Miss Tanaka hoped she was not intruding. Provo was his territory, not her's, and she noted Bradley wasn't even perspiring. His DNA, she knew, might throw up an intriguing cocktail of bloodlines. 'I guess you might be hacked off that I've come uninvited to your piece of the Caribbean?'

'Why should I?' He lifted his shoulders and smiled. 'This here is British territory and neither of us have special rights. In fact, I work as a pool plumber.'

'Do many villains own swimming pools?'

Bradley shrugged. 'Some do. But the majority of villains here can barely afford to feed their families. They're from Haiti, Jamaica and the DR. Pools are not their thing.' Bradley sipped his beer. 'I don't know what I can do to help you, or even why you're here?'

Miss Tanaka would tell him. 'Basically to extract DNA for comparison with samples from a previous situation.'

'Relating to what?' asked Bradley.

'A full range of criminal activity. Going back for years,' she added. 'I understand you were alerted when John Rackham and his party arrived on an unscheduled flight?'

'True, but on learning they just came to promote a rock concert, HQ lost interest. Now you showed up.'

'It's not just a rock concert. It's Sarahanna. She's virtually a goddess.' Miss Tanaka explained. 'Are you an admirer?'

'No, not a huge fan. She's more motion than music.'

Miss Tanaka had never seen Sarahanna perform, but she had listened to her music when hammering up and down Florida I-95. The freeway traffic and life in the federal task force felt so remote now. Here in Providenciales the atmosphere was charged with leisure and pleasure. On the street, cars rolled past slowly while their drivers ogled any action on the sidewalks.

Bradley leaned towards her. 'See that girl and dog over there?'

Miss Tanaka took a peek. On the far side of the road, Rackham's girl was sauntering past the shop windows with her terrier. Toting several shopping bags, the young girl was relaxed and not looking in their direction.

'I saw her earlier,' said Miss Tanaka. 'I'd like to get her DNA. I may get the opportunity now that I'm staying in Rum Cay.'

'If you're at Rum Cay, that should be easy.' Bradley said. 'Does HQ know it's one of the most expensive resorts here?'

'I imagine so,' she said. 'Which explains why I have to succeed.'

'And what crime has the kid committed?'

'None that we know of. However her DNA would be welcome in our CODIS database.'

Bradley appeared less enthusiastic. 'You may get lucky with her DNA, but the British Government are not so gung-ho as Americans about DNA. Visitors are not obliged to provide samples.'

Miss Tanaka noted caution in Bradley's attitude. She didn't expect this from a fellow agent. 'Whose side are you on? We both work for the federal government, don't we?'

'That we do.' Bradley was watching the girl move on down the street. 'But we cannot upset our hosts without good reason. It's not the done thing as the Brits might say.'

'All I need is a sample.'

'So this DNA must be worth some?'

'I guess so,' she replied. 'I'm leading a research program concerning the role of DNA in criminal behaviour. Rackham's case might prove to be a classic example.'

'So you must find a means of extracting DNA without their say-so unless they're happy to donate in the cause of science?'

Miss Tanaka pulled a face. 'Very unlikely.'

'And remember,' Bradley continued, 'these guys are importing a superstar, meaning good news for the island economy and a big party for the locals. Both are more meaningful than test tubes of South American DNA.'

Miss Tanaka decided to paint in the background. 'For the record, Rackham was born in the USA but hasn't lived there for years. He's possibly involved with South American crime syndicates and some significant heists. Down there, however, data records don't match the sophisticated levels of the USA.'

Bradley was listening. 'So that explains why I was tasked to keep an eye on the Rackhams?'

'And why I came to assist in surveillance and find DNA. So far I've established the man drinks rum by the gallon and that's all.'

'You're doin' well,' Bradley laughed. 'I lifted the memory from that young girl's tablet, and it revealed nothing to forensics.'

'And that was odd,' said Miss Tanaka. 'Most girls keep a treasure trove of pictures and emails in their devices. So either it was brand new or they scrubbed it before arrival.'

'So why?' Bradley asked. 'And if we don't know the answer, it's our job to find out.'

'Agreed,' said Miss Tanaka, wiping her brow again. 'Perhaps another beer is the next step forward?'

27

John Rackham on the inspection of runways

I'VE BEEN BUSY all morning. While my girls supervise details at the concert venue Swann should be amusing herself in the Pepper Mills Plaza. Luckily my daughter is not addicted to shopping but she enjoys some independence and self-reliance. Just as well! Her parents, please remember, are walking the narrowest of planks between triumph and disaster.

Helms has returned with a package full of wigs and wardrobe materials. He also laid hands on our Kevlar vests along with a receipt from the airport refuelling service. The cost of refuelling our jet makes my eyes water.

So now it's early afternoon when Helms and I leave our HQ. Chad will remain to monitor the webcams around our quarters. He's crazy about football and as we depart, he's tuning another screen for news about Shakhtar Donetsk, his national team.

Helms follows me down to our private beach, a lovely place at any time of day. The trees and scented undergrowth contrast with the mirrored surface on the sea and meanwhile our weapons cache remains unmolested in the sand below our feet.

'Here comes Javel,' Helms says. 'On time too.'

Time is important to Helms. Being a pilot, he understands there's a finite moment in every gas tank and flight plan when the juice runs out and gravity takes over. He's red hot on measures, distance, weights, all the critical features that keep machines in the sky. Today Helms is working on the plan for his next flight. That's why we're heading back to West Caicos.

Javel brings the Pursuit fishing boat close to the beach, swinging it about so we can climb aboard via the ladder fixed to the stern.

'Weh yuh deal wid, mon?' asks Javel as I join him at the wheel where he stands slim as a post under his stack of wild hair. He's wearing a brilliant white T-shirt and navy shorts. His teeth in his dark angular face flash a welcome. 'Hey, boss. Weh we headed?'

'West Caicos.' I tell him. 'Back to flamingo alley.'

As soon as we clear the headland, Javel leans on the throttles and both Mercuries ramp up, powering the boat onto the plane at a strident 40 knots. Helms takes a seat while I stand beside Javel as the boat pounds over the speckled waters. Below the cockpit coaming is a sliding door which Javel snaps open. In the tiny cabin below our volunteers Able and Ceejay are sitting on the bunk. By the uncertain look on their faces, I feel inclined to enlighten them.

'Only twenty minutes,' I shout as the hull thumps and hammers over the sea. 'Enjoy the ride.'

From Providenciales to West Caicos is ten miles and we reduce power on reaching the shallow waters around the island. En route I've been considering the benefits and drawbacks to our plan. What have we not anticipated? Thinking of the unexpected is essential.

Javel noses the boat into the same beach where the police recently admonished me for abandoning Swann and her damnable dog. Javel is confident the police won't be bothering us today. With a radio tuned to the police channel he knows what's keeping them busy. Today, he reports, they're in the south east investigating a boatload of hopeful immigrants from the Dominican Republic. Javel will use our two-way radio to contact me if the situation changes.

Our passengers come up on deck. Able has a bag of tools and Ceejay is humping a jerrycan of diesel. Leaving Javel in the boat, the four of us jump onto the beach and head into the scrub to emerge on the runway found by Swann. It has no fences, simply a long strip of tarmac with weeds sprouting in its cracks.

I'm also keeping my eyes open for that old black feller Swann claims to have met. Not once, but twice now! I'll admit that Swann's paranormal adventures are getting to me. Along with those unexplained sequences that appear on her tablet, I sense the breath of voodoo witchcraft is shadowing my every move.

For God's sake! I'm supposed to be planning a massive heist and instead I'm worrying about phenomena on an tablet! Can you believe it? I must shape up and cut these spectres from my mind.

Able and Ceejay head off to some deserted buildings where Able knows of an abandoned digger. With tools and fuel, they hope to return it to life.

Helms begins our inspection at the runway threshold. Walking down the centre line, we cast left and right, pausing to kick odd stones and bits of rubbish into the perimeter grass. When we reach the five concrete blocks that straddle the centre of the airstrip, Helms makes a detailed scrutiny, using a tape measure while I record his notes. These dragon's teeth are guaranteed to deliver any aircraft a mortal punch to the belly. When he's done, we continue to the far end of the strip.

'Is it okay?' I ask. 'Is this feasible, or are we wasting our time?'

Helms looks at me and yawns. 'Hell, what do I know? If we don't shift those blocks we'll burn in a fireball. Shift them and we've got a chance. That's all I can say.'

On our return to the concrete teeth, I hear the sounds of a machine starting up. Soon the digger, an elderly JCB, comes onto the airfield, thumping puffs of smoke and lurching on deflated tyres. Able is at its wheel as Ceejay walks beside him. Maybe we now have the muscle to pull the dragon's molars.

'Let's make a start,' says Helms, 'with the bastard in the middle.'

Ceejay uses a rusty cable to connect the digger's arm to the central pyramid which stands five feet high on the tarmac. Able reverses his digger pulling the cable tight while Helms and I stand back in case it snaps. Slowly the pyramid tips and falls with a crash on the tarmac. Able drags it off the runway into the scrub.

'One down, four to go.'

We remove two more, leaving one concrete pyramid on each side of the runway. Helms carefully assesses these two obstacles. 'If a pilot flies over, they may notice we've been at work so let's leave two in place. I figure the wingtips will just clear each block.'

'You figure!' I ask. 'Hell, they might rip the wings off our jet.'

'Only if I hit them.'

'Helms. Hit these, and they'll have to bury us here.'

'Fuck off, Cap'n.' Helms raises two fingers and chuckles.

So we decide to leave the strip with one solid block on each side, hoping to move them later.

'Okay guys. Let's get back. I've seen enough for the day.'

Ten minutes later we're on the fishing boat with Javel as Helms expands on his thoughts. He'll bring false blocks fashioned from cardboard when he returns with our jet. He'll plant these dummies on the runway and park the jet under camouflage netting at the leeward end of the strip. Chameleons enjoy travelling with camouflage to hand, so I add cardboard and/or foam blocks to the shopping list. Dragon's teeth my arse !

28

Annie enjoys a shower

BACK IN OUR villa after a hot day on the stage, I'm enjoying a brief moment of relaxation with Mary. We're in our poolside area under the parasols and I'm drinking lemonade. First I call Swann on my iPhone, telling her to take a cab back to Rum Cay after she's finished shopping. All our calls are made on the basis that someone may be listening, so we confine our chats to family business. All other communications go via Chad's secure network.

'Is it safe for Swann to take local cabs?' Mary wonders aloud. She's wearing white shorts and a floral shirt, both gifts from me.

'Sure it's safe,' I reply. 'She's got Kludo. She's not a baby.'

'I'd kill anyone who hurts her.'

These are strong words. Since Mary never shirks from carrying out a threat, it proves how much she loves Swann. There's a strong bond between them which I encourage. I smile at Mary, admiring her blonde spiky hair. Her eyes, cobalt blue, glimmer with intent. I lean forward, touching her arm as I whisper. 'You won't have to. I would kill him first.'

Mary's lips pucker, as if I'm denying her potential pleasure. 'Better we kill him together.' she says. 'It's going to be okay. I really believe so.'

Mary's desire to revisit the *Amazon Lady* stems from the appalling treatment she received from Dr. Felix and his crew. Her's is a mission of undiluted revenge for which she has my full support. Speaking for myself and JR, our overall objective is driven by commercial survival and profit. To recoup our substantial outlay and to scoop a bonus, we must hit the jackpot and, as gamblers will tell you, jackpots are statistically very rare.

I've been supervising research for many months, collating not only the evidence derived from Mary's visit to Doctor Felix and his floating art gallery, but also hundreds of reported thefts and losses of artworks going back for years. Using the Internet, I've been in touch specialist art galleries and insurance underwriters, learning how the conversion of excess dollars to rare assets appeals to mafiosi and narcos, even though many can barely evaluate an oil painting by Picasso or the tonnage of an oil tanker. For the smartest of such heathen the attraction lies in ownership of assets that accumulate in value while being traded, stored and transported on private vessels like the *Amazon Lady*.

Dr. Felix is one such sophisticated villain. He's a Doctor of Philosophy no less. After obtaining a degree at Bogota University he discovered his path to wealth lay in servicing the profits from the drug trade. Placing high value works of art beyond the threat of seizure is one such service offered by Dr. Felix. His luxury yacht with its Liberian registration provides security for assets of high value but, since we are not guardians of the law, we see here a wondrous opportunity!

Mary wants to review her day's work. 'Jasmin's a fair dancer. She knows how to move like Sarahanna and, if we had more time, she'd probably sing like her too.'

'Not enough time.' I reply. 'Chad reckons the yacht will arrive the day after tomorrow.'

'So tomorrow we should run our tests?'

'That's our last chance.'

Our eyes meet and I know that Mary knows what I'm thinking. We're both thinking the same.

'A shower? Before the others get back?' I make the suggestion.

'You bet. Yes! Let's have some fun!'

This is the moment when humans revert to animal behaviour. When the drive for sex sets free the beast within. We hurry inside our villa, locking the bedroom door and sliding glass doors to the patio. With iPhones switched off it's just the two of us in a world in which we share past, present and future. Let's concentrate on the now, I say, leading Mary to our bathroom suite.

The shower is a gem with a sconce wall that coils inwards and vanishes. Into this vertical conch shell of dark grey slate Mary slides her golden body as she pulls off her T shirt, leaving only a white thong.

I pull off my clothes, tossing shirt and shorts onto the bed as I aim for the shower. I'm wearing a bikini bottom and a gold necklace. I love the feel of gold when I'm being soaped. Too bad JR. You're not in on this!

I hear the pulse of running water as I round the corner of the shower, Mary leaps on me with cat-like pounce. 'You need a good wash, you dirty girl!'

Before I know it, her hands are all over my shoulders, between my breasts, over my hips, between my thighs and round my buttocks. Fluffy soap suds build and then slide down my thighs as Mary kneels below me, working the soap between my legs. She's no stranger to my erogenous zones but in Mary's expert hands, the effect always feels like the very first time.

Now Mary rises from her knees, sliding her hands up past my quivering breasts as she takes my head and slowly bends forward to press her tongue between my lips. A ripple of fire drives through my nerve system, hurling all my senses into a golden haze of lustful abandonment and relief. It's amazing.

'Now, darling, it's my turn,' I whisper. 'Rough and ready if you please.'

29

John Rackham encounters Harumi Tanaka

OUR DAY'S WORK on the runway has been successful, at least as far as Helms is concerned. However I'm not so sure. Leaving the strip with anything solid across its midpoint is not my idea of success, but Helm is the man who'll be flying the jet and I'm not one to contradict a leathery old sky lizard like Helms. Nor do I want details of our runway cosmetics becoming public knowledge.

First stop on our return to Rum Cay is Chad's villa. Here I find the Ukrainian is staring at a football spectacular while keeping one eye on the monitor screens. The girls have returned to the other villa, he tells me, and the GPS indicates that *Amazon Lady* is now 20 miles off Guantanamo bay in south east Cuba. She's still coming our way which is all that matters so I leave Helms to appreciate Chad's monosyllabic comments while I head off to see Mr. Troy.

After my second rum punch it occurs to me that Swann has not reported back from her shopping trip. I ask Troy if he's seen my daughter?

'Yeah, sah. I see her with your dog some time back.' Troy is sure of it. 'She was walking down the lane to salt ponds, sah.'

Five minutes later I'm on the track heading to the salt ponds. I've taken an electric buggy in my search for dog and daughter. Between the palms and bushes are modest plantations seeded with yams, okra, tomatoes, and cucumbers, all cultivated to supply the resort kitchens. It's perfect ecology and I like these electric carts which are now in vogue. I've seen how the jerks in Brazil are chopping up the world's lungs, so I'm backing the green revolution whatever else you might think of me.

Turning a corner, I see the Asian woman hobbling down the track ahead and she is using a pair of crutches. I come up behind her and she turns when she hears me.

'Ni hao.' I say, showing off my language skills. 'You need a ride?'

The young woman looks surprised then she smiles. 'Sure, thanks. I'm on my daily exercise but I've nearly done my quota.'

She steps in, cradling her crutches to sit next to me. Blow me down! She's wearing a Sarahanna T-shirt. My foot pushes the accelerator and the buggy purrs forward.

'So you're here for the show? I guess you're a fan?'

The Asian woman throws me a cute glance. 'You bet. A big Japanese fan and I'm doing a story on Sarahanna for a Tokyo magazine. I think she's a big star.'

'I share that view,' I say. 'She'll set the island on fire.'

We've only travelled a hundred yards when I turn another corner to see Swann walking ahead below the tree canopy. She's on the same track with Kludo trotting beside her.

I push the pedal and the buggy charges on, down the slope until I reach Swann. 'Hi, honey. What are you doing here?'

Swann is staring at a nearby pool. Now she turns to look at me and then more curiously at my passenger. 'I'm exploring, Pa. See how that salt pond is weird. Those ripples on the water? Where do you suppose they come from?'

Looking across the pond's surface, I see swirling vortices that roil like mini whirlpools. 'I haven't a clue.'

'It's tarpon,' says the Japanese woman. 'Tarpon fish that swim in from the ocean using submarine tunnels.'

Both Swann and I are silenced by this revelation.

'Yes, they come to breed in the lake. The hotel brochure says so.'

So typical of the Japanese to actually read all the guff the PR people dish out. 'You're well informed,' I tell her.

'That's what journalists are supposed to be.'

When she smiles, she's quite pretty. Not strikingly gorgeous, but attractive in a subtle alluring way, the Asian way, but smart too.

'I guess so.' I turn to Swann. 'You coming back to the hotel?'

Swann remains on the roadside, undecided with petulance hovering. She's wondering why her father is driving around with a journalist for company.

'Up!' Swann calls to Kludo. 'Up!'

But the dog is not jumping into the buggy. Instead Kludo stands stiff legged and bristling on the verge, his attention focused firmly on the Japanese woman. And he's growling. The last time he erupted like this was at the voodoo witch who found Swann's tablet. My views on that woman and the tablet messages remain very raw.

'I'll walk back,' Swann aims a loaded glance at me. 'No doubt I'll find you in the bar.'

Without waiting, I spin the buggy round and press back uphill towards the resort. Beside me the Japanese woman makes a comment. 'I don't think her dog liked me.'

'He's a rescue dog. Tends to be suspicious of strangers.'

Some dogs smell drugs while others point to cancers but Kludo's innate gift is detection of deceit, falsehoods and fake news. We found him in a backyard alley, rescuing him from a life of mange and hunger. He has repaid us with levels of protection that are both invisible and inexplicable. Dogs can also smell fear but my buggy companion doesn't seem the fearful type to me.

However Kludo did issue a warning. Swann picked up on it and now I'm wondering about this journalist, this fan of Sarahanna whom I found limping down the lane following my daughter and whom I've seen twice in the bar lately. Such issues need answers. Very well, I'll find out soon enough.

Our drive to the hotel forecourt takes us past a hill overlooking the coast. On its peak sits an old stone hut which closely resembles the love nest in that episode of horseplay that I saw on Swann's goddam tablet.

'That hut?' I ask, turning to my passenger who freaked out our dog. 'What does the hotel guidebook say about that?'

'You really want to know?' Her smile suggests she has the answer. She tries to tease me into repeating my request.

'That's why I asked. I don't have time to read guidebooks.'

'You must be very busy.' She looks me in the eye. 'I've told you what I do, maybe you can tell me what you do, Mr...?'

'Just call me John,' I reply. 'I'm a private investor. Boring, dull investments, but generally profitable.'

We have now reached the forecourt where I park the buggy and pass the crutches to my passenger. 'And what shall I call you?'

'John?' she says, stepping out to position her crutches. 'I like that name. He was one of the twelve apostles.'

'Forget the apostles, what about that hut on the hill back there?'

She hobbles around the buggy and offers me her hand. 'I'm Harumi Tanaka and I'd love a rum punch. Then I'll tell you about that hut on the hill.'

She's clever, I know that instinctively. She's playing with me and almost succeeds in controlling the dialogue. Good journalists can do this, but Kludo has never growled at a music reporter. At least not until now. Though my alert bells are ringing, I won't let her realise that's the case.

'A rum punch?' I agree. 'Great idea. Troy mixes the best.'

Miss Tanaka hobbles ahead, in through the lobby doors to the bar area with its view over the lagoon, the reef and the wide Atlantic ocean. Troy sets to work while I help my journalist friend onto a bar stool after placing her sticks against the bar.

'Please excuse my daughter and the dog. On occasion they behave in a very irrational manner.'

'No need for excuses, Mr. John.' Harumi Tanaka gazes at Troy as he applies three brands of rum to the punch before adding grenadine and nutmeg, topping it off with a maraschino cherry and two slices of orange. He pushes the glasses over and beams. 'Enjoy.'

'You bet, thanks. You can start on the refills right now.'

Harumi Tanaka nearly falls off her stool when I order refills, but the Japanese are tough cookies so her eyes open wide and she nods with enthusiasm. 'Do you mind if I smoke? ' she asks.

'Do I mind? Hell no. Here's to your story telling.'

Tanaka rummages in her bag and puts a pack of cigars on the bar. 'From the Cuban cigar shop. Genuine and I love them. Help yourself.'

Now, now! I warn myself. Should any of my gals happen to arrive now, I'll be in trouble. They are non-smokers and broadly disapprove of my occasional cigarette or cigar. If they catch me with this journalist, sinking rums and fumigating the tropical air, they'll kick my arse around the block.

'Help yourself.' Harumi Tanaka strikes a match to light her cigar after removing it from the aluminium tube. She places it in her mouth, between her cherry red lips and sucks till it burns evenly. 'Best Cuban, such a treat.'

I can't let this pass. I slide a cigar from its tube and strike a match. Now I have rum and fine tobacco. What more could I want? And then I remember. 'You were going to tell me about that hut?'

'Oh that,' she says, downing most of her punch. 'That little place belongs to the resort owners who live in Singapore.'

Troy pushes an ash tray across the counter followed by two refills. 'There you are, sir. Troy's double punch.'

'Tell me, 'I turn to Harumi. 'Do you know where Sarahanna was born?'

'Oh Mr. John. A trick question, yes?' Quick as a flash she has the answer. 'Sarahanna is 28 years old and was born in the Bahamas. On Stocking Island I believe.'

'Look who's been doing their homework,' I chink glasses with Harumi who smiles. Right answer.

'You understand that homework is my job,' she says with a modest smile. 'It's the secret of good journalism.'

'In banking we call it due diligence.' Now I'm trying to reclaim the initiative in this discussion. 'But why do the resort owners need an old house like that?'

'Oh, but it must be obvious.' She looks at me through her dark glasses and her eyes are hidden. 'Some people love history. That little house is pure history, maybe the oldest building in the islands.'

'I guess so.'

'In Japan they would never be allowed to knock it down, even if they wanted to do so.' Now she peers past my shoulder, into the hotel forecourt where I parked the buggy. 'Mr. John, I see your daughter and her dog are returning from their walk. I believe she's coming in. They can't let the dog in here, growling like a mad tiger.'

She's right about that. I sink the rum in one and place my cigar in the ash tray. 'Excuse me, please.'

'No hurry. Harumi's going nowhere.' With another smile of the inscrutable kind, she takes a pull on her cigar and blows the smoke right at me.

30

Miss Tanaka gets the DNA

As soon as John Rackham left the bar, Harumi Tanaka carefully picked up his discarded cigar. The bartender was serving customers elsewhere and didn't notice her slide the stub into the aluminium tube, screwing tight the cap before concealing it in her bag. Finally she had the DNA she wanted.

Immediately she took a fresh cigar from its case, snapped off an inch, punch cut the other end and lit it. She drew to liven the flame and then positioned it in the ashtray exactly where Rackham had left his cigar. It was possible that he would notice the deception, but thanks to his love of rum, it might go unnoticed.

Lifting her glass, Harumi Tanaka looked through the window to see Rackham and his daughter were still arguing on the forecourt. The young girl was waving fingers in his face and stamping her foot while the dog sat licking its leg. After a minute of acrimonious dispute, the girl turned and ran towards her villa.

Harumi Tanaka composed herself while Rackham returned to the bar. He beckoned to Troy, rolling his finger, and sat down with a loud sigh on his bar stool. 'Sorry about that. She's got a wicked temper.'

'Every self-respecting girl has one,' she said.

Miss Tanaka watched Rackham pick up his cigar. He inspected it briefly before relighting it with a match.

'You were talking about a famous pirate?'

Miss Tanaka pulled on her own cigar but did not inhale. 'He was something of a legend, so I read in the brochure. He enjoyed keeping two women very happy.'

'Two women?' Rackham speared the maraschino cherry in his drink with a cocktail stick and waved it at her. 'I always offer them first bite of the cherry. Let me do the same for you.'

Miss Tanaka recoiled as the cherry passed below her nose. 'Sorry, John. I don't do cherries. Too sweet for my tooth.'

'I was referring to something else.' Rackham grinned. 'I might get you an interview with Sarahanna, a scoop as you writers call it. That's what I mean by a first bite on the cherry.'

'Oh that's very different!' Harumi gripped Rackham's hand. 'How kind of you, John. You can do that for me?' Had she misjudged the situation when he was only offering to help. 'I'd like that. Very much.'

Rackham nodded, sank more rum and bit on his cigar. 'My wife Annie is managing the backstage requirements for Sarahanna. I'm sure it can be arranged.'

'That would be wonderful,' Miss Tanaka came closer to her quarry. 'The best thing I heard all day.'

'You'll hear a lot more when Sarahanna opens up. You'll get a scoop that will make up for all this hobbling around on those crutches. I understand you didn't need them when you were out shopping today.'

With no hesitation, Harumi Tanaka had the answer to his probing comment. 'My convalescence is nearly complete. I tried shopping this morning without my sticks and luckily I found my knee was surprisingly comfortable.'

Rackham lowered his tone. 'I'm so pleased to hear that, Miss Tanaka. Very pleased indeed.'

She could see stubble on his chin as the glint in his sharp eyes seared into hers. There was no need for DNA referencing with this particular individual. From the cigar stub to the thirteenth ear, this man's bloodline ran straight back to the little old hut on the hill. Miss Tanaka was sure of it.

31

Annie finds her suspicions increase

I AWAKE TO hear hammering on our bedroom door. Also alerted Mary sits up in the bed alongside me. We slip on our bathrobes to unlock and open the door. We find Swann outside, hands on her hips and scowling angrily.

'Yes, Swann? What is it?'

'I'll tell you. While you love-birds have been tinkering in here, Pa's in the bar with a Japanese woman claiming to be a journalist.'

'Maybe she is?'

'What journalist would be wearing a Sarahanna T-shirt and staying in this expensive hotel? She uses crutches to walk around here but discards them when shopping in the Pepper Mills plaza.'

'For God's sake,' says Mary. 'How do you know all this?'

'By using my eyes. That's how! And by listening to Kludo. He growled at this woman, just as he did at the voodoo bitch.'

Mary is clearly concerned. 'So what's this about?'

'Kludo never lies,' I tell Mary. 'I must find JR.'

Minutes later as I hurry to the hotel complex, I meet my husband walking calmly towards me. I tell him straight. 'I'm coming to warn you, my darling. Swann thinks you've picked up bad company.'

My husband kisses my forehead and drapes his arm over my shoulder as we turn back to our villa. 'Swann's right. Kludo didn't take to her. Nor did I when I realised she was lying to me.'

I look around but nobody's in sight. 'Have you jeopardised the plan? That's the only question.'

'No way. Definitely not!' My husband is convinced about this. 'She claims to be a journalist writing about Sarahanna and yes, she's very sharp and may pose a risk, so I've offered to arrange an interview with our star, and that's where it ends.'

'I hope to hell you're right. Otherwise we'll need to revise all our tactics. We're set for rehearsals tomorrow with the marine crew. Then the hardcore action starts next day.'

'Assuming Dr. Felix arrives on time.' JR says. 'Chad reports the yacht is leaving Cuban waters and is currently on schedule.'

That update is exciting. Without *Amazon Lady* our entire operation pancakes, to put it mildly. 'And my news is that Sarahanna is also on schedule. Her manager has confirmed it. We'll be providing transport from the airport, a stretch limo with one of Ceejay's brothers as its driver. So we've got that element covered.'

'A lot of brothers on the damned payroll.' JR's comment reminds me of how much is at stake.

'Too many brothers, but we had no choice.' Now we arrive back at the villa to be met by suspicious looks from Mary and Swann as we enter.

'Her name is Harumi Tanaka,' JR explains. 'Don't trust her.'

'I saw her shopping in the plaza,' says Swann. 'Without crutches and chatting to a man in a bar there.'

'You didn't mention this.' JR says. 'Either that was a chance encounter or they're working together. What did this man look like?'

Swann shrugs. 'A local guy. Mixed race. Curly hair wearing a red shirt. That's all I noticed.'

'You did well, honey. One of these days, you'll make a great...' I leave my comment unfinished.

'Criminal?' Swann finishes my line with a provocative chuckle. 'That's what you meant to say, wasn't it, Ma? The three of you were into mischief long before I was born.'

'In a history going back for many years,' JR adds from the bar where he is reviving an empty glass. 'Harumi Tanaka was telling me about the pirate Jack Rackham who operated from this very cay. Their base was in that stone hut on the hill.'

'And how come Miss Tanaka knows all this?' asks Mary.

'It's all in the hotel guest book,' says JR.

Mary reaches for our copy of the guest brochure and turns the pages thoughtfully. 'No, the Japanese woman wasn't lying.'

'So let's have dinner shall we?' I'm very firm about my decision. 'That's because we have an exceptionally busy day tomorrow.'

32

Rackham – A length of hemp

I TOLD MY gals to go ahead and order dinner. I'll take a shower before following them to the restaurant. To be frank, I like some time to myself after a hectic day. First I had that boat trip with Javel and Helms to assess runway alterations and then came the mind games with Miss Tanaka, the alleged scribbler from Tokyo. She's a tough cookie, that one. The way she stuck that cigar in her mouth! It was provocation unlimited and I fell for it.

Swann has left Kludo with me because dogs are not welcome in the restaurant. She asked me to feed him and left his food on the counter. Alongside it Swann also left her tablet, that fiendishly clever invention from Cupertino which has taken the world and our visit by storm. Chad has examined it three times and found zilch so I've promised we'll buy a new one as soon as we get a spare moment. Meanwhile she prefers this tablet because of the stickers on its case. I won't quarrel with Swann, so you get the picture. I'm a sucker for strong-willed women! And that's what Miss Tanaka said about the pirate in his hill shack.

The quick descent of night always surprises me in the tropics. One moment there's sunshine, the next there's a darkness full of vibrant crickets and insects winging through the inky air. When I went to shower, it was still daylight. Now I'm back in the kitchen and it's nearly night time as Kludo starts to growl.

'Oh, for God's sake!' I peer over the counter and there's Kludo, standing stiff legged and hackled up, growling as if Papa Legba, the voodoo gate-keeper himself, was right there.

'Quit growling!' I shout at the dog. 'Stop it!'

But Kludo stubbornly refuses to obey. Food may divert him so I open the food packet and pour the contents into his dish. But that doesn't do it. He growls louder and walks on stilted legs towards the door. Every hackle on his spine aims for the sky. Any porcupine would be impressed.

'Quit it, Kludo! Now!'

His snarl is resonant, tactile and deeply threatening. Whatever caused his alarm is perplexing. I see nothing beyond the sliding glass doors except insects dancing in the glow of blue light above the pool. Kludo advances at snail's pace while his growl rises in volume at every step.

I step over the dog to slide the door open and Kludo races out into the night, his growl turning to shrill barking yaps. I won't follow because he'll return to base as he always does, but as I turn back into the room, a blast of chilled air flows past me, lifting a vase of flowers from the counter to smash on the floor.

Lost for words, I step over the broken vase and scattered flowers, hurrying to find the rum bottle with my shaking fingers. I feel as if a Richter 9 earthquake has just occurred. 'What in holy shit is happening?'

As the shot of rum hits me, Swann's tablet on the counter self starts and the screen spreads a ghostly radiance into the darkened room. My nerves shred like spaghetti while my knees rattle against each other. I can even hear my heart pounding. I manage to pour another slug before I lean across to look at the tablet screen.

Shown in sepia, I see a courtroom of earlier years with members of the public dressed in clothing of the era. Frock coats, wigs, lace and brass buttons are all there in a scene whose central figure stands in the dock, a chain around his neck linked to shackles at his feet. He's a white man and very similar to the pirate in the old hut, last seen trying to pull his pants on. A man who looks a lot like me!

On either side of the defendant stands a woman, also in chains. To say they are lookalikes for Mary and Annie would be stretching it, especially when both display obvious signs of pregnancy to judge and jury. Behind his desk the judge takes a pitiless view of the prisoner. He waves his hand to dismiss the two women who are led from the dock by guards. Then he dons a black hat and delivers the ultimate verdict for the fate that now awaits the prisoner.

The temptation to smash the tablet into a thousand fragments is over-whelming. But I can't bring myself to do it. Instead I steel myself with another gulp of rum as the next scene sucks me into its savage, spell-binding clutch.

A drummer beats a solemn note as he leads a platoon of marines dressed in tunics and breeches. Behind them comes a horse-drawn cart on which sits the sentenced prisoner, his eyes wide with fear as he surveys the approaching gallows, signifying the end of his final journey. Beside the gallows a hangman stands in a black hood and when the cart halts, he slips the hemp rope around the prisoner's neck. Then the cart moves on, leaving the prisoner to kick in slow strangulation at the end of the noose. The scene fades to darkness as the last drop of rum flows from the bottle to the glass in my hand.

I'm ready to smash the tablet, Swann's cursed gadget, into oblivion, but the screen lights up again to show the hangman taking down the body, removing first the noose and then a necklace from the corpse. Then, drawing a knife, the hangman slices an ear from the corpse which he shows to the cheering marines before fixing it to the necklace with evident satisfaction.

Smashing that tablet is the best moment of my life. I hurl it to the floor and glass, chips and transistors fly all over the floor while I stamp on it furiously. I vow to the Dukes of Cupertino that I will never, ever again watch unsolicited crap like that!

Now Kludo returns through the sliding door, wagging his tail and looking at me as if I've just given him a red raw filet steak. He scents the food I put out and trots over to make short work of it. His transformation from a snarling terrier into a placid colleague leaves me even more confused. Astounded no less.

With no rum left, I've no choice but to put on a clean shirt and hurry through the plantation to the restaurant. I see my three gals at the table and they look up as I enter. Luckily there's no sign of Miss Tanaka. Thank God for that.

'JR!' Annie, ever my caring and perceptive wife, gets to her feet and puts her hands on my shoulders. 'Are you okay, my love? You look as if you've seen a ghost.'

33

FBI Agents Bradley & Tanaka store the DNA

As soon as John Rackham had departed, leaving her alone in the bar, Miss Tanaka stubbed out her cigar and rinsed her mouth with a glass of water. The fumes of Cuban tobacco lingered on her clothes as she signed the bill and, using crutches, hobbled the short distance to her room.

After a shower, she put on clean clothes and using evidence gloves wrapped Rackham's cigar in sterile packaging before placing it in a ziplock bag for the DNA lab in Miami. They had the kit for in-depth analysis with broad access to many databases.

She called the hotel reception to learn that the last flight to Miami had already departed so she'd have to deliver her prize after the concert. Then she realised the refrigerator wasn't working and the precious sample required cool storage. When she called Bradley, he suggested she could use his fridge-freezer.

'I need 4 degrees Celsius, about 25 Fahrenheit,' she told him.

'I'll try,' he said.

'You're an engineer, so please help me on this.'

The taxi ride took twenty minutes from Rum Cay to Bradley's home beside the Leeward Channel. In the evening air, Harumi Tanaka noticed how the local people stood outside the highway stores, chatting and laughing. Many would be talking about Sarahanna and even the taxi radio was playing one of her hits.

'What you make of Sarahanna?' Miss Tanaka asked the driver.

'She's hot. Real hot. All the island be going to see her.'

Miss Tanaka paid off the cab outside Bradley's house. When the cab's tail lights had vanished she found the entrance and two dogs began barking as she approached. The door opened and Bradley came out. 'Hi Harumi. Now where's that sample?'

The freezer thermometer was reading 22 Fahrenheit when Miss Tanaka deposited the DNA package in the cabinet.

'I worked hard for that,' she told him.

'In a five-star bar? Yeah, that's a tough assignment.' Bradley's comment reinforced her opinion that he wasn't too impressed by her achievement.

'I had to smoke a cigar and drink two rum punches.' Miss Tanaka continued. 'Rackham puts them down like nine pins. Have you any cold water. '

'These islands run on rum and beer,' said Bradley as he took water from the freezer. 'You get anything else from Rackham?'

'That he'll arrange an interview with Sarahanna when she arrives. He thinks I'm a journalist from Tokyo.'

'Did you ask him why he's doing all this? That would be useful.' Out on his verandah, Bradley invited Miss Tanaka to sit down. He lit an insect repellant candle and slumped into a wicker chair. 'Why is he doing this?'

'Because he's promoting a show.'

'A show?' Bradley raised his dark eyebrows. 'If that's what you call it… A star like Sarahanna normally commands a huge fee for a performance. We have twenty five thousand islanders on Provo. Even if every islander goes to the show, Rackham must charge at least twenty bucks per ticket to recoup costs with any decent return.'

Miss Tanaka sipped water and did the math. 'So?'

'Would you invest in such a promotion?' Bradley asked. 'Many islanders don't have the cash for that kind of expenditure. They keep spare dollars to paint fingers nails or to add chrome to their cars.'

'I take your point,' Miss Tanaka agreed. 'I told Rackham about the 18th century, when pirates bearing his name cruised these seas as their hunting ground. It's my guess the cigar's DNA will prove that Rackham's genes have not improved in three hundred years.'

Bradley was dubious. 'I guess that might be the case. So how do you plan on improving his genes?'

'That's the entire rationale for the research programme. The agency wants answers for that very question.' Miss Tanaka felt she should change the conversation. 'So, Sutton Bradley, do you live here on your own?' she asked with a smile.

'Just me and two dogs.'

'Don't you find it lonely? So far from Miami and the USA?'

Bradley cocked his head. 'Nobody asked me that till now. Yea, I like it here in the islands, just keeping my eyes open for potential trouble. Being lonely is no problem. I'd feel more isolated in the suburbs of Miami and Fort Lauderdale. Here most locals are happy to chat and share a joke.'

'Maybe that's what Rackham wants from the show,' said Miss Tanaka. 'I found him very willing to talk. He has an attractive manner.'

'Maybe that's the answer to all your research.'

'What do you mean by that?' she asked.

'If he's a gangster and you're a law officer, in theory your offspring would be neutral. Bad genes balanced by good ones?'

'That's an interesting concept. I'll think on it.' Miss Tanaka felt it was time to return to Rum Cay. The thought of having offspring with John Rackham had not occurred to her. 'I should call a cab. I want to be on the first flight tomorrow.'

'You're welcome to stay,' said Bradley, 'but I only have one bed.'

'Kind of you to offer.' Harumi Tanaka raised her eyebrows and smiled. 'But I'll head back to Rum Cay, thanks all the same.'

Bradley shrugged. 'Up to you.'

Half an hour later when a taxi had returned her to Rum Cay, Miss Tanaka began to feel lonesome. Bradley was an interesting young man and they both shared similar lifestyles. Maybe she should have accepted his invitation? She would think about that another day.

34

John Rackham tests team & equipment on the spit

THIS IS AN important day for my crew. At last we're preparing to engage in serious business, starting with a visit to our beach at dawn where we recover our weapons from the sand, transferring them directly to Javel's boat. Swann will entertain herself at the villa while Chad and Helms fulfil other duties.

The pace, and shred of nerves, starts building.

Javel points our boat to the south and the engines sing as twin falsettos, driving the vessel onto the plane with a broad fluted wake astern. We head over the banks of the vast turquoise lagoon that extends for many miles across the archipelago. Some believe the higher temperatures of these shallow waters create a pillar of heated air which deflects hurricanes as they whirl across the Caribbean. Chad has checked with the Hurricane Centre to ensure no tropical cyclones are rolling our way in the immediate future.

Shortly the dark profile of Providenciales island sinks below the horizon and then we're on our own, gliding over a mirror surface at 35 knots. The early sun guides us to an assignment which entails weapon checks, crew choice and initial briefings.

Detailed briefings will not be given. That's for good reason. I cannot risk any information leaking to the authorities or to crewmen on the *Amazon Lady*. I'm told she sailed 200 miles overnight and will arrive later today in local waters but there's another reason for a reluctance to share details. We don't yet have a complete plan. How could we? When storming a superyacht crewed by feisty Columbians, anything can happen.

The location for our training program is West Sand Spit. The tide is low when we reach the long flat mound of golden sand that rises just two feet above sea level. Javel explains that nobody knows why the sand accumulates here as he drops anchor twenty yards from the spit and kills the outboards. We jump from the boat and wade ashore, taking scuba tanks, supplies of drinks, food and accessories. We're all wearing swimsuits,

T-shirts, wraparound shades and baseball caps. The sun ricochets from the sea, dazzling, hot and bright. A few hundred yards away, the sea of turquoise changes to the royal blue of the Atlantic. That's where the drop-off dives deep towards the ocean floor. The memory of my recent visit to that shelf beside the abyss is one I'm keen to forget.

It takes some time to free our weapons from their waterproof packaging. I remind you that both Annie and Mary are born-again gun fighters who handle weapons as lovingly as mothers fawn over new infants. While they examine the tasers and 9mm Beretta PX4 Storm pistols, I squeeze a small wad of plastic explosive into an empty coffee cup and attach a remote controlled detonator fuse. Taking this test device in a polythene bag I jog to the end of the spit and scoop out a hollow to conceal it. While I'm doing this I'm thinking about the Japanese woman, and how she almost had me believing her bullshit. Thank God for Kludo is all I can say.

With the test bomb planted I rejoin my girls who are cautiously examining a pack of Flash Bang grenades. I select one of these at random and I hurl it along the beach where it explodes with a deafening crash.

'So we know they're not duds,' I remark as soon as I can hear again. 'The best visiting cards ever...'

While we pause for chilled beer Javel wanders down the spit to hammer a post bearing a cardboard target into the sand

Suddenly Annie and Mary are at my side, both of them licking at my ears, one each.

'You girls okay?' I ask. 'What did I do to deserve...'

The next thing I know is that I'm looking up from the sand, gazing past the tanned thighs of my two ladies to their smiles of satisfaction and achievement. I'm also aware of Javel howling with laughter. He steps past the women, leans down and grabs my arm, pulling me upright to stand again.

'What was that?' I splutter. 'What the fuck happened?'

'The test worked,' replied Mary as she holds a tiny aerosol spray. 'The zonk spray took you down faster than we thought possible.'

Now I get it. My two demon women have just tested the secret weapon in our arsenal. We call it zonk spray because the latin names of the ingredients are too bizarre to remember. One sniff and down you go but at least they sank me on the sand, I'm pleased to note. A soft landing for the guinea pig. It's a close range weapon, I should tell you, since if the attacker also gets a sniff, he or she will also drop like a nine pin. The attacker must resist breathing while the vapour does its job before evaporating. It's clever stuff that Chad found via the black web. And apparently it works!

Javel is still laughing at the sight of my collapse to the sand. 'You get good dreams now, man.'

I confess it has left my head feeling rather fuzzy but he plants a can of beer in my hand and joins in the laughter of the two devil girls. 'We're all set, man.'

It's hard not to love Javel, especially when he laughs. He's a black saint and I can sense shivers of sexual expectancy pulsing down the spines of my girls. Javel may be a Rasta, but he's one helluva good-looking sailor. I trust him to ferry me anywhere on water , just as I trust Helms to spirit me anywhere by air.

Javel swings his dreads and stares across the lagoon. Then he nods and points. 'The troops they be coming.'

In the distance, I see a dark speck on the lagoon. It must be the boat bringing our volunteers, nevertheless we remain wary until we can identify it clearly. We may plan our attacks with subterfuge, but we don't appreciate others launching attacks on us out of the blue.

Minutes later the boat arrives and our volunteers are wading ashore. Along with Boxman, Ceejay, Able and Le Sage come several new faces whose demeanour suggests they've spent most of their lives behind bars.

'Good to see you guys,' I begin. 'Please line up while my friend Javel checks you out. All weapons and cell phones to be declared now. We promise to safeguard and return them later, and after we've agreed wages and terms.'

The men shuffle into a line, standing barefoot on the sand. Behind them the two boats bob and turn at anchor while Annie and Mary size up the newcomers. This might spark trouble. Two white women and a bunch of black dudes!

Javel frisks each man, taking cell phones and three blades in the process.

He places each item in a clear plastic bag. Meanwhile I pull out a stack of $100 bills to demonstrate good faith.

'All of you will have an equal share, so there's no need for argument. Each man gets a thousand dollars here and now but your man Le Sage will keep all this money safe until you return. If all goes to plan you'll each receive a bonus of four thousand bucks.'

The concept of five thousand dollars brings some joy to these deeply suspicious and wary gentlemen but I detect a warming sentiment as I count out the dollars, placing the combined total in a bag with their cell phones. 'Over to you Le Sage.'

Making this deposit to one of their brothers should fortify the goodwill until Ceejay chooses to upset the party. All this, you'll remember, is taking place on this glistening heap of tidal sand surrounded by the vast wide open spread of blue sea. The only escape is via the outboard boats lying at anchor nearby.

Ceejay steps forward. He's taller than me and I don't like the look on his face. 'You messin' with my woman.' He snarls at me. 'Who's to say you're not messing with us too?'

Ceejay's face radiates deep-rooted rancour. He's a big dude with shoulders like a silverback. I imagine he's won a few fights in his time, which is why we want him on our side.

'Who says we're messing with your woman?' asks Mary as she steps towards Ceejay. The top of her head reaches to his hairy chest. 'Jasmin's doin' real well and dances like a dream. We like her a lot.'

'That's ma point! She's liking you a lot more than me!'

'There's no accounting for personal tastes, Mr. Ceejay,' Mary says. 'If I was your woman, I'd run a mile.

That's when Ceejay grabs Mary by her neck, lifting her feet from the ground in a dangerous manoeuvre. It's time for me to step in. Pulling one of the berettas from the bag I aim it at his head until he drops Mary but I catch her wink as she skips back to me. 'Let's see who shoots best,' she mutters.

I lower my weapon and turn it around, offering the butt to Ceejay. 'If you can shoot better than her, she's all yours.'

Ceejay assesses the weapon and takes it while Annie points along the spit. 'Hit that target and yes, you can keep her.'

Ceejay positions his feet, takes aim and fires one shot. Mary raises her binoculars to view the target, shakes her head and then swiftly removes the gun from his hand.

He was never going to hit it. Mary had previously inserted a blank as the first round in all the magazines. For our pop-up pistol range in the Atlantic desert, do you really believe we'd allow Ceejay and his mates any opportunity to jump us? Not a chance.

While Mary reloads the weapon, I locate a small helium gas container and a pack of balloons. I attach a red balloon to the nozzle and inflate it. Tying the knot I release the scarlet balloon to the sky. As the target skeets up on the wind, Mary fires a single shot and hits it. One shot, just like that! The punctured balloon falls into the water.

The effect of this brilliant display of pistol skill is spectacular. Ceejay and the men stand mute on the sand, increasingly uncertain, in awe perhaps, about these women and their abilities.

'Fine shot!' I praise Mary. 'You'll be leading the charge when we go visiting.'

But now Boxman has a question. 'What's this visit, Cap'n? You said not'ing 'bout that.'

Annie has been rehearsing answers for this inevitable query. In her usual upfront manner my wife faces the recruits. 'There's a man I know who has taken something that I treasure dearly. He has a yacht in these waters so we plan, with your help, to go aboard it and reclaim what he took. Simple as that.'

'That don't sound simple,' decides Boxman. 'Could be plenty dangerous?'

'And so it might be.' Annie sounds serious. 'But we have the weapons, skill and advantage of surprise to achieve our objective. After taking what we need, we shall leave the man on his boat and depart from the islands. You will then go to Le Sage and claim all the deposited money and your cell phones. Le Sage will remain stationed on another vessel near here.'

Le Sage is no fool but his role and reputation seem to satisfy the men. Le

Sage, son of the voodoo bitch, nods as he stands in line, broadly agreeing to the proposal. It's a fair deal for all.

Now I check my watch which I synchronised with the timepiece worn by Helms early today. Precise timing is important now.

Out beyond and behind our volunteers, who are all facing me, I spot another dark speck just above the horizon. It tells me that Helms is on schedule and about to make a high-speed run over the spit. At low level the jet will deliver a significant shockwave. We're not telling our recruits about this imminent surprise. We need to test their ability and reaction when under stress.

The speck rapidly assumes the profile of an approaching jet. Even though I see it coming, there's a natural tendency to duck and hold my ears when, seconds later, our jet screams low overhead at five hundred miles an hour. The silver dagger clears the spit by fifty feet creating a whirling slipstream with a following blast of sound as Helms points the jet towards the south.

On the sand our recruits are either on their knees or holding hands to their ears. Strangely, the only man standing is Ceejay and he's grinning at the others. 'Woeh, man. That was truly joyous!'

After that little stunt, Helms will continue on his flight to survey the *Amazon Lady* whose position is now some 80 miles from the islands. He'll take aerial photos before returning.

Soon every recruit regains his feet and composure. With hearing and dignity restored, Mary steps forward to complete the address.

'We'll be operating in two teams. One team will remain on land. The other team will form the boarding party. You can decide which to choose. If you don't like the deep Atlantic, then volunteer for the land-based team. Either way, both teams rely on surprise for success. We will give the orders and you may be asked to seize some crew, but only to capture and secure them with tape like this.' She holds up a roll of silver duck tape. 'You may carry blades to cut the tape but you cannot harm these people except in self-defence you understand? You will ensure captives are kept out of action until we achieve our objective. Is that understood?'

Her message is heard and broadly understood by our rent-a-thug crowd. Mary walks up and down before the men. 'Okay,' she says. 'There's a pack of beer for the first man to reach the end of spit. Let's see you run!'

I feel proud of Mary. After her show of pistol skill, she has won massive respect from this crew of rascals. Barefoot on the spit Mary cuts a classy figure in her white shorts and blue T-shirt, her blonde hair flickering on the trade wind. I may love her, but somehow she feels happier and safer with Annie than with me.

And for God's sake why do I keep thinking about that Japanese girl? Wondering how it might be to be have Miss Harumi Tanaka and Mary in bed together? You can say I'm a crazy fucked-up feller, but I'm human too.

Inspired by the lure of a liquid prize, our local champs are now racing along the spit. It's two hundred yards to the end and when the first of them is nearly there, I hit the electronic trigger. A pulse flies to the detonator in the plastic explosive and whoosh!!! The sand erupts, shattering the peace. Overhead the terns and frigate birds veer from their flight paths as Javel throws back his thirsty roots to roar with laughter. 'Eeh man! That stopped them. Eh not so!'

Annie and Mary can't help but join in Javel's convulsions. The men have turned back towards us, a perplexed and confused bunch as we ever saw. Javel stoops to our Eski and tosses a beer to each man as he returns.

Ceejay is not impressed. 'Why yo do that? he shouts, crowding into my personal space. 'Yo damned near blow me to hell!'

'But I didn't.' Putting my hand on his shoulder I push him away. 'If I wanted to send you to hell, I'd have done so by now. But remember this. Never give us reason to leave similar, or even more unwelcome surprises, in your neighbourhood. Okay?'

'We get the message,' says Ceejay. 'Don't mess with Mr. Rackham and his gang.'

'That's exactly the point. Don't forget it.'

Half an hour later, we've cleaned the spit and boarded our respective craft for the journey back to the islands.

35

Miss Tanaka returns to Miami

MISS TANAKA WAS relieved to find Agent Bradley waiting at the check-in for the early morning flight to Miami. He was carrying a plastic bag which, she assumed, contained the cigar butt once held between John Rackham's lips.

Bradley was peeved. 'So why the urgency?'

'I don't know.' Miss Tanaka replied. 'HQ called last night, ordering me back to Miami. Such a shame when I was just getting to know the island.'

Bradley passed over the bag 'Here's your sample with icepacks to keep it cool.'

Miss Tanaka smiled. 'Thanks for all your help. I'll be in touch.'

Then she was on her way to security where she placed the bag in a tray on the conveyor for hand baggage, cell phone and crutches. She walked through the screening arch to keep pace with her belongings. Then the security officer beckoned to her. 'I need to check this bag, ma'am.'

Miss Tanaka opened her shoulder bag and showed her FBI pass to the official. 'This is government business and this holds important evidence. May I request you not to open it.'

The security official chewed gum and contemplated the FBI badge. 'What evidence, ma'am?'

'An important item the FBI needs for tests in Miami.'

On the screen the image of the freeze box and the aluminium tube remained annoyingly static while the officer squinted at the screen. 'Some items here contain liquids which are not permitted aboard the aircraft.'

'Yes, I'm aware of the TSA 3-1-1 liquids rule but this lies within those limits.' Miss Tanaka was stretching the truth but the plea, backed by the FBI pass, finally worked in her favour.

The officer flicked a shoulder. 'Okay. I let it pass.'

Shortly Miss Tanaka was again looking down from her window seat onto shanty townships, the luxury hotels of Grace Bay and finally the shimmering coastal beaches as the airliner climbed towards its cruise altitude.

The cabin was half full with businessmen, real estate traders, Canadian tourists and a handful of wealthy black women aiming for a shopping spree. When the jet found its cruise level, the cabin staff offered coffee and tea. Then most passengers, including Miss Tanaka, dozed off to the soothing rumble of the engines.

She woke as the wheels hit runway 26 at Miami International. Across the airport a dull smog, thick with humidity, contrasted to the cleaner air of Providenciales.

Miss Tanaka sailed through Immigration and Customs, no questions asked. Her car was waiting in the park and she took I75 directly to HQ where she deposited Rackham's cigar at the DNA lab. If a match existed between the thirteenth ear and the cigar, the expert analysts would find it. She then took the elevator to the director's floor.

'So, how was Rum Cay?' Jenkins began.

'Beautiful place, beautiful people.'

'Don't get too used to the five star lifestyle.'

Miss Tanaka nodded. 'Point taken.'

Jenkin's office reflected its occupant, cool, uncluttered and woefully short of charm. She recalled the buggy ride with Rackham, the subsequent rounds of rum punch leading to the cigar theatricals. Staring at the director she felt that Rackham was the more attractive man. Rackham, maybe a rogue, was more exciting.

'So you have left the DNA sample with the lab. They'll inform me when they get the results.' Jenkins said.

'There may be finger prints too.' .

'I imagine so.' Jenkins nodded. 'And you met with Bradley?'

'He was very helpful.'

'And you're both still convinced that Rackham's presence is primarily for a concert featuring Sarahanna?'

'We found no reason to suggest otherwise.'

'Other than it makes no financial sense.' Jenkins sniffed as he referred to some papers on his desk. 'Bradley reports the show is likely to cost several hundred thousand dollars. Since we understand entry tickets are effectively free, are we to believe Rackham is doing all this for charity?'

'I didn't ask him.'

'It seems unlikely. He might win friends in the islands by presenting them with a sexy superstar, but his presence is unclear, particularly as we have now identified the two females in his party.'

'I saw them,' she said. 'Who are they?'

'Neither woman features in federal databases so we initiated a search with some South American colleagues. The blonde woman is known to Columbian authorities as a sex worker. The other woman is Rackham's wife and mother of his daughter. Mrs. Rackham used to deal in fine art and antiques in Buenos Aires. She moves in elite circles and knows plenty of high rollers.'

'Is either woman on a wanted list?'

'That's not yet determined.' Jenkins fingered the PC keyboard as the mugshots of Annie and Mary came up on the screen. 'Just imagine living with those two!'

'A striking couple,' said Miss Tanaka. 'I guess you realise they both have the same names as the women who lived with Rackham in 1720?'

Jenkins leaned back in his chair, clasping his hands behind his head. 'Yes, we had noted that. If true, it amounts to one of the most extraordinary anomalies in recorded criminal history.'

'Mary and Annie have been common names in use for centuries. Mary, possibly more so, since she was the mother of Jesus.'

Jenkins shrugged. 'And none of that's relevant. We still have no clue to their motives for promoting this concert, no valid reason to alert the local authorities.'

'So, what next?' asked Miss Tanaka, hopeful that he might offer her coffee. She was feeling thirsty after the early start to her day.

Jenkins swung his computer screen towards Miss Tanaka. Now it showed blurred images of two men. 'Bradley took these long range photos a few days ago. This man is their pilot, William Helms, a former pilot in the Australian special forces, experienced in a wide range of aircraft, with three ex-wives, six children and of no fixed abode. He probably needs a fistful of dollars.'

'So that might provide motives. Who's the other guy?'

'We're learning about him. We believe he's Tomas Chaderlitz, a Ukrainian national with proven skills on the darkest web. If it is Chaderlitz, he qualifies for extradition to Brazil. He broke out of jail and the Brazilians will welcome back to custody. Alternatively we could offer him a job in our cyber unit here.'

'I didn't meet either man. They've taken two villas at Rum Cay, so I guess they must be in residence. I did get to meet Rackham's daughter and her dog. The girl is more cunning and manipulative than most teenagers but her dog is something else.'

'I don't follow,' said Jenkins.

'You would if you met it. Real nasty.'

'The dog may not merit attention but others in Rackham's crew do justify interest. Be careful since we're not yet operating on an approved basis.' Jenkins sat motionless. He stared at his screen, apparently evaluating his options before turning to Miss Tanaka with one of his rarer attributes, a smile.

'I want you to fly back today. Liaise with agent Bradley. See what else you can dig up. You never know in this business, but history has been known to repeat itself.'

36

John Rackham – My Fury with Chad

I'VE JUST PUNISHED one of my crew. And you can guess who…

I found him sprawled on the sofa, wearing T-shirt and shorts. His mouth was open, his head thrown back with one arm dangling towards an empty bottle of Stolichnaya lying on the tiled floor while a hard core porn video was running on his TV.

Chad did not hear me arrive. Nor was he aware that the alarm on our local movement sensors was buzzing. Our HQ's integrity was therefore jeopardised by his total lack of discipline.

There's a general disorder in the kitchen, with half-eaten pizzas and empty bottles to amplify my foul mood. I fill a jug with cold water and return to our geek as he lies inert and senseless, blissfully unaware that I'm about to grip his testicles and squeeze them without mercy. Simultaneously I pour a jugful of water over the ghastly expanse of his shaved skull.

Chad wakes up howling.

'Holler as much as you like, buddy. I'm going to teach you a lesson.' I tip more water over his head and increase my grip on his Ukrainian nuts. 'You cannot behave like this! Do you hear me?'

Chad cannot hear since he's making too much noise.

'You have compromised our security! You're drunk on duty! You are a low-life stinking bastard who doesn't know his own luck.'

Realising that Chad's howls might alert other residents, I remove my hand from his jewels and return to the kitchen to wash my hands and refill the jug.

On my return to his room, Chad is whimpering. With water dripping from his skull, Chad is nursing his groin as he grits his teeth and sobs. 'I'm sorry, boss. I'm sorry.'

I throw a second jug of water at his head and shoulders. 'Sorry! I've spent a fortune setting this up and you're putting all of it at risk. Do you get that, Chad? Or must I crunch your nuts again?'

'I get it, boss. I do. I'm real sorry.'

'You'll be even more sorry when I return you to the cell block in Manaus. They want you back, Chad, because you left prematurely, before you had finished your visit to their foul, crowded, stinking, asshole of a prison. The reason you were there in the first place was because you overdosed on your spending habits which made the authorities wonder why you were inexplicably driving around in juiced up cars. Can you remember all that?'

'Yeah boss. I remember.'

'Then you need to revive that memory of life in that prison, Chad. Very fast and permanently. Because if you don't obey my orders, Helms will drop you off in Manaus!'

'Heh, what's goin' down here?'

I turn to see Helms has just returned. He's in his pilot shirt, dark glasses riding on his crewcut with his flight bag in his hand. He's staring at the miserable creature lying on the sofa.

'What's the problem?' he repeats. 'I heard the bastard hollering a hundred yards away.'

'He fell over that bottle and whacked his scrotum on the sofa.'

Chad is making strenuous attempts to recover, probably realising that I'm serious about my threats. Helms, you see, is no whacky piss artist. He drinks in moderation and flies jet aircraft, so he's not on Chad's side. 'Get cleaned up, Chad,' he says. 'I need you to download my camera.'

I take two beers from the cooler and beckon Helms outside after he has handed over the camera. 'Next time Chad won't be forgiven. We'll return him to Manaus. Drunk on duty. A bad dude.'

Helms rubs his jaw pensively. 'You're right, boss. But maybe he's been taking his cue from you.'

I protest instantly. 'That ain't fair, Helms. I may love rum, but I never collapse on duty, especially when guarding the base.'

We tap cans and drink. 'So how did it go? Your fly-past on the spit was outstanding. They never heard you coming. You nearly ripped their heads off.'

'That was a game we played with the Taliban. Full gallop at turban height to drop hot gifts and vanish.' Helms chortles at the memory. 'But makes a helluva mess if you screw up the altitude.'

The beer tastes good as my temper cools. With goddam Chad I lost it big time and his nuts will feel like hot peppers for days. 'So you got lucky in your recce for the target?'

'You bet!' Helms crow's feet crinkle. 'I climbed to 5,000 feet where I successfully identified and photographed the Felix yacht to the south-west, about 80 miles from Turkey Chaos.'

I gather this is Helm's pet name for the islands. 'Let's take a look at your aerial shots.'

We sit in the evening sunshine, both realising the deadline is imminent. *Amazon Lady* is only hours from landfall and the action on which rides a ton of money will shortly begin.

'Then I put the bird down on the West Chaos airstrip. Had a cross-wind on the approach but nobody had moved the dragons' teeth. The wings cleared the blocks by a whisker. Just as well we walked the course.'

'Too right.' The thought of my jet whacking into a pillar of solid concrete sends another shiver down my spine. 'So what else?'

'I parked at the end of the strip. After shut down I spread the camouflage netting as agreed. From the air you won't see much of the jet unless you're really eyeballing. Then I set up the new dragon's teeth, locked the jet and waited till Javel came to ferry me back. A good day, I'd say.'

So you now understand why I lost it with the Ukrainian. Helms is a professional fighting man who can be trusted to deliver. Chad, on the other hand, may be equally skilled, but his head revolves in a Stoli cyber space, somewhere well beyond my grasp.

Helms wants to know about my day. 'Did the locals enjoy the rehearsal?'

'My God, they loved how the girls used the hardware. When they saw Mary shoot, the entire mob came onside in seconds. We had a grand finale after warning them to stay silent and not to leek our details before, during or after the event, on fear of fatal punishment. When I triggered the explosive, they believed me. All very dramatic.'

Helms finds it entertaining. 'I'd like to have seen that.'

'Haven't you seen enough bombs and explosions?'

'Too bloody right.' Helms chews it over. 'But some of us got hooked on war games and I guess I'm one of them.'

While I consider his honest view on warfare, I'm thinking about my own addiction to drama. Helms, it seems, is reading my mind.

'How about you, JR. Don't you want to retire in style? You're not obliged to go seeking trouble.' He pauses. 'Or maybe you are?'

'It's odd you should mention that,' I reply. 'You've heard about these strange videos on Swann's tablet?'

'Yeah. Annie mentioned unexplained stories and Swann's ghosts. If this is where old Jack Rackham kept his sheilas in the past then old habits die hard. Maybe this place is your destiny?'

'I guess we all get to destiny sooner or later.' I'm thinking of that video on the cursed tablet, when my ancestor slid from a horse-drawn cart to twitch for the final minutes of his life on the end of a rope. The memory strikes at the pit of my stomach. 'Helms,' I say. 'No more talk of destiny. We're here for a purpose. Let's see if Chad has something to show us.'

Back inside the villa, our sulking geek has unloaded the camera memory. His screen shows the *Amazon Lady* steaming over the waters of the Atlantic. He has enlarged five shots and opens each image for more detailed inspection.

We see immediately the yacht is a significant piece of marine real estate with four decks above the waterline. According to yacht websites, the *Amazon Lady is* valued in the 150 million dollar range. With crew, dock, maintenance and ancillary costs, it means Dr. Felix Roblado is loaded, dare I say over-burdened with wealth. That thought gives me good reason to feel no guilt for what we're planning. This fat feline from Columbia has caused enough pain to fellow humans in accruing the wealth to own this huge asset, not to mention those other assets on board for which we have developed an acute desire.

Chad enlarges the images. We see passengers on the decks and below the awnings. I note life-rafts tucked along both flanks of the vessel but there's no sign of activity on the foredeck or bridge where the officers are shielded by darkened window panels.

Chad zooms onto the helicopter deck astern of the midships. Lying there, on the painted H symbol, is a woman in a topless bikini sunning herself on a lounger. Maybe she's also been branded like other women who have played with Dr. Felix?

'Good photos,' I say to Helms. 'You did well.'

Helms helps himself to another beer before slumping into a chair. I amble over to Chad and grip his shoulder. 'Right, my friend, time to send another message. Tell them Sarahanna is arriving tomorrow and is hoping to see Dr. Felix at her show.'

Chad taps out a draft email to send to *Amazon Lady's* server which I quickly approve. After he has sent the email, Chad aims his sunken rose-tinted eyes at me. 'I'm sorry boss. Real sorry.'

'Sorry for what?' I ask him.

'Sorry I drink all vodka. Nothing left now.'

'And Chad, my friend, I'll tear off your balls if you ever do that again!'

37

Annie believes that we are being watched

A BIRD IS singing outside our bedroom window. The repetition of its song may be charming, but it's also irritating because I need more sleep. I was awake for much of the night while my mind roved through the options for the job ahead. Then, just when slumber finally arrived, this feathered alarm starts to chirp, warble and trill like a nightingale on acid to advise me that D Day is here.

The bird has also woken Mary who's sleeping alongside me. She switches on and off easily and always appears rested. Now Mary's eyes open and blink while on the other bed my husband continues to snore softly, his head thrown back on a single pillow.

'Tell that fucking bird to shut up,' Mary whispers.

'Let the birdie sing. It's better than his snoring.' I yawn and swing my legs off the bed. 'I'll get some coffee.'

Out of bed, I slip into my robe and head for the kitchen as Kludo wanders in from Swann's bedroom. He also yawns and stretches before I release him into the yard. There's a fresh feel to the air and when it sees me, the bird flies away leaving an empty silence.

Half an hour later, breakfast arrives with room service. The Filipino waitress lays out fruit, eggs and pastries, which we ordered mindful of the super energy needed for our assignment. Only Swann remains in bed so we talk quietly in guarded terms.

'I hope Le Sage enjoyed his sleepover,' says Mary sipping her coffee. 'I'm glad I didn't spend a night on that wreck.'

Mary is referring to the isolation unit we found for Le Sage. Compared to our luxury quarters, his couldn't be rougher. It was Mary's idea to put Le Sage on an old wreck, a tribute to dodgy seamanship, which sits at a jaunty angle on a shallow reef one mile offshore. Among its withering bulkheads reside colonies of screaming seabirds but the rusted bridge and captain's quarters remain largely intact. We imagine Le Sage has made himself comfy with the large duvet we provided but we also left him with the stash of dollars, the initial deposit to guard for the crew, an FM radio and three day's supply of essentials such as food, water and beer.

'He'll be fine,' says JR who now joins us. He runs his fingers over his stubbled jawline. 'Folks from Haiti are tougher than tungsten. Three days on a wreck doing fuck-all, and getting paid. Sounds like a dream job.'

'Can the men trust him?' I ask. 'Not to vanish with their wages?'

'It was their decision.' JR loads a forkful of scrambled egg. 'They trust him because they believe Le Sage has the puissance. Because his mother is that old witch at the Conch Bar, nobody's likely to step on their toes in a hurry, are they?'

'I wouldn't,' says Mary. 'She's pure evil.'

'Forget her.' JR reaches for some toast. 'I shall miss all this when we're back in Brazil. I like how these guys do breakfast.'

Mary picks up a glossy mag, one of those featuring royalty and celebrities. Sometimes she finds ideas for future operations in their pages since people who parade wealth and assets tend to attract our expertise. This is exactly what Dr. Felix Roblado has succeeded in doing. He has homes in Columbia to entertain guests, but not many go aboard his yacht. Our Mary is among the chosen few.

Over the months we've analysed the entire structure of the *Amazon Lady*, studying the original designs of her architects and builders in the Netherlands. Chad managed to unearth the layout of her electronic systems.

However at this moment, we need super luck and plenty of it. Plus we need a superstar and, of course, a superyacht.

Helms arrives as we wind-up breakfast. He has the latest updates on two of those requirements. 'Sarahanna and her people will be arriving at noon on schedule. She'll have a retinue of six and they want a brief visit to the show venue before they have lunch.'

'No problem,' I say. 'I've reserved rooms for Sarahanna.'

'And the yacht?' asks JR, passing a coffee to Helms. 'She should be here by now.'

Helms nods. 'She is. Lying out beyond the reef at Grace Bay. Chad is monitoring their RT. Everything suggests Felix is on board.'

On hearing this news Mary's eyes narrow, like a panther contemplating a juicy peccary. 'Bring it on, Roblado.'

'And the weather is good,' Helms adds. 'Ideal I'd say.'

JR is happy. 'So we're all set. Sounds too good to be true.'

My husband's guarded optimism is typical so I make the point. 'We planned it this way. Being on track is no accident.'

Yes, the easy part has been achieved. To entice a yacht owner to leave home to play with a superstar is nothing new. We believe Sarahanna is entirely unaware of her unique and adoring fan from Columbia because we've never informed her of his adulation. Nor will we. Sarahanna's single task is to do what she does best. To sing her heart out. And for that she'll receive her agreed fee.

Except she won't be getting it in bank notes.

On one of our previous raids at the ranch of a cocaine merchant near Bogota, we relieved the gentleman of his finest emeralds and some of these will go to Sarahanna in lieu of dollars.

Like many celebrities and royalty Sarahanna adores gemstones. In her case, it's a major passion. Negotiations with her manager were easy once we agreed to pay his cut in dollars while Sarahanna was happy to take raw emeralds for several reasons. Columbian stones are generally the best and they can be imported into the United States duty free. Only when cut and polished do the taxes kick in so she's bringing her own gemologist to check the goods.

To be frank, I'm not big on adornments. I wear the gold wedding ring JR gave me when we tied the knot in Montevideo. My right ear lobe has a golden stud, matching the one in Mary's left ear. We find bracelets and necklaces are awkward in combat so we wear them sparingly. In short we won't miss our green gem stones. Sarahanna is welcome to them.

As I think about waking Swann we are disturbed by the sudden arrival of our Ukrainian. Chad is milling his arms, discharging like an angry drone.

Helms and JR are studying a map and my husband responds instantly. 'What's up, Chad? You've left our HQ unattended. That's unforgivable.'

I jump up from my chair and step between JR and Chad, placing a hand on my husband's shoulder. 'Steady, luv. Allow Chad to explain why he's here.'

Chad's slavic features look grey in the tropical sunshine. His face is loaded with perspiration and he stammers in confusion.

'Now Chad,' I offer him orange juice. 'Speak slowly and tell me the problem.' Chad responds to my gentle persuasion while JR and Helms remained twinned in fury. 'What's the matter, Chad?'

Chad drinks some juice, straightens and wipes his brow. 'I go into the FBI files, looking for mention of Turkey Chaos. They have two agents here watching us. One we do not know. The other is a Japanese woman here in the hotel.'

JR freezes. His unshaven jaw sets to stone while Helms takes a deep breath and holds it. Mary studies her finger nails before she makes the first comment. 'Maybe I should pay her a visit? I could persuade her to lose interest.'

'The FBI would alert every cop on this island.' I tell them. 'No, Mary. Not your best idea. There has to be another way.'

Helms glances at his watch. 'We don't have much time. Sarahanna arrives in three hours.'

Then we get another surprise. From the corridor in our villa comes my lovely daughter wearing her green floral bikini top with matching pareu. Unlike Chad, she's as calm as I've ever seen her, with a cocky smile and no apology.

'I've been listening in.' Swann admits to eavesdropping. 'Kludo warned us the woman was dodgy and I thought so too and now Chad has proved it.'

'Okay. So where does that take us?' I ask. 'We've invited her to meet Sarahanna for an interview before the concert and there's no crime in that.'

'True,' Swann agrees. 'But perhaps I can look after her – while you're on your other business?'

'You realise that FBI agents are not known for kindness?'

Swann smirks as she sits down and reaches for a bowl of muesli. 'I watch *Law and Order*, don't I?'

'We're not talking television dramas, honey.' JR is clearly concerned about allowing Swann to spend time with Miss Tanaka. He looks as though a heart attack is imminent. 'What do you think, Annie?'

'Swann's quite capable of entertaining your Japanese friend.'

Mary and Helms nod, appearing to agree with the proposal.

'Then it's a done deal,' I declare, suddenly feeling very proud of my only child. 'Just so long as Swann knows nothing else about our vacation here. She cannot be involved. Understood?'

'Some holiday,' says Swann as she starts on her breakfast. 'All I need now is a federal agent to share it with.'

38

Miss Tanaka returns to Rum Cay

MISS TANAKA ARRIVED back in Providenciales on the evening flight and reached Rum Cay as dusk fell. Finding no sign of the Rackhams in the public areas of the resort, she ordered a caesar salad with a glass of Chardonnay before retiring to her room. She had made two international flights, met with executive director and delivered one cigar stub. A fair day's work for a special agent.

Next morning Miss Tanaka opened her verandah door, allowing the air conditioning to blend with the early morning heat. She would have a light breakfast before treating herself to a massage in the resort's wellness centre. Travel hassle was reason enough to visit the resort spa which was just five minutes walk from her room.

'Would madam prefer a massage with Abhyanga?' asked the white-coated Filipino receptionist.

Miss Tanaka wasn't too sure. 'What exactly is that?'

'Massage with warm sesame oils, Madam.'

Harumi Tanaka shook her head. 'No. Just the standard massage, please.'

While the masseuse went to work on her back, neck and temples, Miss Tanaka lay naked and face down on the table, wondering how to handle her interview with a major star. What questions would Sarahanna appreciate? Though trained in interrogation techniques, reggae and rap were not Agent Tanaka's regular topics. Perhaps Sarahanna had her own views on massage?

'Madam has such beautiful skin.'

Miss Tanaka woke up, realising that the massage had induced a light doze. She dressed, tipped the masseuse twenty bucks and strolled back in the growing heat of Rum Cay.

Back in the main hotel, Miss Tanaka felt that an iced lemon drink might be in order. She wasn't surprised to find John Rackham and his daughter were already in the bar. The pair sat facing the ocean with a rum special and a cola respectively. When Rackham glanced in her direction, Miss Tanaka waggled her fingers in a return of greeting.

Rackham rose from his chair and invited her over. 'Hi, Miss Tanaka. You're very welcome.'

But as Tanaka walked over to join him, her cell phone chirruped. 'Excuse me,' she said as she looked at the screen. 'It's my editor. I'll join you in a moment.'

Out of earshot, at the edge of the infinity pool, Miss Tanaka took the call from the lab assistant at Miami HQ. 'We have the results on the sample you delivered yesterday.'

'Okay, ' she said. 'And?'

'We believe your subject's DNA overlaps with the original sample, the ear DNA that you first delivered. It's not the strongest result, but it's clearly positive.'

Miss Tanaka felt elated by the news. A proven link was exciting and successful. It showed how the Rackham DNA had survived for over three hundred years.

'Please forward the results to Director Jenkins and tell him I'm with the subject at this very moment. Thank you.'

Turning back to the Rackhams, Miss Tanaka was pleased that her call had been both discreet and brief. Rackham had abandoned his daughter and was now walking towards her.

'What a lovely day,' Harumi Tanaka said, closing her cell phone. 'My editor had some ideas for the interview with Sarahanna.'

Rackham grinned. 'I was going to say that Sarahanna will be free this afternoon. She's due here at noon for a basic rehearsal. Then she'll have time-out before hitting the stage this evening. I've asked my daughter, Swann, to liaise with you. Is that all right?'

'Absolutely. Thank you so much.'

Rackham gave her arm a squeeze. 'No trouble. I hope we may get together after the concert for another cigar? Back in the bar here? Is that okay?'

'I'd love to,' said Miss Tanaka.

'A small favour. Don't tell my daughter.' One of his eyes winked as his grip tightened on her arm. 'Just between us, okay?'

'Absolutely.' Miss Tanaka blew Rackham an air-kiss as he released his grip. 'So kind of you to arrange the interview.'

'I've got a ton of duties,' said Rackham. 'See you later.'

After Rackham departed, Miss Tanaka strolled over to Swann's table. The girl looked pretty in her green bikini and sarong. Miss Tanaka felt envious as she stopped at the table. 'Safe to join you?'

Swann was reading a magazine. She looked up. 'Safe? What do you mean?'

'The dog?' Miss Tanaka explained, noting how Swann's smile and eyes were so similar to her father's. No DNA needed to prove a family link there, she thought as she peered below the table. 'I don't see him today.'

'Kludo? Oh, I left him in the villa. You're quite safe.'

Miss Tanaka sat down and beckoned a waiter. Rum Cay always had hovering staff on hand. 'Your father says you've kindly offered to help with Sarahanna and the interview. To be honest, I'm a bit nervous about it. She's such a big star.'

'Big, beautiful and brilliant. She's a real star,' said Swann.

'I've just spent an hour in the massage clinic. I need a drink and what would you like?'

'Thanks. I'll have a cola zero.' Swann closed the pages of her magazine and smiled at Miss Tanaka. 'Was it a good massage?'

'Fair to middling. Next time I may try the Abhyanga.'

'Yeah, that's better,' said Swann. 'The one with hot sesame.'

39

Annie visits the wardrobe department

CHAD'S DISCOVERY ABOUT confirmed FBI interest in our noble gang gave me a shock. The thought of spooks hanging around us in Rum Cay almost spoiled the start to our great day. Luckily my daughter, as they say, is a chip off the old block. When Swann volunteered to spend time with Miss Tanaka, I felt very proud of her.

So we left Swann on the job at Rum Cay and now we are in our SUV driving to the show venue where we find Walter Schulz has a case of stage fright. The imminent arrival of a super rapper to entertain a horde of thousands appears to daunt him. This is surprising, as he knows the business so well, but he's done a good job. The stage, lighting and sound systems are primed and as for the Portakabins where Sarahanna and her retinue will decamp, they're ready with preference supplies in each room.

My husband tells Schulz we must reserve one cabin exclusively for our daughter and a Japanese journalist and that we'll be providing security guards for their protection. My daughter, I tell him, goes a bit loopy when pop stars are around, so we must keep her safe. Schulz will deal with these requirements, so he says.

Back in the SUV with Helms at the wheel, we now head to South Dock Road, an area of shanty homes, street dogs, discarded cars and rusting white goods. We've seen many similar locations in South America but here it's equally unsightly. Nevertheless Helms finds our destination and we descend to make our way past curious street kids into a dilapidated warehouse.

Waiting inside for us are Jasmin and her man Ceejay. Both are being fitted by our seamstress Nana, an enormous woman who comes from the Dominican Republic. She's in her 50's, dark-skinned with a huge smile, as wide as her hips.

'Hello my lovelies,' Nana greets us. 'You folks getting busy for Sarahanna, yeh?'

'You bet,' JR replies while he assesses the outfits we have ordered. 'You've done well, Nana. Let's see how they fit.'

Ceejay and Jasmin watch as we try on our respective uniforms. I sidle over to Jasmin and pull on a loose fitting Muumuu. 'How does this look?' I ask her.

Jasmin tries not to laugh. I can't tell her that the copious folds of the garment are to hide my bullet-proof vest and pouches for my firearms and ammunition but Mary and JR nod approvingly. They're also trying on uniforms that Nana has copied, based on the reconnaissance photographs I took at South Side marina. The police shoulder badge and chest insignia are convincing additions to the disguise. JR and Mary will wear these uniforms and they'll be carrying sidearms in regulation holsters.

'You look so good in uniform,' I purr, giving my husband a hug. 'And as for you, Mary, in officer kit… you look ravishing!'

Both are equally amused by my compliments. 'And now for your wig,' I tell Mary after adjusting the pleats on her navy shirt. I assess the wig we found for her. 'Let's see how it looks.'

Mary pulls on the wig, an Afro frazzle with a streak of purple on one side. 'Yeaa!' says Mary as she faces the mirror on Nana's wall.

JR is less impressed. 'She's very pale. She might be recognised.'

If a crewman on *Amazon Lady* sees through Mary's disguise it would create significant problems. 'With make-up I can turn her to the colour of Dijon mustard.' I tell him.

Mary shrugs. 'I guess you'll have to.'

Nana has done a fine job. Our wardrobe is soon approved as ready for use, and throughout Ceejay has been watching from the warehouse sidelines, arms folded on thick biceps, his face loaded with suspicion when he sees the police uniforms. I must change his attitude swiftly.

'Mr. Ceejay,' I say as I stride over and peer up at him. Last time we tussled, he was defeated and ridiculed before his friends. Nor has he forgotten how we shoot, so he's watching with caution now.'I need your permission, Mr. Ceejay.'

The Trinidadian chews his lip. 'Permission for w'at?'

'I need to borrow Jasmin for a day. I'll look after her personally until she returns tomorrow. This evening you'll be working with Mary. When she gives you an order, you must carry it out. Is that clear?'

'Sure that much is clear,' Ceejay says with a derisive sneer. 'But I don't agree. I don't want you messin' with ma woman. And why must I take orders from Mary? You ain't payin' 'nuff dollar for that.'

So it appears we have a problem.

Mary cups her hand around my ear and whispers. Then she finishes by inserting her tongue into my ear, so typical of her naughtiness.

'I'll ask him.' I reply, reaching out to take Ceejay's wrist. He thinks I'm about to deck him again. He's very tense.

Meanwhile Mary delivers her idea to JR's right ear also sealing it with a loving lick. JR nods and comes over to join us.

'For your wrist, Mr. Ceejay.' JR traces his finger around Ceejay's muscled wrist. 'How 'bout you keeping my fine Swiss watch until we get Jasmin back to you. Is that a fair deal?'

Ceejay's no slouch when it concerns bling. He's got anchor chains of gold around his bull neck with bracelets, ear-rings and a fat nose stud. JR slips the watch from his wrist and places it on Ceejay's wrist.

'You like it?' JR asks. 'Now will you lend us Jasmin and help us with all we want. Is that a deal or not?'

The offer of the expensive timepiece is like winning the lottery. Suddenly Ceejay's mood switches. He begins to smile.

JR repeats. 'So that's a deal?'

Ceejay can't believe a swiss angel has just landed on his wrist. 'Ya, man. You can take ma woman. Ya keep her. No problem.'

I give Jasmin an appropriate smile. Poor girl. She has just been traded for a stolen wrist watch! For a feminist that's a capital offence. For me, a realist who loves men and women equally, it's a case of manifest effrontery.

'And you will carry out our orders?' I repeat.

'Sure, ma'am. Anything you want.'

JR and Helms gather up the wardrobe bags and head for the door. Helms looks outside, checking to see if it's clear, then nods.

'Very well. Ceejay, you'll go with them. We'll take Jasmin from here.' I give Nana a thousand dollars and then follow the men out to the street.

Parked behind our SUV there is now a full stretch limo, one of several available for rent on the island. We've hired two for the day. Both come with drivers who are friends of our Boxman. Standing beside the limo the uniformed driver is keeping onlookers at bay as we make our way to it.

Jasmin, bless her, is overcome by the sight of the stretch limo and the growing crowd of curious folk. 'What's that for?'

'It's for you, darlin'.' Gripping her shoulder, my enthusiasm fills Jasmin with confidence. 'Ceejay gets a watch. You get a limo. And you also get to meet and play with Sarahanna. So let's take a ride.'

40

John Rackham needs a chicken's leg

MY GIRLS WENT off in style. In this shanty town their limo is a rare sight with its dark windows and zappy chrome wheels. They'll head to Rum Cay where Annie will give Jasmin a full makeover using her cosmetic artistry which more than equals her skill with a pistol. After the makeover, we'll have a passable body double for Sarahanna.

The star, the genuine Sarahanna, will soon be landing in her private jet from Nassau in the Bahamas. She'll arrive to a full gale welcome at Provo airport where local dignitaries and adoring fans will greet her, providing the fanfare of revved-up drama that top performers rightfully deserve.

All that ballyhoo will be managed by Walter Schulz. He's an expert in preening egos, and knows what accessories to provide in dressing rooms. Schulz can handle the inevitable histrionics that follow such folk around so I'll leave that to him. Sarahanna will have the finest memory of her visit to the islands, won't she just? It falls to me to ensure that she does.

Now that I've lost my watch to brother Ceejay, I'll take my time-checks from my iPhone. However Ceejay is a changed man. Funny how a lump of Swiss metal can boost social standing, isn't it? I was quite fond of the watch, liberated from a Lebanese trader whose illegal profits we pruned some years ago. The schmuck was selling hardwood by the ship load along with rare jungle animals while he wallowed in a grotesque mansion in Brazilia.

Enough of past history. We must confront the present as we drive to our next destination. Ceejay is lounging in the back of the SUV gazing at the watch on his sturdy wrist. At least he's happy as we take the Leeward Highway to the eastern shore.

We assumed from the outset that our SUV will be fitted with a transponder to provide data of its whereabouts to the hire company. Yes, Chad could have disabled it, but what's the point on an island this small? Our operations mainly take place at sea using vessels whose transponders will be disabled. Similarly when Helms parked our jet on West Caicos, his transponder did not record the change of location because he disabled it after leaving Providenciales.

All these considerations occupy my thoughts after we learned that the FBI have infiltrated our base thanks to that sweet-talking, cigar-puffing bitch. Now we must be especially alert. The cheek of the woman! Then Swann astonished us by offering to chaperone the Japanese spy, in an attempt to keep Miss Tanaka from reporting our activities. Swann says she will disable the woman's cellphone by some ruse and how she does that is beyond my control.

Meanwhile the local police, according to Chad, remain ignorant of our plan apart from detailing a sizeable detachment to patrol the show. And that's exactly what I intended.

Listening to the car's radio it's obvious that every islander intends to attend the show of the decade. Apart from a few dribbling expats and some big mamas with kids, the entire population will be worshipping at the altar of Sarahanna while we set about relieving Dr. Felix of his valued collection.

It takes fifteen minutes to reach the Leeward Channel. Here we park the SUV at the ferry station leaving its key under the floor mat as we don't expect to need it again. The hire company will find it soon enough I imagine.

Leeward Channel links the huge turquoise lagoon to the south with the Atlantic Ocean to the north. One shore of the channel hosts a marina for pleasure yachts. On the opposite shore lies a wide mangrove swamp, an impenetrable mass of vegetation, home to mosquitoes and birds of weird feather. Further beyond lies the island of North Caicos which is our immediate destination using the public ferry.

In the ticket office, I ask for three return tickets. To create a memory for the ticket agent, I specifically ask for First Class tickets. The agent stares at me disbelievingly. The ferry has no such facilities, she says. We must take our seats with the general public who travel between the islands. That explains why I'm now seated beside a cheerful woman who is travelling with five chickens in a wicker basket. Helms and Ceejay sit opposite me, the latter still gloating over his windfall and Helms inevitably nursing a beer.

'Excuse me, ma'am,' I say to the island lady. She's wearing a home-made dress of scarlet floral print. 'What are you planning to do with those chickens?'

She gives me a funny look and giggles. 'Same as you, man. If they don't lay me eggs, I eat them.'

'And what d'you know about voodoo and chickens?' I note that Helms raises an eyebrow as we wait for her answer.

This time the lady doesn't laugh. The chickens cluck and cheep while she recoils. 'Why for you ask me that?'

With a brief shrug I tone it down. 'I heard a chicken's foot can keep enemies away. Is that something you know about?'

Serious now, she stares at me lowering her voice to a whisper. 'Only if you scratch de enemy with de claw!'

'Well now, that's very interesting. Thank you ma'am.

The ferry skipper comes on board. In blue shirt and shorts, he has long braids and hops up to his midships cockpit where he fires up the four outboards. Adjusting his wrap around shades he stoops over the wheel as the engines kick in. Soon we're sweeping down Leeward channel, passing the mangroves and conch beds at top lick. This skipper's a mean navigator, flying round marker buoys at each bend in the channel like he's driving a Formula 1 at Monaco. The speed with the wind racing through my hair is exhilarating. This is the stuff, goddammit! I'm ready to board *Amazon Lady* right now.

Twenty minutes later we step off the ferry onto the sparsely populated island of North Caicos. As we disembark, I have an idea.

'How much for one chicken?' I ask my mama friend.

'Ten dollar for one chicken,' she replies.

'Okay. But kill it now and give me its foot.'

Now her eyes pop. 'What for you want the foot?'

'You already gave me the answer.' I flip her a $10 bill. She sets the crate of clucking fowl on the jetty and plants her hands on her hips. 'Okay. Which chicken?'

Even Ceejay has stopped admiring his new watch. Like Helms he thinks my behaviour is very odd. I count four red chickens with their sharp eyes blinking up at me but only one is needed for sacrifice. 'The white one there,' I tell her.

She tugs the bird through the flaps of the crate and offers it to me. 'Your chicken, sah.'

I take the bird and pass it to Ceejay. 'Now wring its neck and cut off one foot.'

Without hesitation Ceejay twists the bird's neck and then, to my horror, bites off one foot with a single crunch of his molars. 'Your foot, sah.'

'Give the bird back to the lady.'

Holding the foot in his teeth, Ceejay passes the dead fowl back to its previous owner. Then he takes the foot from his teeth and spits out some feathers.

'It won't lay eggs now,' I tell her. 'So take it home for dinner.'

The mama has a meal to add to her windfall and meanwhile I pocket the chicken claw that may be worth more than any watch.

We take a cab from the arrivals jetty and drive along the northern shoreline. Passing the occasional roadside shack I see straightaway this is nothing like Rum Cay. Here the locals sweat hard for a living. No bars here where fellers like Troy can mix me a punch, but that changes when we reach Dragon Quay resort some 50 mins ahead of schedule. At the bar, overlooking a stunning beach beside a dark cave, I can lap up a drink or two while we wait for Javel to show up in the Pursuit fishing boat.

Without a map of the islands you need to appreciate the geographic aspects to the plan. In short we've left a trail to the Leeward Highway and then to North and Middle Caicos, the least inhabited island in the archipelago. From here we'll return to Providenciales keeping out of sight when possible.

Plenty of action, you may agree, but all designed to keep hounds off our scent with detours and false trails. It's a practice we've developed over the years and it has served us well to date. So here's to another rum punch, if you please!

Helms stays shtum in the interim. I know he disapproves of my love affair with rum. He's an airplane jockey and has never been known to zoom around the heavens in a haze of alcohol. Ceejay, on the other hand, takes his lead from me. He enjoys rum refills until I notice he still has a feather stuck in his teeth.

God, what a revolting sight! I can't imagine how Jasmin feels when she's lying akimbo under this thundering Trinidadian. I sneak a look at my watch on his wrist then, raising my eyes, I see the Pursuit rounding the point. Thank God for Javel. He's on time.

At this hour, the sun is high and merciless while we wade out to meet Javel. He holds the boat offshore, killing the engines while we climb the ladder. The boat's cockpit is covered, hidden from the punching power of sunlight, and we gather in the shade as Javel sets the boat in motion again.

'Where to, boss?' Javel asks, as we pull away from Dragon Cay.

'Let's visit Le Sage. We don't want him getting lonely.'

In no time we're scooting over the lagoon waters. By using the trim tabs the hull rises to clear any coral heads that are visible below the surface. Twice the shadow of a shark races from our path, but there's no sign of other fish even though many thousands reside down there. Javel hands the wheel to Ceejay and then comes to sit with Helms and myself.

'I see he has your clock, boss?' Javel rarely misses a trick and wants to know why.

'I had no choice. We need his woman more than the watch.'

Javel is not a talkative type and pretends to ignore the news.

'If we find what we want on *Amazon Lady*, I'll get one for you .'

The offer cheers Javel and at this rate the Swiss will be selling watches faster than they make them. With the engines running at full speed, it's hard to hold a conversation but it's my guess we're all reflecting on our futures.

At least I am and it amounts, I have to admit, to a bad case of stage fright. I often get this before the action kicks in. Of course it may be natural, but Annie and Mary don't appear to suffer to the same extent. When they go to battle stations, they charge in with their eyes on fire. They dismiss considerations of risk, while I tend to reflect otherwise. Is this a failing, a weakness in my character?

Again I must admit it. The saying that those who live by the sword die by the sword may be valid. That video on Swann's tablet, of that rope around the prisoner's neck before he drops, fires a frisson down my spine to shred my nerves. No wonder I needed the chicken's claw.

Soon a brownish fleck appears on the horizon. As we approach it enlarges into the profile of a rusting hull, a dead ship which has become a corroding coffin on the reef.

Javel resumes control as we slow down, listening to the burble of the engines as we edge slowly towards the hulk. Now I see smaller fish darting between the corals while the seaweed moves to and fro with the flow of water below our hull.

'Le Sage! Are you there?' I shout. 'We've come to visit.'

Several seconds pass and then Le Sage shows his head in the hatch on the stricken vessel. Javel stops our engines and we stand off. In the silence, there's no need to bellow.

'You doin' okay?' I call out.

Le Sage comes into the sunlight to rest his elbows on the taff rail. Wearing spectacles and a faded baseball hat, he reminds me of a schoolmaster watching a game. He's lucky. There are no Columbians on this ship and his worst fear would be a hurricane blowing up a deadly swell to wash his rusting home into the deep.

'You got all you need? Enough beer and water?'

'Yeah, man. I could use some jerk chicken,' he replies.

'Should have told me earlier,' I laugh. 'You'll get no jerk today, Le Sage. We'll be busy for the next twenty-four hours.'

'The radio says Sarahanna has just landed.' Le Sage shouts, meaning he is happy with his FM radio.

Now Ceejay breaks his silence. 'Yo still have ma dollars?'

Le Sage is insulted by this question from the Trinidadian. 'What d'ya fuckin' tink? I don't see no shops here.'

Le Sage knows how to handle our big feller who can't wait to get his hands on the spending money. But it's good to hear Sarahanna's arrival is confirmed. We can start the countdown on our operation.

'Take care, Le Sage,' I shout. 'Specially at night. Don't use a flashlight unnecessarily. Sharp eyes might see you.'

'I hears yo. I be careful.' He raises a clenched fist in a panther salute. 'And yo be careful, my brothers. Be lucky.'

You see what I mean? Here's Le Sage, our bank clerk, who is safe-guarding tens of thousands of dollars. He's thinking of our welfare while Ceejay, the big mother from Trinidad, is only thinking of himself. Reminds me of some American politicians.

Someone once told me the black population in the Caribbean reflects the genetics of the original Africans who settled there, generally against their will I may add. One day I'll find out if there's any truth to this. Somebody who studies DNA may know.

Helms points to the sea floor ten feet below the hull. 'We need to salvage the equipment,' he says. When we left West Sand Spit yesterday we care-fully re-sealed our equipment inside the scuba tanks and dumped them in shallow water near the wreck. Now we need to recover and prepare the kit for our final appointment.

We left a plastic float tied to the equipment. Javel soon locates it and the line tethering it to the submerged scuba tanks. Using a gaff, up comes the float, followed by the tanks and we're in business.

I look at my men. 'When we drop Helms ashore, we'll take on other crew before holding position outside Southside marina until we get the call from Annie. You guys ready?'

'Okay.' They reply. 'Yea man! We's ready!'

Armed with a chicken's foot to soothe my nerves, I'm also primed to go.

41

Agent Bradley investigates more boldly

BY MIDDAY, AGENT Bradley was concerned. Having heard nothing from Miss Tanaka, the lack of communication implied she might be in trouble. He was at Tommy's, the downtown bar where news and views were traded by locals and visitors alike. This morning only one topic filled the air, the imminent arrival of the superstar. Cars rolling along the strip boomed her reggae from customised speakers. T-shirts, cap and balloon salesmen were doing great business, promoting the brand of Sarahanna. An unofficial public holiday had self-declared.

Bradley accepted that silence during a surveillance operation was often necessary but Miss Tanaka's silence had endured too long, especially since the stated purpose for Rackham's visit was imminent. Again he tried to contact his fellow agent, tapping out a text to say he would be attending the gig. Did she want to join him?

With no response, Bradley tapped out another text, asking his handling officer in Miami if there was any news of Agent Tanaka? Back came one word. *Negative*.

Finally deciding it was time for proactive action, Bradley returned to his pick-up truck and drove to Rum Cay, noting a greater volume of traffic than was usual for the time of day. His radio soon provided the reason. Sarahanna had touched down and was now confronting fan frenzy at the airport. Bradley felt he might learn more via the radio than from Miss Tanaka. FBI officers were trained to assist each other and if Miss Tanaka had gone missing it was his duty to find her. At the gates of Rum Cay, the security guard stepped from his kiosk to enquire about the reason for his visit.

Bradley tapped the side panel on his truck. 'Gotta fix a pool pump.'

The guard was dubious. 'What pool pump on which villa? You have a procurement number?'

'Heh, man. I dunno.' Bradley searched around the cab for his clipboard.

'Don't know where I put it. Somebody mentioned the Rackham villa. Guess it must be urgent, since he's promoting the concert today.'

Bradley was achieving little with the guard. The man stood his ground, refusing to lift the barrier. 'No procurement number. No passage.'

In the USA Bradley would have whipped out his FBI badge to gain access, but here on territory ruled by the British, he would need a better reason. He heard the honk of a car pulling up behind him. In his wing mirror he saw it was a stretch limo and on impulse, he sucked in his breath and swore. 'Shit man. That's Rackham's superstar arriving and there's a bad fault in their pool system. I could lose my job and Rum Cay might upset a major client.'

The barrier flew up allowing Bradley to gun the pickup towards the main hotel complex. In his mirror he watched the limo follow astern until it turned into the principal forecourt. He drove to the service area to find a parking spot. Bradley had successfully forced entry. Now he had to locate Miss Tanaka.

Bradley knew Rackham's entourage occupied two luxury villas over-looking a secluded beach. Bradley took his tool bag from the pickup locker and checked that his T-shirt was clean with company name and logo visible. In any luxury resort, trespassers were obliged to step carefully.

Taking a guess at various pathways Bradley set off on foot aiming towards the coast. The natural beauty of the resort enhanced the atmo-sphere for wealthy clients and no doubt helped the staff to enjoy their work. One of them, a Filipino housemaid, was singing to herself when Bradley met her on the pathway. He told her he was looking for Mr. Rackham's villa. A fault had been reported in their pool system. Could she help?

'Very private people. Down there, first right.'

Bradley thanked her and soon reached the first villa, a secluded clap-board building under palm trees. There was no sign of the residents and the windows were shut. Bradley pushed the doorbell and a dog barked, furi-ously leaping at the french window, teeth bared and ears flattened. For sure it was the same terrier he had seen at the Conch Bar. Bradley peered through the window and saw a cluster of packed bags on the floor, suggesting their owners would be on their way after the show. Bradley would not confront a terrier with such brazen teeth, so he moved on, whistling as he went.

Fifty yards on, he arrived at the second larger building, much of it hidden in lush foliage. Again he pushed the bell, but without response. Presumably the residents were dealing with the limousine and its celebrity occupant at the main complex. Still whistling he walked around the building and there beside the pool he found Miss Tanaka relaxing on a lounger.

Rackham's daughter was sitting on the poolside, feet in the water. She was surprised to see him. 'What are you doing here?' she shouted. 'This is a private villa.'

'I know that, miss. But I'm here to fix the pool.'

'I don't think it needs fixing.' The girl stood up.

'All pools need maintenance,' explained Bradley. 'It won't take a moment.'

Bradley put down his tools and dipped a pH tester for a sample measurement. 'No problem. I'll just check the filter.'

He walked around the pool examining the water. A dark rectangular object lay at the bottom of the pool in the deep end. 'So what have we here? Looks like a cellphone?'

The teenager was following him. 'Yeah. Because that's what it is. It belongs to this lady here and I dropped it by accident. She lent it to me because mine's not working. I feel dreadful about it.'

Miss Tanaka's eyes met Bradley's but her smile was clearly false. 'Never mind. These things happen.'

Bradley shrugged. 'I'll get it.'

Peeling off his T-shirt and shades, Bradley kicked off his flip-flops and dived into the pool. Swimming down, his eyes felt the sting of chlorine as he reached for the phone. In a few seconds he was back on the surface holding the phone above his head.

'There you are, Miss. Dry it carefully. Maybe it will recover.'

Miss Tanaka took the cell phone and thanked him. 'How kind of you.'

'No problem, ma'am. Pleasure to be of service.'

Swann walked up to Bradley and stood for a moment appraising him closely. 'You're something rather special. Pity we haven't met before. We might have got along very nicely.'

42

Annie is meeting the star

I WASN'T HAPPY about leaving Swann in the company of an agent of the FBI, and a Japanese one at that! We all know the Japanese are clever individuals who generally achieve their objectives and my daughter has not yet developed those same skills. Swann has grown up in wealthy neighbourhoods and though she has an ambivalent view of her parents' sexual peccadillos she has no experience of our business practice and we've kept it like that on purpose.

That explains why Chad and Helms reside in separate quarters and why Swann has been under our close supervision much of the time. That's not ideal for a precocious teenager, but in the hope that Swann could handle Miss Tanaka, we decided to run with her plan.

Meanwhile the game is on and running as I wait with Mary and Jasmin at the main hotel entrance to Rum Cay. We watch the stretch limo carrying our famous guest complete a wide circle before it stops. There's a magic in the air, a suspension of time, as the chauffeur leaves his seat and opens the limo door.

First we see long shapely legs followed by Sarahanna's legendary body. The star pauses to thank the driver, then she pulls down her shades and sallies over towards me as I step forward to greet her. 'I'm Annie Rackham.'

Sarahanna is all smiles 'So you're Annie. It sure is good to meet you after all the chit-chat.'

Her voice is a mix of smoke and sorbet and we punch fists in welcome. No wonder Dr. Felix Roblado has fantasies about this woman. She's a pure sex bomb. Her hourglass frame only just fits inside a tight leopard-skin dress tied at her waist by a glittering scarlet sash. Her legs shimmer black and bare all the way down to gold ankle chains and platform heels. How she can walk is a miracle, but now she leaps at me with arms outstretched and I hear bangles crashing as she hugs me tight. 'Yo' sure a fine woman, Ms Annie. I'm super happy to be here.'

'What a lovely compliment. Thank you Sarahanna! Welcome to Rum Cay and the Turks!' What do you say to a superstar who's kissing you all over and reeking of expensive fragrance. Amouage if I guess correctly?

After the bear hug, Sarahanna steps back to size up Mary. 'My God, but she's so sexy too!' says the star launching at Mary for another bearhug. Mary's features disappear behind the star's wild black mane where multiple highlights sparkle in the sunlight. When Sarahanna turns back to me, I note prominent cheek bones and a magnificent wide forehead over dominating dark chocolate eyes.

'And this is Jasmin, our assistant,' I wave towards Jasmin. The poor girl melts nervously as the rapper supremo swivels to wrap Jasmin in another joyous embrace.

Then Sarahanna stands back and looks Jasmin over. 'If I didn't know better, I'd say you was just like my sister.'

'That's neat,' I say. 'Jasmin's been acting as your body double during our rehearsals.'

'Well, honey. Am I the honoured sister! You are so-o lovely!'

Jasmin nearly faints with embarrassment. Shanty girl meets megastar and they adore each other! By now the star's entourage has unwound from the limo. The chauffeur oversees baggage transfer to the porter's trolley while Sarahanna introduces me to her manager Ron, a runty dude with wrap-shades covering most of his unshaven face and white frizz of hair.

'We need to talk,' Ron insists without even offering a fist. 'I want to talk like now!'

I don't take kindly to bossy assholes. They can ruin a woman's day, however I need to keep this game in play. 'Come inside,' I say. 'And bring your client with you.'

Without waiting I stride up the hotel steps into the lobby. Behind me trails Sarahanna, her manager and a woman not yet introduced. We sail through the lobby where the desk staff stand in awe. They get plenty of famous folk at Rum Cay but Sarahanna's different. She's one of their own, born in the Caribbean, and she's here to entertain the island's entire population.

I've reserved a business suite for all meetings and media interviews so

I lead the group to this suite where I offer hospitality. Mary and Jasmin remain with Schulz who has arrived just in time for the greeting.

Sarahanna asks for Coke Zero but Ron only wants money.

'My client has come a long way from the Bahamas,' Ron begins. 'Before she puts a single toe on the stage, I must have her fees, my fees and,' he adds, ordering his own drink. 'I want a beer.'

At least these folk don't share JR's shameless love of rum. I put the order through by desk phone as Sarahanna kicks off her stilts to settle on the sofa and you know how cats lie down to relax. Her manager Ron, on the other. hand, is hopping like a cat on a hot plate. After the drinks have been delivered, I open my bag to show him a wad of $100 bills.

'There's the fifteen K we agreed on.' I dunk a bundle in his open mitts and he starts counting. 'It's all there.'

Then I turn to Sarahanna who shrugs. 'He never says thank you. I guess he don't know manners. So where's my slice of the mango?'

Again I dip into my bag. This time I pull out a suede pouch. Undoing it I walk over to Sarahanna and tip the contents, a shower of small greenish pebbles, onto the sofa table. 'These uncut emeralds come from the most desirable mines in Columbia. Their transparency, colour and carat value are estimated at around $100K. Take a look.'

Sarahanna's talons zone in on the largest gem, She holds it against the light and a purring rumble comes from her glossed lips. 'Yeah!! Fabulous. But, Annie darlin', I brought my gemologist with me. She can look them over, if you don't mind.'

'Of course. She's very welcome.' I reply.

Now the third person in the retinue settles down and puts on a headband magnifier. As she starts work on each emerald, Sarahanna fondles the largest gem and continues to purr.

Having counted his cash, Ron comes over to check Sarahanna's goods, a changed soul it seems. He must have thought I was going to scam them on the concert deal. I can't blame him, but the guy's has no manners whatever he thinks. And now he's chewing gum, openly masticating in a constant rolling motion of his jaws. It's a revolting display, a gross lack of courtesy to myself and to the clientele and classy atmosphere of this resort.

Now the gemologist perks up. She has examined the emeralds which have been several hundred million years in the making and how's that for provenance? 'There's no problem,' she says. 'This is a very fine collection.'

Sarahanna and Ron absorb her opinion and the atmosphere improves with the good news.

'So you guys are paid up and ready for tonight?' My smile remains passably genuine. 'I've arranged rooms for you here. I'll see you at the venue.'

Sarahanna sits up and beckons me over. She has flawless make-up and a bewitching smile. 'Thank you Annie. Thank you so much. I'll sing till my tonsils burst this evening. It will be my pleasure.'

'The louder you sing, the more they love it.' I kiss the star on both cheeks and even Ron sheds a smile while he churns the gum.

Leaving Sarahanna and Ron to their own arrangements, I press on with our real plans. Getting rid of gems and cash is easy. Anyone can do that. The hardest part lies ahead, how to effect seizure of so much more. Back on the forecourt, I tell Schulz that Sarahanna is fully paid and primed. All systems are *go*. I'll catch up with him later.

'But there's one more thing. I'm leaving my daughter Swann with our private security team in a Portakabin on site. I want the doors kept locked throughout the concert, is that clear?'

Schulz hears me but his brow creases. 'Why's that?'

I look around, lowering my voice. 'Threats have been made. I don't want my daughter held for ransom. Is that good enough?'

Schulz nods vigorously. 'No. We don't want that.'

'No sir, we don't!' I leave Schulz and the limo driver to assist with Sarahanna's requirements while I prepare the next operation. I join Mary and Jasmin in a guest buggy and, with Mary at the wheel, we skim on electric power, down through the garden groves, past the old pirate hut on the hill, and back to Chad's villa. He opens the door as we arrive. Kludo rushes out to greet us before lifting his leg in the undergrowth.

'There was a visitor,' Chad tells me. 'Kludo barked but the man didn't see me. He didn't come in and I have him on CCTV.'

'Let me see.'

I follow Chad into the villa where he points at his computer screen.

'This man.'

Chad may suffer from simplistic English, but he certainly knows his digital skills. I watch the replay to see a stranger walking towards our villa where I know that Swann and Harumi Tanaka are spending the afternoon.

'Well done Chad. You did well.'

'And then I look in FBI files. 'Chad loves to boast about his hackery. 'This man works for FBI. I know this is true.'

So now I'm concerned. Worried may be too strong a word. If the FBI are sniffing around, that's what they meant to do. We are promoting a gig on an island beyond the FBI's direct control and that's the sum of it so far.

'And the yacht?' I draw up a chair beside Chad. 'How's the traffic on that channel?'

Chad's very alert today. Doubtless JR's warning and threat of more testicle damage made their mark. He points at his screen. 'The *Amazon Lady* has moved to the west, but there's little radio traffic.' Chad pulls up a map of the island. A red marker shows the yacht's position which actually suits our purpose even better.

'Okay, so now we must send Dr. Felix an email to say Sarahanna is looking forward greatly to meeting him. What time would suit him best?'

Chad taps out an email. His fingers move with the speed of a concert pianist. I check the text, nod and off it goes.

'Let me know when they reply.'

I return outside to update Mary who is helping Jasmin to savour the change of pace. Limo travel and meeting Sarahanna in a five-star hotel is a long way from the hell shed which she shares with Ceejay. She's loving it all, so she tells Mary.

I leave them and drive to our villa, making a silent arrival to ensure surprise when I walk into the pool area. Swann's sitting at a table close to the Japanese woman. Both look up as I approach. I lean down to kiss Swann's head as any mother might. 'Hi honey. I see you've got company.'

I shake the hand of the FBI agent with the warmest welcome I can fake. 'So you must be the journalist my husband mentioned?'

'That's me.' Miss Tanaka is a convincing liar. 'I'm so hopeful for my interview with Sarahanna.'

'Sure. No problem. I've arranged a car to take you to the concert where she's very happy to do your interview. Is that okay?'

Miss Tanaka beams. 'Thank you. How kind.'

'Listen, Swann,' I say. 'When you go to the concert you must take Kludo. Keep him on his lead and very close. There'll be a huge crowd. We don't want to lose him. Understood?'

'Yeah Ma. I get it.'

'Okay. See you there. Miss Tanaka, please help yourself to the bar and if you want some food just call Room Service.'

'How thoughtful.' says the FBI agent. 'How very kind.'

'I just want to keep everyone happy. See you later.'

And off I go. Back to the buggy and to Mary and Jasmin. The hours are ticking past as the sun tips to the west. I can feel the adrenalin surging into my bloodstream. Things are falling into place but the challenges, the really serious ones, still lie ahead. This, says my husband, who is a mastermind of unorthodox enterprise, will be the most challenging operation of our career.

Now we shuttle in our electric buggy back to the hotel. This time I'm riding with Jasmin, checking her make-up as we travel. The colour of her eye shadow and lipstick appear identical to Sarahanna's, and don't forget I've been up close and very personal to the star herself. Jasmin is wearing a leopard pattern dress, which as our research indicated, is the performer's preferred outfit. I'd say Jasmin looks about 80% identical to Sarahanna.

Now to Chad. We've discussed his outfit and have settled on the uniform he wears as No.2 on our jet. This means he's in a conventional white shirt with epaulettes, blue trousers, black shoes. His flight bag contains the radio suppression kit and he has a set of tools in a second bag. With his Serengeti dark glasses and polished skull, our Ukrainian looks quite the part. Helms joins us, drinking water today from a plastic bottle and wearing flight overalls.

Mary and I are wearing what might pass as stylish tourist kit. My lovely Mary looks very hip in a loose white cotton trouser suit. The turquoise belt echoes the stripe on her trainers. Somewhere hidden at the base of her sinewy spine is a Beretta close range pistol, loaded and ready for action.

With her blonde hair and blue tinted shades, she's more than an eyeful.

I'm wearing the moo-moo mentioned earlier. Underneath is the stab and bullet proof vest in kevlar, rather and sweaty in this climate but essential for close-combat protection. I too am wearing trainers. They provide good grip and look ultra-cool to the various gentry we're about to visit. We aim to dazzle, don't we?

Now we transfer from the buggy back to the second limo that we've hired. I'm riding shotgun alongside the driver. Once the door closes with a soft click we're on our way.

'Where to, ma'am?' The driver asks.

I look at my watch. We're on schedule and we know that JR and his crew are in position, trawling for imaginary fish in waters just beyond the marina entrance. After a deep breath, I reply. 'Southside Marina. Let's go.'

Fifteen minutes later, the stretch sidles innocuously down the hill towards the marina. At this point, our limo is visible to our fishing crew who can now prepare for their role in a pincer action.

Our limo driver knows what to do. He drives past the police launch which, thankfully, remains on its regular mooring against the harbour wall. We see two uniformed guards aboard, both armed and standing at the head of the gangplank. They certainly noted us when we passed by. Now our driver reaches the end of the road where he turns before cruising slowly back to the gangplank where we stop.

It's for Mary to launch the action. She opens her door and steps out. Lowering my window I watch her stride in that beautiful white trouser suit to the gangplank.

'Excuse me,' she shouts. 'Can you guys tell my driver how to find Rum Cay? We're lost and Miss Sarahanna here needs to get to her show immediately.'

Hearing the star's name the two guards react as anticipated. Like eager cats. Their fellow officers may be attending the concert, yet the legendary singer is right here, behind the darkened glass of this limousine. One guard comes down the gangway.

'You got Sarahanna in there?'

It's my turn to get out. I smile at the guard as he approaches. 'Sure. And if you ask her nicely, she'll give you an autograph.'

Beyond and behind the police vessel, I see our fishing boat approaching the mouth of the marina, but the guard is beside me now, bending down to ogle Jasmin as she lowers her window. The other guard sticks to his post and remains on board while Mary skips up the gangplank towards him.

'I'll get an autograph for you too,' she offers.

In the back of our limo, Chad is activating the radio jammer and Jasmin sits pretty and obliging, as any good celebrity should. She's following my instructions to the letter.

As Mary reaches her man, I leap on my guard, taking his arm into a lock that makes him howl. 'I'm sorry sir, but it's my duty to protect Sarahanna.'

Mary has decided to use the zonc gas on her target, giving the guard a blast which renders the poor man unconscious in a single inhalation. As he falls, Mary guides him to a soft landing and removes his weapon while I simultaneously disarm my victim. Out come the plastic wrist-ties and in thirty seconds both police guards are in our bag. Too damned easy!

As I walk my captive up the gangplank towards his companion our rein-forcements come aboard from our fishing boat now moored on the far side of the launch. JR bursts into the wheelhouse while Ceejay goes to the stern. First we must ensure no other officers are on board. When I try the sliding door to the wheelhouse, I find it locked. 'Is there a key?' I ask my captive.

'No.' His reply comes with a painful grunt as I tweak his arm. 'No key.'

He's doing his duty. But refusing to help means we must search the guards for keys, cellphones. holsters and ID cards. JR waits impatiently as we go to work, then using a jemmy he forces open the cabin door and steps in. I watch him go below, first to the galley area and then to a primitive bunk room. Luckily both areas are unoccupied.

JR completes the search and his grin is emphatic. 'Easier than we thought. Now let's see if this sucker starts.'

He has found a set of keys hanging from a hook on the wheelhouse bulkhead. He tries them one by one, seeking the key for the starter switch. We've discussed the possibility that the launch may have alarms to prevent unauthorised access and alert police HQ if something is amiss. It falls to Chad to analyse these hazards, so he continues with his jamming skills while JR finds the correct key and fires up the twin diesels. Bursts of black smoke rise from the exhausts before the engines settle to a steady note. JR stoops to examine the gauges. 'Plenty of fuel,' he reports.

'And no alarms,' concludes Chad while Mary and I strap duck tape to the guards' mouths. Mary's victim is regaining consciousness, his eyes spread wide as he realises what occurred during his blackout.

'You did your job and we did our's,' says Mary. Her concern is genuine and she dabs the man's eyes with a Kleenex. 'You'll be safe if you follow instructions. Understood?'

Both policemen nod with reluctance. Their peaceful afternoon watch has been shattered by the arrival of a pseudo Sarahanna with Team Rackham. It was too damned easy.

After securing both prisoners in their own bunk room, we complete the transfer of our crews. Helms heads to the weapons locker and jemmies it open. 'Eureka! We got lucky! Some useful kit here. This Sig P228 might be handy, don't you reckon?'

'Whatever weapons this ship carries, the *Amazon Lady* will have more of the same,' JR reminds us. 'And she's no hospital ship, that's for sure!'

Javel has moored his fishing boat alongside and he hops on board for a quick inspection. 'Irie. Ya Mon. She okay.'

'Now listen up,' says JR to Javel, 'I'll command this launch and you will follow at a distance in the Pursuit. Understood?'

The game plan is set and the crew all know what is expected of them. It has taken fifteen minutes to complete our takeover of this Government asset. From now on we're in deep shit, particularly if there are witnesses. We look around the marina, but as anticipated, it appears to be deserted. Nevertheless we can't assume our raid has gone unnoticed. As I hurry down the gangplank to collect bags of uniforms and equipment from the limo, I remember how Swann saw an old man during our recce but I don't see him now. I pass the bags to JR and cast the mooring ropes free from the bollards.

Back in the limo, I reclaim my seat beside Jasmin. She's not too happy now, so I give her hand a warm squeeze. 'You did fine, Jasmin. You really did! One more job and then you're done. You're a fantastic girl, Jasmin.

Just like Sarahanna.'

My praise does the trick and a smile returns to Jasmin's pretty but now more troubled features. Helms and Chad climb in and we're off to our next target, leaving the police launch and our fishing boat to head for the open sea.

From this point on, the action is bound to be unsettling, if not bloody and confusing for all concerned. But that, I have to tell you, is the basic nature of our business.

.

43

Miss Tanaka and Swann – A double act

TOWARDS LATE AFTERNOON, Miss Harumi Tanaka was struggling to maintain the charade with Swann, trying to show no visible signs of impatience. The teenager was a smart cookie. Miss Tanaka had no doubt about that. Swann's theatrical skill had been demonstrated when the iPhone had been dropped 'accidentally' in the swimming pool. Now the young girl was verbalising her fantasies about the pool man who had recovered it.

'I mean, he was gorgeous, wasn't he? I kinda like that in a man, the half-way mix between black and white – the mulatto look, if you know what I mean?'

Miss Tanaka's smile was sardonic to say the least, but she had to agree with Swann. In his white shorts, Bradley did cut a neat figure.

'Muscled, gorgeous and clever, that's what I saw in him.' Miss Tanaka pulled off her dark glasses looking directly at Swann. 'He must be about thirty five. I bet he gets lots of girls in his cleaning business. He's welcome to clean my filter any time he wants.'

'That's grotesque!' Swann hissed. 'I would never talk about him like that.'

Miss Tanaka tossed her shoulders and lay back below the parasol. This teenage girl chatter was wearisome. What mattered was the pursuit of her duties as a Federal agent. That's why both she and Bradley were paid, to deliver the goods one way or another. However the goods, whatever they were, now seemed further beyond reach than before. She hoped a development of some significance would move events beyond this current melodrama.

Then she heard a shout from an approaching visitor. Hotel staff were instructed to signal their imminent arrival to these private villas. 'Hello. I have a delivery.'

'Come on,' shouted Miss Tanaka.

The delivery was for her. Watched keenly by Swann, Miss Tanaka tore open the padded envelope after the hotel porter had her receipt signature. Inside the envelope was a cellphone complete with charger kit. A note was included. '*You can't go to Sarahanna's gig without a camera, so borrow this. Pin is today's date. Have fun. xx*'

'Well, that settles it.' Miss Tanaka said. 'He made up his mind and it's two kisses for me.'

'Fuck no,' said Swann as she read the note. 'I won't give up that easy. Let me see it. I don't know that model.'

Miss Tanaka shook her head, clutching the gift to her chest. 'Sorry, I'm not falling for that again. You're very clumsy with other people's property.'

'I apologised, didn't I? I didn't mean to drop it. Would I do that on purpose?'

'Unlikely, but some people do strange things. I'm a journalist and I understand how people react to changed conditions.'

The teenager sat down on a sunbed, drawing her bare knees up to her chin with a pout on her young lips. Miss Tanaka felt sure Swann was dreaming up another ruse to prevent her using the new phone. Bradley had been resourceful in sending a replacement so quickly. Tanaka turned it on found the camera app and framed Swann's face in a shot. 'You look more pretty when you smile. Please.'

Looking at the image Miss Tanaka could see a family likeness and she still hoped to take a DNA sample from Swann but how would she do that? Maybe an opportunity would occur at the concert. 'Isn't it time to be going?' she asked.

Swann looked at her watch and swung her legs down. 'Yeah. My Ma is sending a car for us, but first we must get Kludo.'

Miss Tanaka wondered how to handle the dog's hostility. She stood up, gathered her stuff and set off following the young Rackham towards the second villa used by the gang. Hopefully she find uncover useful clues there.

As expected, the sole resident was delighted to see Swann but Kludo's pleasure turned to intense hostility with stiff legs, raised hackles and menacing growls in Harumi Tanaka's direction. Swann hooked a leash to the dog's collar, and attempted to calm her pet with loving strokes and murmurs. It would be easier to tame a tiger, thought Miss Tanaka, as she made a quick appraisal of the villa's interior. Hardly a luxury villa, she decided. More like a military barracks. Emptied bottles and discarded wrapping paper reminded Miss Tanaka of prisons she had visited when training for the FBI. Human detritus was never a pretty sight. She noticed travel bags ready for collection, as if the residents were preparing to check out. She would report this assessment when she next made contact with Jenkins or Bradley.

'When will Kludo realise I'm your friend?' she asked.

'You must be joking.' Swann raised her eyes in exasperation. 'He knows we both fancy the same man. He's protecting my interests until we sort that out.'

A car with Able at the wheel, drew up near the villa. It was their transport to the show andnMiss Tanaka walked over to take the front seat beside the driver. The terrier jumped into the back seat with Swann. On the car radio, the commentary was entirely devoted to Sarahanna and her imminent performance.

Arriving at the venue, Miss Tanaka saw immediately that thousands of happy islanders were assembling to see the reggae goddess. The atmosphere was tangible, ripples of music and action radiating into the evening air where hues of sunset sparred with the flash effects of the stage lighting. The car passed behind the stage where huge speakers thumped bass rhythms from a warm-up band hammering on steel drums as the crowd went halfway to crazy.

Swann and Miss Tanaka were escorted to a Portakabin beside the main stage. There Able told them to wait inside so that Sarahanna could do the interview before her act. Miss Tanaka felt this was increasingly unlikely but she would maintain the charade.

Swann attached the dog's lead to the handle of the freezer as she pulled out two cans of cola. 'So let's get in the mood,' she tossed a can to Miss Tanaka. 'Party time at last! Isn't this cool!'

Ten years previously Miss Tanaka might have shared in the excitement. The walls of the Portakabin seemed to flex to the music but thankfully it had air-conditioning because the windows were sealed. She tried to open the door but found it locked so she was now effectively a prisoner. She wondered if Bradley knew of her changed circumstance if the location of the replacement phone was discoverable. Bradley had even installed a photo of himself as a screensaver. Naked from the waist up his smile was salacious. She showed it to Swann. 'Now isn't that a hunky feller?' .

'A man we must agree to share,' Swann replied. 'My parents are very happy with such arrangements, so we can do the same.'

Swann busied herself with a TV monitor on a side table. The image showed the stage and ranks of an audience whose enthusiasm continued to build towards the main act. Finally the dog stopped growling. Kludo lay on the cabin floor closely watching Miss Tanaka, a silent dog on a short fuse.

'You're full of bright ideas.'

'So is that a Yes or No?' repeated Swann impatiently.

Miss Tanaka was texting HQ detailing her location to Director Jenkins. FBI agents had been known to adopt unorthodox activities in order to secure their objectives but this story would certainly entertain Jenkins and her colleagues at the FBI.

'Yes. Get your friend in here. let's ask if he's up for a threesome.'

44

Annie explains how to capture a helicopter

IT'S BEEN AN hour since we left Sarahanna with her entourage at the concert venue. Using our own communications tailored by Chad, I learn that JR is now at the helm of the police launch, heading towards the open ocean, followed closely by the fishing boat under Javel's command.

The line has been crossed. We have seized government property, a highly reprehensible crime, so we must keep ahead of any imminent reaction from the authorities. With the approach of nightfall both vessels will show no lights out on the dark waters of the Atlantic where, in any event, there's rarely any nocturnal traffic. Their presence could be detected by radar, but few aircraft are likely to attempt visual searches until dawn tomorrow.

Most fortuitously and due to Sarahanna's divine presence, the locals and their police force have enough to occupy them at present without searching for purloined government property. Yes, we might add kidnap to that list. There are two police guards on board, held against their will with wrists tied by plastic but if they behave, they'll be set free by dawn tomorrow.

The launch and fishing boat are now heading around the island to the last known position of the *Amazon Lady.* She's currently lying at anchor off Grace Bay where visiting superyachts often linger, close enough to make shore visits but beyond the unwanted attention of tourist tykes.

With our two vessels on the water I must now add the final, and arguably the most crucial piece, to the game plan. We need an aerial weapon and surely this is best supplied by our prospective host. We must seize the helicopter belonging to Dr. Felix!

So now we're riding in the stretch limo to a location not too distant from the show venue. It's a flat piece of ground ideal for helicopter operations but crucially outside the view of concert goers, meaning that the audience are unlikely to notice our aerial activities. Chad has contacted the yacht and sent the GPS coordinates of the landing place to their pilot. The Colombians have approved and that's the best we can do for the present.

Too many *ifs* and *buts*, I hear you thinking. *What if* the helicopter is not operating? *What if* they change their plans? What can we do about altered situations? We can develop options and alternatives for ever, but ultimately our success relies on readiness and swift adaptability. But here's what we plan to do. Let me run you through it while we drive to the landing pad for the helicopter.

Dr. Felix suffers from megalomania. He has everything that money can buy and, like most rich folk, he uses his money to fortify personal holdings and position. Thanks to Mary's previous intrusion into his domain we know a great deal about this scoundrel and his lifestyle and over the months since her visit, we've conducted intensive research on the *Amazon Lady*. We have details of her deck plans, her gangways, lifts, AC systems and crew quarters but, most importantly, we have Mary's first hand account about the accommodation for the owner and his principal bodyguards.

Let's be clear now. These henchmen are Columbians, most of them battle trained during FARC's territorial wars around Florencia. For such men and women, the killing of an enemy is as easy as stepping on an ant. Guns, RPGs and IEDs are daily toys of choice. To them dollars mean far more than human rights. Kill or be killed is their simple creed. Such are the guardians of *Amazon Lady,* the crème de la crème of lawless professionals. Even Bond might suffer insomnia if contemplating action against such characters.

This means we must reduce the risks to improve our chances and fortunately the naval architects have helped in some respects. The *Amazon Lady* has four decks for guest and crew accommodation. The lowest of these decks, just above the waterline, is assigned to the yacht's crew. Chefs, maids, deck hands and cabin staff are confined on this deck in small egalitarian cabins with communal areas for recreational use.

Across the stern of the yacht lies an open deck which serves as the main entry point for the vessel. When the owner and his chums want to play with jet skis and speedboats, they seal the doors to the crew quarters. These leisure craft are stored on racks and rollers behind watertight doors which are kept closed when sailing in rough weather. You may know that car ferries have the same features.

On the second deck above the waterline are larger cabins where the gun slingers and their whores enjoy debauchery without upsetting the sensitivities of shipmates on other decks. To restrict casual movement, the access gangways and elevators are controlled by doors with coded keyless locks. Only by punching in the right code can a door be opened. Chad, with his cyber kit, knows how to unscramble and change these codes and he'll control all such doors to coincide with our arrival.

The two upper decks are almost exclusively used by Dr. Felix, his Captain and the senior officers. Here also, access doors are code controlled to the bridge where the yacht's movements are supervised by watch officers. Now for a word about the crew.

The Captain is a surly old bastard from Bogota who, in the 1980's, trained with Pablo Escobar in the Islas de Rosario near Cartagena. Having married a sister of Dr. Felix Roblado, the Captain is considered one of the family, though his spouse has since died from breast cancer. The Captain now lives alone in some style close to the bridge. He's on call when needed, as is the helicopter pilot whose cabin sits on the top deck next to the hangar and adjoining flight deck. These upper decks are 'no-go' areas for most of the crew and we will ensure it remains that way.

Now picture this. The third deck, the deck below the luxurious quarters, is where we must focus our attention. Here lies the art collection, most of it consisting of rare, unique and high value items. All are displayed in a spacious gallery with a controlled internal access. Our task is to break into this marine coop, seize the goods and vanish before dawn. Amen.

If only it will be that easy!

Messages begin to arrive as we reach the landing ground. Beside me in the limo, Chad recites them in his charmless tone. 'Dr. Felix Roblado will not attend show. Instead he will send his helicopter preferring to invite Sarahanna for drinks on the yacht.'

'Tell him, that's fine. Miss Sarahanna is happy to accept.'

Chad sends our reply. 'Miss Sarahanna very happy with your invite but must be back by ten for her performance.'

I can see through his plan. If Dr. Felix attends the concert, he'll have to mix with thousands of islanders all juiced up on rum and reggae. Hardly an ideal location for a neurotic art dealer whose real motive is to host the performer and dope her into a sexual liaison.

It's a calculated gamble on our part, but so far it has worked in our favour. Roblado's hope is that Sarahanna will take the bait and even enjoy his special gift of hospitality, a hot branding iron on her rump after mating with him!

'How d'you feel about taking a helicopter ride to a lovely yacht?' My question is directed at Jasmin who sits beside me in the silky interior of the limo. 'We'll be with you. Also Ceejay will be there with the brothers. We'll make sure you're safe.'

Jasmin is getting a buzz about this spate of action in her hitherto bland life. She has just met the greatest of reggae stars and witnessed the seizure of a police launch just so that her boyfriend can brandish a swiss watch. She must be thinking what next?

'Okay,' Jasmin murmurs after a thoughtful silence. 'I've never been in a heli-chopper. Is it safe?'

'Ask my friend here. He'll be flying it.'

Helms may be recalling the last time he flew a whirly into a potential death trap but his dismissive humour is loaded with Australian nonchalance. 'Safe as this limo, Miss Jasmin. But we'll need to change the pilot first.'

At the helipad I'm pleased to find Boxman and his men are already in position. They have parked two pick-up trucks just outside the H-circle. Each vehicle is loaded with loose gravel, as JR requested, and I get out to check that both trucks are equipped with coils of 9.5 mm. climbers' rope.

'All looks set to go.' I tell Boxman, noting that all his colleagues appear eager and primed for action. 'When the chopper lands, make sure you park behind it, where the pilot cannot see you. Understood?'

They nod. 'Yeah, we get it. We stay out of sight.'

'Then my friend Mr. Helms will take these ropes to the chopper skids and attach them with shackles. Understood?' I show them the shackle clips at the rope ends. 'While Mr Helms does that, you stay in your cabs with the engine running until he spreads his arms wide. Then you drive one to each side of the circle, keeping the ropes tight, and wait till we have removed the pilot. Is that understood?' I open my hands waiting for their answer.

'This is plenty dangerous,' decides Boxman's colleague.

'What? Sitting in your cab while we tie your truck to a helicopter? That's not dangerous. The weight of your truck with ballast will prevent the chopper from lifting off. It's that simple.'

I try my best smile, but they're not easily convinced.

'We'll handle the pilot and the chopper. Afterwards you may have some guests to guard. Keep them tied up but alive until we order their release. That's all you need to do. Is that clear?'

But these brothers are still holding back. Perhaps I've pushed them too deep? I must drive home my point. 'It should be easy. You have enough money on deposit with Le Sage, haven't you?'

'Yeah, guess so.'

Reluctance is in the air, but so is the chopper. Chad reports that he has now tuned to the yacht's airborne channel to learn that the chopper pilot has left the yacht.

'Chad, ask JR for his ETA at the yacht.'

Chad passes my message and back comes the reply. 'Twenty minutes.'

We're using encrypted messaging. 'Tell JR to press on. We'll report when we have seized the chopper.'

Dr. Felix may be in a state of excitement, but so what? We too are in a similar position, ready for his helicopter to come buzzing in. Helms knows that landing a chopper on a ship at sea is never easy and when night closes in, the task is even more demanding. The sooner we kick off, the better.

I leave Helms to further inspire the pickup drivers. Back in the limo I settle down and refresh my make-up, watched closely by young Jasmin who leans towards me.

'Is this really safe?' she whispers.

'Depends on what you call safe, luv.' I keep smiling while I touch up my lip liner. 'We all face the devil one day and Ceejay will be real proud of you, I know he will.' I continue smiling if only to reassure myself. 'You just stand beside the limo as the chopper comes in and I'll tell you when to join me. Okay?'

Jasmin nods.

'And you're ready with the jammer?' I look to Chad.

He has the jammer set on his lap and he's wearing earphones. He may be a weird but he's worth his weight in emeralds when digital mischief is needed. He also nods. 'All set.'

'Good on you, Chad. Keep me posted.'

The minutes tick by as the evening light fades away. We listen to the heavy beat of music coming from the distant show ground. Briefly I wonder how Swann is coping with the FBI agent, but our man Able has reported no problems as he stands on guard outside their Portakabin door. At some stage, when we've secured our objectives, I'll ask Able to get Swann and the dog out of there while leaving the Japanese woman locked inside. Her blatant attempts to ingratiate my husband have annoyed me and knowing that federal agents of the United States are nosing around is rarely helpful. It will only be a matter of hours till the police hear of their missing launch and then the chips will really fry. We must move fast.

Now Boxman hears it. He's sitting in his truck cab with the window open and he raises a finger. Chad has heard no R/T traffic but that's not surprising since Columbian pilots won't talk to the local ATC unless necessary. We anticipate that the chopper will land with at least one armed passenger since that's normal practice and we expect it to be flying low, to stay below the radar sweep from Providenciales airport.

Over the racket of reggae flowing from the concert, we hear the chuff, chuff of whirring blades and suddenly here it comes, rising up above the coast to make its hovering approach. The pilot will see the limo parked beside the H pad as he's expecting. Pickups are standard vehicles in most parts of the world, so he won't be too surprised by their presence.

The chopper descends, throwing up a tsunami of dust and sand around the helipad. I step from our limo and wave at the pilot, raising my thumb and smiling. I'm so pleased to see you is my message as I run out to meet the aircraft. While the pilot opens his door, I see Helms moving in from astern, out of pilot's view though not out of danger. He must pass close to the perilous tail rotor as he shackles the skids with ropes to both pick-ups.

As requested, Jasmin pokes her head from the limo's window while I tap on the pilot's knee and shout. 'Please shut down your engine. Sarahanna can't breathe in this dust. Her voice is important.'

I can see the pilot close up. Definitely a hard man, facially scarred and not used to obeying women. He looks across at his partner whose baby face is betrayed by killer eyes. I can't see where his hands are, but he'll be my immediate target so I raise my fingers and smile. I beckon to Jasmin who comes from the limo after Boxman opens the door for her. Meanwhile having run around the nose of the chopper, I remove the zonk aerosol from my pocket. It's almost invisible in my hand as baby face opens his door. Instantly I spray him and I see the snub nosed gun in his hand. He's a sonofabitch, a thoroughbred criminal who gets one snort in both nostrils while I hold my breath. As the gunman pitches forward, the pilot reaches for the cyclic and collective controls while pumping in full power. I jam my elbow against the cabin door and step onto the skid simultaneously. Now I'll ride this chopper as it leaves the ground and I aim my spray at the pilot. He shakes his head as the rope anchors catch, restraining the chopper with the sudden jolt almost dislodges me.

'Put her down now!' I yell. I aim the aerosol at the pilot's head. He's no pushover, that's for sure, but he has to comply when I send a blast of zonk into his nostrils. This time he inhales and stoops forward on the controls. The chopper blades are still whirring as it hits the ground with a heavy thump but Helms is there immediately, opening the pilot's door and reaching for the principal controls. I unclip the harnesses on both men and haul them out. In twenty seconds I've bound their wrists as Chad comes to help me.

'Did they make any calls?' I ask him.

'They had no time for that. I suppress radio but could not hear.' Chad chuckles as we bind the pilot's feet. He enjoys action beyond his digital world on moments like this. In fact I feel very proud of him. Now the victims begin to recover and Boxman and his brothers haul them to the limo where they further bind and gag them. Then they unhitch the lines to the chopper while Helms settles at the controls. When I beckon Jasmin she comes running through the dust and downdraught to jump into the rear seat.

Goddamn it! I believe we've done it! Chad takes his computer bag and suppressor kit to follow Jasmin into the aircraft. Finally I climb in beside Helms. 'Let's go!'

Seconds later we lift off in a suitably orthodox manner climbing away from the H-pad where our team of snake charmers can be seen securing the Columbians inside the limo. Shortly we are flying close to the concert venue where my daughter is hopefully coping with the joyous outbursts of humanity. The lights around the stage flare high towards the sky. Though we can't hear the music, we can see thousands of deliriously happy fans down below.

If Sarahanna is doing what we asked of her, then it's the best we can offer the good people of Turkey Chaos.

45

John Rackham heads for the Amazon Lady

AN ENCRYPTED MESSAGE from Chad informs me that Annie and Helms have overcome resistance to take control of the helicopter and are now airborne. They are poised to land on *Amazon Lady* as soon as our police launch is also in position. It sounds too good to be true, but my wife has a lethal disposition. What Annie wants, Annie gets! And the same goes for Mary. That's why these two women complement each other so perfectly. Empowered women pack more than double the punch when they come in pairs. I'd rather face a pack of tiger sharks.

This police launch, kindly on loan from the Turks and Caicos Government, is a lively piece of equipment. Spurred on by twin Perkins diesels the vessel soars over the pink sunset waters of the Atlantic as happily as a hare sprinting over fields of young wheat. Standing at the wheel of this fine vessel I admit to enjoying the ride. Whoever is the regular Commander has a great job. Let's hope he's raving to Sarahanna's performance while we borrow his baby.

A glance at the GPS tells me we have three miles to go before we reach the *Amazon Lady*. I can see her hull and we're closing at 30 knots. In minutes we'll be alongside.

Mary joins me in the wheel house. She has changed into her police uniform, a blue shirt and slacks with brocade and ID labels stitched all over, but her golden hair has vanished. Now it's hidden under a silver grey afro wig which may prevent her being recognised by Dr. Felix and his shipmates. In my case, they've never seen me, so the ruse is less risky. I'm wearing a uniform, but with more stripes on my shoulder tags as I'm now the Captain of this boarding party even though we'll be acting as government officials performing their legal duties.

Mary slips an arm around my waist tightening her fingers on my gun belt. As commanding officer of this marine patrol boat I'm entitled to carry a weapon.

'You look good in uniform,' Mary says. 'And I love your Glock.'

'Go Glock yourself,' I reply.

'I've checked our prisoners,' Mary continues. 'I gave them water and told them they'll be free within hours.'

Naturally we've debated how to dispose of the launch and its crew, just as we've thought long and hard about the fate of the *Amazon Lady*. Plans have ranged from pointing both vessels on autopilot at the open ocean, or aiming them at the reef and letting them grind their bellies on the coral. The latter option is too drastic, leading to ecological issues with leaking oil and debris so we finally decided to leave both vessels at anchor. When the authorities reclaim either vessel, they can liberate their crews simultaneously.

Mary has been reading my mind. 'But first we must complete our business,' she says. Then she leans against me and does her heavy breathing feline act in my ear. My hands may be on the wheel of this speeding police launch, but I'd prefer they were patrolling down Mary's body to that naughty zone where she loses control.

We both accept that the imminent reality of finding the *Amazon Lady* across our bow may lead to moments of life-changing importance. We could just as easily swing this craft around, head back to Southside marina, moor the boat and vanish empty handed. But that's not our style and we've no time for such thoughts. I reach for the VHF radio and turn up the speaker volume. I'm not anticipating much traffic at this time of the day. '*Amazon Lady*,' I say. 'Calling *Amazon Lady*. Come in please.'

Seconds pass. Some clicks indicate my call has been noticed.

'*Amazon Lady*,' I repeat. 'Calling *Amazon Lady*. Come in please. This is PV218, Marine Unit Providenciales police calling *Amazon Lady*.' I'm speaking in the lilt of the local dialect which I've been practicing. '*Amazon Lady*, Come in please.'

'This is *Amazon Lady*. Calling PV218. Pass your message please.'

I have my script ready as Mary squeezes my waist. 'I am Commander of PV218, Marine Unit. We are coming alongside and wish to board with your permission. We need to speak with your Captain please.'

These might sound like regular marine communications, but nothing is regular on a vessel like *Amazon Lady*. I can now see the faint shape of a helicopter in the sky above the shoreline. Our skylark is closing in as the radio crackles.

'This is Captain of *Amazon Lady*. I copy your message.' His voice has a strong Spanish accent. 'We have Liberian registration and are not obliged to accept boarding. Over.'

'Understood. This is an important communication that must be delivered in person regarding the arrival of your guest. Over.'

This creates a brief silence. I assume the Captain is talking with his security people and maybe to the owner. The crew have sailed a long way to host Sarahanna so it does concern them.

Throughout this interchange, our launch has been splitting the sea, leaving a slash of white foam in our wake. I switch on the blue lamps which flash intermittently on the wheelhouse roof. This is a new one for us. Blue lights and uniforms, can you believe it?

'*Amazon Lady*. We will come to your stern boarding platform. I will board with just one officer. Our launch will stand off nearby.'

'You may board at the stern. Permission is granted.'

Surely a posse of Columbian gunmen can cope with two Caribbean policemen? That's what they'll be thinking as I pass the wheel to Ceejay. He's in uniform now, has a loaded weapon on his belt and is driving the boat. Amazing how he's happy to take my orders now after all the previous shenanigans. Giving responsibility to a man can make all the difference.

'After we've gone aboard, you wait alongside. Be ready to retrieve us when we call. Javel is following behind. Okay?'

'Yeah, mon. Understood.'

The *Amazon Lady* looks increasingly impressive as we approach. Her top deck rises 40 feet above the waterline. She's at least eight times longer than our launch as we power around her stern to reach the boarding platform. The weather hatches that protect the interior are open with two guards in position on the platform. We assume they're armed and we can see the CCTV cameras that will be relaying images to the bridge, but also to Chad's computer. He's well prepped on the yacht's systems and will supervise and over-ride cameras and alarms when applicable. As I have indicated, without Chad we'd have little to no hope of surviving this venture.

The guards offer no welcome as Mary and I jump onto the boarding platform. I nod to them, tuck a briefcase under my elbow and offer a brief salute. One guard points to an open doorway and we move on, leaving our launch behind but I can hear the helicopter making its approach to the landing pad above which means Anne and Helms must have seen us. Chad will have initiated radio suppression so that communication between helicopter, yacht and shore is now a meaningless splatter of sound. Chad will have screwed the ship's electronic locking systems. Occupants of the lower decks will find digital locks no longer respond to their usual codes. That discovery will rattle them, so we must move fast.

Following Mary up the gangway to the upper decks, I'm aware of the guard following behind. He's a professional and keeps his distance, watchful as a hunting jaguar. At the top deck we encounter more guards. Seeing us in uniform and apparently on a mission dear to the owner's heart we are given sullen nods and finger directions, propelling us towards the bridge. Here in the subtle lighting of the yacht's nerve centre, we find the Captain and three officers with several more guards in the corners. A bank of TV monitor screens shows the boarding platform, engine room, galley, gangways and helipad where the chopper's skids are hovering above the deck. Helms loves a challenge and he's doing brilliantly.

The Captain and his men are fascinated by Mary, who looks dynamite in uniform. 'I need to speak to the owner,' she says.

'That's not possible,' the Captain replies. 'The owner is busy elsewhere.'

'We understand he has invited the singer Sarahanna to visit,' I say. 'And that's why we've come to warn you.'

'What warning?'

I take my briefcase from below my elbow, reaching inside for a primed M84 flash-bang which I hurl to the deck, covering my ears and closing my eyes simultaneously as does Mary who anticipates the action.

BAAAANNNGGGGG!

The flash-bang's detonation is massive. I can see the burst of light through my raised hands and closed eyelids while my ears ring to the blast of 170 decibels whacking through the confined atmosphere. Thankfully

Mary and I are both wearing ear plugs.

Forewarned we may be, but only by seconds. The scene moves in slo-mo as we consolidate our surprise attack. Mary's gun is out and aimed at the most dangerous gunman. She knows him from her previous visit and when the poor guy returns to consciousness after the explosive shock, she's right there, whacking his head with the butt of her gun while she removes his weapon. As he tumbles to the deck, she swivels to face the other guards. 'You're dead if you try!' she snarls in Spanish.

God, am I proud of this woman! I level my Glock on the Captain and his three shipmates. As I do so, I can see on the monitor screen that Annie has just thrown her flash-bang at the deck guards on the helipad. It's an encore performance for Annie. Helms is winding down the helicopter while Chad applies codes to lock all doors leading to crew and guard quarters. Thank God we did our homework otherwise the crew's retaliation would turn us into kebabs across the decks.

Mary is swift with plastic wrist ties. One guard tries to pull his weapon, so I place a shot in the bulkhead beside him. It strikes with a spark and rico-chets into his shoulder. Down he goes to be tied up by Mary. Meanwhile the Captain and his officers are watching in suspended horror, all stupefied by the first explosion. One young officer dives towards Mary who places a kick in his groin that would drop a fighting bull. He goes down howling.

'You'll never get away with this,' I hear the Captain saying, just before I treat his stomach to the butt of my gun.

'We're officers of the law,' I say, striking him again. 'Our job is to uphold the law.'

It takes us a minute to secure the bridge. It's a long minute I'll confess, but defeating our adversaries is essential. Another guard is about to resist when Mary treats him to her aerosol anaesthetic. The guy doesn't have a chance.

Our next task is to secure the hatches to all decks and gangways. Again our research pays off. On the main control panel I find the relevant controls for these crucial items and soon we have sealed the *Amazon Lady*, excluding the helipad and boarding platform where Ceejay is maintaining position in the police launch, under orders to repel anyone who dares to ignore his warning. The TV monitor on the helipad shows me that Annie is facing resistance up there. I see her firing two shots at a guard who collapses on the deck. Dead or wounded? I've neither time nor motivation to care. We did try to discourage resistance, didn't we?

The Caribbean sky has grown dark and along the coastline the lights of hotels and apartments blocks are glowing. Further down the coast brighter radiance lights the sky. That's where Sarahanna is doing her best to help us. She's keeping the local police happy with her eye-popping cleavage and snakelike legs in that scanty costume of glittering leopard lamé. The thought nearly stops me from recalling exactly why I'm here.

'Now where's Dr. Felix?' Mary leans over the Captain who is gurgling in shocked outrage. She screams in his ear. 'Tell me, how do I find Dr. Felix?!'

46

Miss Tanaka at the Concert

THE RAUCOUS THUNDER of Sarahanna's gig continued for over an hour. Miss Tanaka listened stoically to the change of rhythms while young Swann jigged mindlessly around in time to the music. It was totally surreal to Miss Tanaka, as though she was dreaming. No surveillance operation could be more bizarre.

While she watched the pirouetting teenager, Miss Tanaka occasionally glanced at the dog that lay resolute and unfriendly on the floor. It was Kludo who was in control and how would Bradley terminate her forced detention? Surely Miami HQ had received her text message and was aware of the situation? How long would the farce endure? But why was it necessary for Rackham to incarcerate her in the first case? There had to be answers to these questions.

But none came to mind.

Undoubtedly developments would occur, but in the interim Miss Tanaka was obliged to tolerate the ceaseless racket from the nearby stage with wild bursts of applause as each number finished. In a brief silence between songs a text pinged on Miss Tanaka's cellphone. Bradley wrote to say he was up for a threesome and would meet after the gig. *Position fixed* said the final sentence.

This was comforting. Bradley had been in touch with HQ so her confinement was unlikely to continue much longer. Miss Tanaka put a question to Swann. 'How does it feel to belong to a family of famous pirates?'

Swann stopped gyrating to stare at Miss Tanaka. 'I don't follow. Pirates? What do you mean?'

'Back in 1700, a pirate named Jack Rackham lived on Rum Cay, the very same cay where you've been staying. Your family is descended from him.'

'You're kidding me?' Swann frowned. 'That's three hundred years ago. Anyway, there must be many families called Rackham.'

'But your's is linked to *the* Rackham of Rum Cay. And I can prove it.'

'Oh yeah? And how's that?'

Miss Tanaka opened her bag and took out a screw-top bottle. 'Spit into that. From the DNA in your saliva, the laboratory will provide the proof.'

Swann hesitated. 'What laboratory?'

'Any DNA lab. They're everywhere. Just spit and when I get the results I'll email them to you.'

After a brief hesitation Swann unscrewed the bottle and spat into it. 'There you are, a sample of pure Rackham spit!'

Miss Tanaka smiled. Extracting DNA from her father and condemned ancestor had been far more challenging. 'Write your email on the label.'

The teenager took a pen and scribbled on the label.

'SwannR@rackunited.com.' Miss Tanaka read aloud and then put the sample in her bag. 'Might be fun, don't you think?'

'I can't see why. We all have DNA, don't we?'

'But not everybody has pirate DNA,' said Miss Tanaka.

Swann was not listening. Outside the Portakabin a massive applause preceded Sarahanna's delivery of her final number. Swann pulled up a chair and sat down beside Miss Tanaka. 'I gave you what you asked for, so now you can do something for me. I want to know if you believe in ghosts?'

'Ghosts?' Miss Tanaka frowned. 'What sort of ghosts?'

'I've seen ghosts here. And my father has seen them too.'

Miss Tanaka nodded. 'The faculty to experience apparitions may run in your DNA. Where did you see these ghosts?'

'One was near the old township and another was down at the marina. Both times it was the same ghost. A nice old black man.'

'The old township?'

'Yep. It's called Yankee Town where they used to farm sisal and cotton. There's an old steam engine there, and that's no ghost.'

'How fascinating. I'll look into that.' Miss Tanaka continued with the theme. 'And what sort of ghosts did your father see?'

Swann shook her head, suddenly more serious. 'His weren't so good. He saw them in my tablet so he said. But I don't think manufacturers ship ghosts with electronic products, or do they?'

Miss Tanaka laughed. Having finally found a level of intimacy with the youngest Rackham, she didn't want to lose the advantage. 'Ghosts don't live in tablets, so whatever your father saw must have originated in his mind.'

'Even his own execution?'

'His own execution? How was that?'

'He was hanged. They put him on a horse cart with a rope around his neck and it left him dangling. That sort.'

'How dreadful! How horrible for your father.' Miss Tanaka seized her own throat and began gagging. 'Get me a drink. I think I'm going to faint.'

Swann stood up. 'It was only a dream.'

'A coke or water, please.' Miss Tanaka continued to gasp.

Swann ran to the door and thumped her fist on it. Three sharp knocks. The letter S in morse code.

The door opened and Swann hopped out followed by the dog. Then the door closed shut behind them, leaving Miss Tanaka on her own. She went to the door and tried the handle. It was, as she expected, firmly locked.

The charade was over. While Sarahanna began her closing number, Miss Tanaka opened her cell phone to make direct contact with agent Bradley.

47

Mary gets her revenge on board *Amazon Lady*

SO FAR, LUCK'S been on our side.

The *Amazon Lady* rides at anchor on the Atlantic as we set about the plunder of her treasures. We have positioned Javel's fishing boat and the police launch on either side of the superyacht so that their crews can maintain watch on the portholes and hatches on each deck in case of counter-attack. Currently the yacht's crew remain in detention thanks to Chad's skill with their electronic locks. We can't be sure that no manual override exists, but we know that Dr. Felix, like most yacht owners, is suspicious of his crew and guards. Transporting valuable and desirable assets around the high seas creates temptation for all desperados which explains why access to the art gallery is via a single doorway inside the personal suites reserved for Dr. Felix.

The helicopter deck is near these suites so that his guests can come and go with minimal delay. But now the helicopter is in our domain and the TV monitor shows Helms in the pilot's seat, sipping cola, while Chad sits beside him ensuring control over the security and suppression systems. To which should be added control of the air conditioning.

Artworks of great value must be kept in regulated levels of humidity and temperature, especially when the overriding atmosphere is salty, warm tropical air. The AC ventilation system has backup pumps and units similar to those used in hospitals but most ventilation require air intakes and on the *Amazon Lady* these intakes are up near the radomes, those bulbous covers that protect the yacht's navigational equipment. Annie will soon empty a canister of CS tear gas into the intake of this ventilator system. It's like popping a milk bottle into the lips of a hungry infant. Then, after a while, we know what comes out of infants. Something very smelly and undesirable. Something in the human form of Dr. Felix.

Both JR and I have put on our gas masks when the yacht's owner finally staggers from his private door onto the bridge. I have my Beretta and taser ready, in case he comes out shooting, but Dr. Felix is no cinema hero. When the door to his quarters suddenly opens he emerges, holding his eyes and gasping, only to see his principal officers and guards are all subdued and held at gunpoint.

I cannot resist the opportunity to use my taser gun. Using its laser sight I aim the probes at the Felix groin and fire, allowing him to enjoy an intense whack of high voltage. It brings him down on the deck where he screams like a child having its teeth pulled. I step over him to padlock one of his wrists to the leg of a heavy table. Then I check him for hidden weapons before pulling the electrodes from his thigh.

I lean toward him. 'Dr. Felix. So good to see you again.'

He's a small man whose pallid skin is pock-marked from juvenile chicken pox. His teeth are especially foul and ill-cared for. Presumably, like many bullies, he's fearful of pain, even at dental level. With greying hair and spectacles, he may look professorial, but his eyes are weeping from the gas and his face is streaked with tears and fury. He splutters with three simple questions.

'We meet again? Who are you? How dare you come on my yacht like this?'

I won't provide answers until I complete a security check on his clothing, seeking the single item that will give us entry to the gallery on the third deck. I know where to find it having seen him use it on my previous visit. Around his scrawny neck is a gold chain on which hangs a thick gold crucifix. I know this is the key to his gallery. It emits a radio pulse to release the gallery locks, but we have explosives if we need to blow the door. Pulling the chain from his neck I pass the crucifix to JR who, to my complete surprise, pulls a chicken's leg from his shirt pocket, scraping the claw across the forehead of Dr. Felix.

'Who are you?' yells Dr. Felix as the blood flows.

I smile and reply. 'We met at Baranquilla last year. I've come aboard to repay your hospitality.'

He makes no sign, no reaction, no indication of recognition. He just stares at me with his ghastly mouth wide open. This reminds me that I have another gift for him, a small piece of durian fruit which I've been keeping in a sealed bottle. Durian has the foulest stench you can ever imagine and I have the greatest pleasure when I shove this morsel into his mouth, holding it there while he attempts to vomit.

We've been aboard for fifteen minutes and we must complete our business swiftly. Night has fallen outside and through the bridge windows the lights of Grace Bay hotels reflect upon the sea. The moon will rise before midnight and we must be gone by then.

Leaving JR and his men to guard the prisoners, I hurry to the private quarters where I spent so many hours previously. They remain unchanged from my last visit with gleaming surfaces, polished leather, fitted lamps and blatant opulence that create an atmosphere of sterile wealth. I pause outside the bedroom where I was repeatedly raped and branded while Dr. Felix roared with laughter at my suffering, but there's no point in reminiscing, so I run to the door leading to the helicopter deck. It's the one door which I know has a manual lock.

Throwing it open, I find Annie standing there, her Glock at the ready. Beyond, in the waiting helicopter Helms and Chad raise their thumbs to indicate all is well. Annie joins me and together we return to the hardened glass door leading to the gallery where JR is unloading tools and wrapping for the artworks. Standing by are two brothers to transport these to the helicopter.

Holding the gold crucifix I wave it over the door lock to the gallery and hear a satisfying click as the mechanism responds. With one push the door swings open. JR applies a lash to its fittings, holding it open as we hurry down the stairwell.

I see immediately that nothing has altered since my visit. Lit by ceiling LEDs, a sterile atmosphere permeates the gallery which contains several dozen oil and watercolour artworks in various dimensions. Annie knows where to concentrate our efforts. Starting with the Concert by Vermeer, I also see two Rembrandts, one Cezanne and a Caravaggio, all previously filched from their original owners and now decorating the panels of this uniquely private marine museum. We're aware of the many millions of dollars offered as reward for their safe return. These rewards may be paid by insurers or the original owners but of one thing we're sure. Dr. Felix

Roblado has no legal right to ownership of these masterpieces. We must relieve him of these items as swiftly as we can. Later we'll have time to admire the paintings.

We start by spraying any CCTV cameras that could be recording our actions, not that such actions will make much difference to the outcome. Then I photograph each wall of the gallery and each individual work of art. Click, click, click! I place sticky labels on those we must free first to complete our inventory, JR leaves us to maintain supervision of the prisoners, the yacht and the escort vessels. Using power tools we unscrew the perspex and protective glass frameworks on each painting. These fixings are less formidable than those used by public museums and they dismantle with relative ease. After carefully prising free each frame, we place it on a sheet of bubble foam spread on the floor. Each package, I reckon, might be worth at least several million dollars.

It takes an hour to complete this phase. The brothers transport each package to the helicopter placing them carefully on the rear seats after Chad has moved his operation elsewhere. He reports the suppression kit is functioning well, effectively squashing pleas for help that the entrapped guards and crew might be hoping to send to the outside world. Chad also reports the concert is winding down after overwhelming success. Annie asks him to text Swann telling her to leave as agreed. It means abandoning Miss Tanaka in the Portakabin using any excuse she can engineer to make her escape. As long as Swann is escorted by Able she'll be safe.

Finally the principal artworks are aboard the helicopter, Annie joins Helms as he winds up for take-off. Soon the roar of rotors deafens us as I head back to the gallery for a second sweep of the assets. Standing in soft downlights are a number of fine bronze sculptures, two Faberge eggs and a huge gemstone set in a collar of bright diamonds. They will all find a place in my holdall.

This is fun, the climax to months of planning and research, the greatest raid of our career, the GOAT deal as we know it, Greatest Of All Time. At any moment the situation might change, reversing our flow of premium luck. Let's face it, there'll be a rash of infuriated Columbians on this yacht when we finish, not to mention all the ballyhoo involving syndicates and previous owners of the sequestered pieces. In short, tonight's raid on the *Amazon Lady* will soon be global news and by this time tomorrow insurance agents will be in fevered excitement along with the museums and collectors who may entertain hopes of recovery.

It will take Helms thirty minutes to unload our first and most valuable consignment. Then he'll be back on the rear deck to load the remaining booty but before leaving I have some unfinished business. Our brothers must be relieved of their weapons to be left with Javel. Each man gets given a generous dollar bonus as they transfer to the fishing boat and we will leave the police launch moored alongside the *Amazon Lady*. At first light shore dwellers will see the launch and officers will ultimately be despatched to investigate. They can release the prisoners as they choose. My God, just imagine the comments when the duck tape comes off.

Before leaving, I make a final check of our prisoners on the bridge. They're a sorry bunch in their white uniforms with epaulettes of custard braid. They won't be collecting a bonus, while our brothers will hopefully be enjoying the fruits of their labours. Then I stride over to the dismal little creep who owns this yacht. I pull off my wig and fix it on Dr. Felix's scrawny skull. His face reflects grey while the horrible taste of durian fruit lingers inside his mouth.

'You asked who I am? So let me remind you.'

It takes me seconds to unhook my belt and drop my police uniform trousers. I pull down my white panties to reveal the naked flesh of my buttock where he can see the scarred brand on my skin.

'Yes. Dr. Felix. You did that to me and I will never forget it or forgive you.'

I see his eyes rolling in silent misery as I hear the approach of the returning helicopter.

'There will be no Hasta La Vista,' I assure them. 'You're lucky we decided to spare your lives. If you ever come after us, I promise you'll not be so fortunate next time.'

Five minutes later, JR, Chad, myself and Helms lift off the darkened deck of the *Amazon Lady*. None of our navigation lights are showing but below we can see the wake of our unlit fishing boat moving like a silver snake across the sea as it speeds, like us, away from the scene of our success.

Later Helms will fetch Swann and Kludo from the helipad near the concert ground before he dumps the chopper in the sea off West Caicos. As it spirals to the ocean floor, we will rescue him with a rib and outboard we left prepared near the airstrip. All of this must go to plan, so we hope.

JR reaches for my hand, holding it with a squeeze. 'That went okay, didn't it?'

'Awesome!' I reply. 'Just terrific!'

48

Miss Tanaka meets Sarahanna

WHEN SARAHANNA'S FINAL melody had drifted away into the tropical night, her audience reluctantly returned to the reality of life without their superstar and prepared to make their way home.

Behind the stage complex, Miss Tanaka was still waiting with frustration for her release. Using her replaced cellphone she had called Bradley twice but without response. Either she hadn't heard his reply in the drenching sound or he was beyond signal reach. She left messages asking him to contact her immediately however the silence persisted. She considered calling Miami HQ, but they might not appreciate her reporting lost contact with a fellow agent. It was too early for that, she decided, as she peered through the tiny sealed window, watching the audience disappear into the night.

Then Bradley materialised from the shadows. Suddenly he was in her field of view, and carrying bolt cutters. A minute later, the cabin door opened.

'They put a tough lock on that door,' he explained. 'I had cutters in my truck, but it was a mile away. Sorry for the delay.'

'But why was I locked in?' Miss Tanaka asked. 'The girl said she was going to find Sarahanna. So she locked me up instead.'

'She was never coming back,' said Bradley while inspecting the padlock he had just severed. 'They had to keep you away from their business.'

'They?' Miss Tanaka retrieved her bag and accompanied Bradley out through the show ground. Lighting engineers were shutting down their systems. Mounds of rubbish, cans and empty bottles littered the path back to his truck. 'The question is why did the Rackhams think it was necessary? It was just a reggae concert.'

'So it appears,' Bradley agreed. 'A mega concert by island standards and Sarahanna gave it her best. But did you actually see any of the Rackhams during the show?'

'How could I? The daughter chaperoned me throughout and the guard on the door stood firm, for my safety, so he told me.'

'Hard to believe,' said Bradley. 'Most islanders are peace lovin' enough. No way they'd be after you.'

Ten minutes later, they reached Bradley's pickup. He tossed the cutters and severed padlock into the back.

'Your place or mine?' he said, opening the passenger door.

Miss Tanaka looked at her watch. It was nearly eleven and the moon shed a silvered reflection over the sea. A wide arc of lights twinkled around Grace Bay as the audience returned home. 'I doubt we can achieve any more tonight, so drop me at Rum Cay and we'll talk tomorrow?'

'That so?' Bradley laughed. 'I was hopin' for a threesome.'

'Dream on, Agent Bradley.'

As she lowered the pickup window, Miss Tanaka heard the unmistakeable sound of a helicopter moving in the darkness. 'Stop! Do you hear that?'

Both agents listened, searching the night sky for any sign of the machine but they saw no red beacon lights usually displayed by aircraft at night. Gradually the thrumming beat of the rotors faded.

'It was a helicopter, I'm sure. We should make enquiries.' Miss Tanaka was convinced that various ploys had successfully distracted their investigations. 'Air Traffic might have something to say.'

Agent Bradley chuckled. 'Harumi, we're not in Miami, ya' know. ATC may be closed now, so leave that till tomorrow.'

Bradley dropped her at the main gate of Rum Cay where a driver ferried her to the hotel in a buggy. Miss Tanaka found her way to the bar hoping that the Rackhams and Sarahanna might be winding down after the show. Wasn't that standard practice for performers after a hard night roaring and grinding before their fans?

Miss Tanaka saw no sign of the Rackhams in the bar but there was no shortage of activity in one corner. The star herself was lounging in a jump suit of red silk, surrounded by animated members of her crew, all celebrating the success of the concert. Miss Tanaka did not delay She went straight over.

'Excuse me, folks. I was promised an interview with the great lady. I'm from *Giza* magazine, Tokyo.'

Her intrusion had been blunt and smiles turned to frowns. One man, a minder, got to his feet and spread his hands. 'Miss Sarahanna ain't doin' no interviews tonight. I's sorry but that's how it is.'

'I understand. Then how about tomorrow morning?'

'Miss Sarahanna don't do interviews in the morning. We's taking wings back to Bahamas for another show. That's all I know.'

Harumi Tanaka smiled. 'Tell her I only need five minutes and a few quotes. Japan is waking up to Sarahanna. They love her music so this is a big opportunity for her. I'll be at the bar.' She found a bar stool and smiled as Troy made her a nightcap.

'How was the concert, Miss?' the barman asked.

'Truly stunning. Sarahanna's fantastic. I was hoping to get an interview for my magazine.'

'And you're in luck, it seems,' said Troy. 'She's coming over.'

Miss Tanaka turned to see Sarahanna striding on high-heels towards her. The star reacted graciously as Miss Tanaka congratulated her. 'What a wonderful show. I loved every minute.'

'Honey, I loved it too, but I'm so sorry. I know Annie Rackham promised you an interview, but shows have a way of snowballing, know what I mean?'

'That will do for one quote,' Miss Tanaka pointed at Troy. 'You want a drink?'

'A punch, if I may. Easy on the rum.'

Sarahanna planted her shapely backside on the same bar stool where Rackham had smoked his cigar. Then she fixed eyes loaded with rainbows of wild make-up on Harumi Tanaka. 'You workin' late honey.'

'You know how it is for the wicked. No peace.'

Troy placed the drink before the star and grinned. 'On Mr. Rackham's bill. For you, ma'am.'

Sarahanna lifted the glass with a glance at Troy. 'Sometimes I get lucky, but Mr. Rackham, where is he now? He didn't even come to the show. Standard practice for the promoter to attend, but Mr. Rackham was long gone before I opened up.'

'A busy man.' Miss Tanaka tried to smile. 'I hope he paid you?'

'Oh, sure, honey. He did, so he did. I don't sing for free these days, but when I was young all I did was sing for free, so life has a way of balancing out, don't it just?'

Another quote. There was a lot more to Sarahanna than glamour, Miss Tanaka decided. 'So tell me, did you ever work for the. Rackhams before?'

The star's gaze wandered. 'No. Never even heard of them. But he did what he promised and that's all me and my manager Ron want. He called up out of the blue. Said he had a job for me and that a big fan of mine would be paying, so here I am.'

'A big fan? You must have scores of them?'

'He's from South America. I don't speak much Spanish but I think he's called Felix Robado, or summat similar.'

Miss Tanaka's smile remained constant as the information rolled in. 'And did you get to see this gentleman at the show?'

'He may have seen me, but I wouldn't know him if he was sitting on my knee. T'ing is that all fans they blur together when I'm on stage. I'd be terrified if I saw them individually.'

Yet another quote. 'Well thank you so much, Sarahanna. May I ask for a photo of us here at the bar, and then I will not trouble you anymore? You've been so very kind.'

Sarahanna lifted a scarlet fingernail and a minder loped over to use Miss Tanaka's iPhone. 'You're no trouble, ma sweety.'

The minder took three pictures and then passed the iPhone back to Miss Tanaka.

'See you in Japan one day?' said Sarahanna as she turned towards her party. 'Send us a copy of your story, won't you?'

'You bet,' replied Miss Tanaka. 'I'll be happy to do that.'

49

Bradley and Miss Tanaka get airborne

LYING SOUTH OF the Tropic of Cancer, daylight arrived at six in the morning as Bradley sat on the steps of his home watching his dogs devour their breakfast biscuits while he drank his coffee.

He had not slept much, possibly three hours at the most. He couldn't isolate any single reason because there were more than a few. Together they had kept his brain racing all night. For example, the show had been a musical extravaganza that would become legendary in local history. Sarahanna had blown so many fuses with the extraordinary power of her personality, her feline dance routines and her vocal energy. All of it would be unforgettable.

Then what about that incident, when he had dived into the Rackhams' pool to retrieve Agent Tanaka's cellphone? He had enjoyed being teased by the teenager but her blatant and suggestive comments to goad them towards of tripartite sex had been explicit. Erotic thoughts had kept his imagination on fire all night.

And as for Miss Tanaka… well? Bradley concluded she was a some-what mysterious individual. Rather chilly and analytical, but certainly a good officer. Hard working, resourceful and committed, she had all the attributes the FBI required. Bradley hoped he too was similarly qualified. As an offshore watchdog the job had its merits but maybe he was growing soft and less committed than at the outset?

Bradley knew that life was difficult for many islanders. It could be hard work in the service, hospitality and construction sectors. Often these were thankless jobs whereas for the tourists and the business community island life was generally more rewarding. In a world of differing values it was not surprising that some might succumb to corruption and dream up dubious projects. Bradley was supposed to monitor such activities, but this morning he wondered if it would forever be his destiny.

Bradley chucked aside the coffee dregs as one dog ambled over to offer friendship of the canine kind, where differences of colour, creed, wealth and human values never mattered.

'I'll tell you this, old son,' said Bradley as he stroked his dog. 'Yesterday I met a dog who really didn't like me. Not at all!'

Then his cellphone rang. Bradley flipped open his shirt pocket, and removed his phone. 'Bradley Pool Services.'

The call was from his handler in Miami. It was unusual to have contact with HQ so early in the day. He listened while the instructions flowed via WhatsApp from Florida.

'Okay, sir. I copy all that and will report.' Whilst those were the words he used, his mind was thinking holy shit! He returned the cellphone to his pocket and stood up to check the weather. Riding the trade wind as it blew from the north-east were numerous gulls and terns heading out to sea. He clipped his dogs to their chains, locked the house door and climbed into his pickup.

He had learned that Miami HQ had been alerted to the presence of a major international villain. The name Robado had been provided by Miss Tanaka after her interview with the singer Sarahanna. However Miami had no criminals named Robado on their data base, but there was a Felix Roblado and if this was the gentleman in question, then HQ wanted immediate confirmation. Roblado was a Columbian national who regularly sailed a large yacht in Caribbean waters. Bradley was ordered to charter a local aircraft and conduct an immediate survey of local waters.

Bradley knew that the US Coastguard maintained a Hercules surveillance aircraft on Grand Turk with a standby crew ready to address irregular activities such as smuggling, illegal migration and marine emergencies. Today his handler in Miami reported the Hercules was out of service due to a fault with its fuel system.

In any event, Bradley's first duty was to join forces with Miss Tanaka who had also been in touch with Miami. She was currently travelling by taxi to the Leeward Channel ferry station where the SUV rented by the Rackhams had been located via its transponder.

The ferry station was barely ten minutes from Bradley's home but there was no sign of Miss Tanaka or her taxi when he arrived. Here he called a local friend, a pilot who owned a four seater Cessna 172 and was easily persuaded to get airborne within the hour. When asked about reasons for the flight, Bradley explained his fellow passenger was a photographer who enjoyed sight seeing at that early hour of the day.

Meanwhile Bradley busied himself in preparation. He took the long range lens and camera from the steel locker on his pickup, loaded fresh memory cards and found relevant maps and binoculars. At the Ferry Station he bought a coffee from a bleary-eyed saleswoman who doubled as ticket agent. The woman told Bradley she'd been to Sarahanna's gig and was still thumpin' to the memory. 'Beyond doubt. Best ever.'

He was back in his pick-up when the taxi arrived with Miss Tanaka. In T-shirt, jeans and trainers, his fellow agent was looking remarkably fresh and focused this morning. Bradley wondered if she ever fell short of this standard? He rather doubted it.

What's new?' he asked.

But agent Tanaka was not listening. She was already striding towards the black SUV tucked among the vehicles that remained parked while their owners visited North Caicos. Bradley followed behind and watched as she made a quick inspection of the SUV, around and beneath it, before opening the passenger door.

'Why the caution?' he asked. 'This is just a rental car.'

'They may not be Chicago gangsters,' Miss Tanaka replied, 'but I like to be careful.'

They completed the interior search in minutes. Finding no clues they returned to the pickup and drove to the airport while Miss Tanaka updated Bradley about her interview with Sarahanna.

'That's when she mentioned this individual named Robado or Roblado. I gather he's a fan from South America who showed up for the gig. A long way to come for a song. Finding it suspicious, I mentioned it to Jenkins.'

'You were right. But a long way for the best concert ever.'

'Yes,' she replied. 'For a concert not attended by its promoters. I mentioned that anomaly when I called HQ.'

'HQ never called me so early and you certainly don't let the grass grow. I've found a local pilot to get us airborne.'

At the airport, Bradley's pilot friend was waiting with minimal security and paperwork. The trio walked to board the pale blue Cessna 172. Bradley took a rear seat advising Miss Tanaka to sit beside the pilot, a local islander, who sported curly grey hair and a matching moustache. He shut his door and handed out headsets. 'Welcome aboard folks. A lovely day to join the birds.'

'Let's start with a run along Grace Bay,' Bradley suggested. 'To take a look at any vessels standing off the reef.'

The pilot adjusted his headset, giving Bradley a knowing glance. He wouldn't be asking awkward questions. 'Okay Brad. Let's go.'

The Providenciales runway was built for long haul jets so the Cessna had a long run to the holding position. When cleared for take-off, the pilot applied full power and soon they were airborne, climbing up over the perimeter fence, across the narrow waist of the island towards the sweeping arc of Grace Bay.

Among the world's finest beaches, Bradley tried to imagine how Grace Bay would have looked before the coastal buildings had been added. Looking over the shoulders of the pilot and Miss Tanaka, Bradley then sighted the profile of a large yacht anchored off the reef. She was lying in lucid waters out beyond the rolling surf, a perfect anchorage for seafaring billionaires.

'Let's head for that,' Bradley said. 'An overhead pass and then maybe a full circle at low level.'

'Whatever you want.' The pilot adjusted course as Bradley prepared his camera. 'We'll go over at 500 feet.'

Soon Bradley was staring down directly on the upper decks of the superyacht. He tapped the camera trigger five times before the pilot banked to hold a slow turn around the yacht. He saw a name on its bows and while the camera recorded it he turned his attention to a smaller vessel lying alongside the larger vessel. He recognised it immediately as the local police launch but seeing no signs of human activity on either vessel he found that suspicious. At this hour of day, somebody should be visible.

Miss Tanaka made another comment. 'The yacht is flying an emergency flag. X in red means they need assistance.'

Bradley was impressed, having forgotten the codes for marine flags. 'Well, they seem to have already attracted police assistance.'

The pilot continued the turn as Bradley took more photos. After a full circuit, he climbed to 1000 feet heading along the coast towards the Leeward Channel. Here Bradley looked down on his own home, vacated only an hour previously. He wondered if his dogs were behaving themselves as they flew above, turning south west to follow the more barren coast overlooking the shallow waters of the Caicos Banks. Bradley remembered his brief discussion with the Haitian saleswoman at the Conch Bar. He had often found her a useful source of local gossip. Hadn't she mentioned that her son had been talking with a Jamaican about wrecks in the area? Bradley tapped the pilot's shoulder. 'Let's take a look at the old wreck down there. Close up if you can.'

Again the Cessna dipped its nose as the pilot aimed for the rusting hulk. The rocks that held it fast were visible in the clear water and nearby Bradley noted several smaller craft of local fishermen. He took more shots as they flew low above the surface as several fishermen raised their arms.

'They seemed surprised to see us,' Miss Tanaka remarked. 'And did you notice how some hid their faces?'

Bradley hadn't noticed, but his camera would have done so. 'So what does that tell you?'

'That they didn't want to be photographed.'

'Maybe after fishing all night they were tired,' the pilot added, pushing the throttle forward so the Cessna climbed again.

Minutes later the Cessna was overhead Southside Marina and here the three occupants in the Cessna could see the flashing blue lights of police cars. They were clustered around the empty berth where the police launch was regularly moored.

'Do we tell 'em where to find it?' the pilot asked.

Miss Tanaka turned to Bradley. 'Or should we leave that to our senior colleagues?'

Bradley understood her reasoning. They were still operating without the consent of the local government and their accumulating file on the case was not one they were authorised to share.

'I take your point,' Bradley replied. 'I'll ask base.'

Using his cellphone, Bradley called Miami to convey his concerns over the police launch and superyacht which was apparently requesting assistance.

In distant Florida at the FBI headquarters in Miramar, Bradley's contact listened to the report. Impressed by the speed of their response Bradley was told to wait while tactics were discussed internally. In the meantime, Bradley should send any images showing the name and flag of the vessel requesting assistance.

Bradley quickly chose the best images. On the yacht's bow was the name *Amazon Lady*. Another showed the V assistance required flag. He forwarded all these images to HQ via his cell phone.

While doing so, Bradley overheard Miss Tanaka questioning the pilot. 'Do you know of a place called Yankee Town?'

'You bet.' The pilot nodded. 'The old colony on West Caicos. They lived there in days when sisal was the only route to a meal.'

Miss Tanaka turned to Bradley. 'We should check Yankee Town while we're up here. Young Swann said she'd been there.'

Bradley was less convinced. 'Sorry, but I don't see the relevance. We need to resolve problems here on Provo before visiting old sisal farms. Besides, nobody currently lives there.' Miss Tanaka's suggestion did not seem logical.

'You say nobody lives there, but Swann met an old man there.'

'The girl's full of nonsense,' said Bradley. 'We both know that.'

The Cessna was humming along 1000 feet above the commercial docks. Down below he counted three container ships unloading goods from Florida. Then Bradley's cellphone beeped with a call from HQ. He clamped the phone to his ear and listened to Director Jenkins who had assumed command of the situation.

'We've determined the *Amazon Lady* belongs to a Dr. Felix Roblado from Columbia. The British have agreed to send a patrol ship to take a look since the yacht is in their territorial waters and they may deploy marines to go aboard. Columbians, as you'll appreciate, can be touchy about visitors. In short, it might be dangerous.'

'Understood,' said Bradley. 'So what should we do?'

'Standby for further instructions. Out.'

Bradley tapped Miss Tanaka on the shoulder. 'HQ says the yacht will be checked by the Royal Navy, so we're off that hook.'

'Then let's take a run over West Caicos? I've got a feeling about it. Why did Swann go there? Surely not to visit to Yankee Town?'

'You've got a feeling?' Bradley repeated with scepticism.

'I'm a specialist in DNA and psychological behaviour,' replied Miss Tanaka. 'Given all we've discovered so far, it's highly probable that Swann's family did not come here just to promote Sarahanna. They didn't even attend their own event. It's my guess they were out on the Atlantic paying an unscheduled visit to the *Amazon Lady*. We heard that chopper last night. With no navigation lights, so a stealth operation could have been in progress.'

Bradley looked at his watch. They had been airborne for forty minutes. He tapped the pilot's shoulder. 'Hey, you got enough fuel for a run to West Caicos and back?'

The pilot looked at his gauges. 'Yeah, man. No problem.'

50

FBI and the Royal Navy

At FBI HQ in Miramar the ongoing drama in the Caribbean was now under the supervision of senior FBI staff who recognised intuitively that the case was highly unusual.

The situation began at 7 a.m. with a call from the Department of State in Washington. They had been informed by the Columbian Head of Mission, also in Washington, that an unauthorised act of extreme violence had been reported. The private yacht owned by one of Columbia's foremost citizens had been raided by pirates masquerading as police and the yacht was riding at anchor off Providenciales. The Columbian Government would welcome any relevant information from the Department of State.

This interchange followed diplomatic tradition. State would contact their people in Florida who had contacts with many territories across the region. From their reports, the summarised feedback would flow to the Department of State who would then select what might be suitable for release to the Columbians.

The FBI officials knew instantly that the case merited investigation. Had they not pre-empted it? In fact more details were currently incoming from two agents touring the dawn skies in a light aircraft. These agents had inspected the *Amazon Lady* as she lay at anchor beside a police launch. The yacht's signal *Assistance Required* had evidently brought response from the local authorities.

American intelligence soon delivered more information. The so-called foremost citizen of Columbia was an odd way to describe an individual whose case file was consistently linked to trouble. According to intelligence, Dr. Felix Roblado had been heavily into mischief for a decade, though many of his alleged crimes had been dismissed due to lack of hard evidence. Briefly, Roblado was a very fat cat with a very thin dossier.

The *Amazon Lady* was by no means Roblado's major asset. He had plenty more to crow about including a substantial portfolio of real estate.

Rumours also persisted about priceless artworks on board his yacht. Specific items were not however identified, while other sources indicated his possible part in opaque deals with military and civilian associates from South and Central America whose identities also featured on their watch lists.

Of more pressing urgency was the position of a large yacht with a patrol launch so close to the reef. It was a poor choice of anchorage regardless of any other reasons. Both vessels were inside British Territorial waters and the US Coastguard reported that a Royal Navy warship was on patrol near Grand Turk.

A radio call was made to the warship's commander, Captain Barnet. He confirmed that, if officially ordered to proceed, his ship's airborne unit was standing by, ready to offer robust assistance with marines boarding both vessels if conditions allowed. To Captain Barnet it amounted to a standard SAR mission. In any event his warship would set course immediately for Grace Bay while his helicopter unit would fly on ahead.

Such resolute action had been the benchmark of the Royal Navy for centuries and the FBI directors in Miami knew they were in safe company. Now they would await further diplomatic input and reports. If the Colombians were seeking practical assistance from the Americans and the Brits they would get it. Later the details be investigated more closely.

As he glanced away from his colleagues to look out across the contrived landscape beyond the glass windows, Executive Assistant Director Jenkins was fretful. Something here worried him. At present he was acting liaison officer with his airborne agents but meanwhile something else snagged in his memory. He searched for a hint, just one link to this missing item. Then after a minute it came to him. He turned to his fellow officers.

'I've got it. Agent Tanaka, as you know, is one of our best DNA specialists. She also studies the psychological elements in generic patterns of human behaviour.' Director Jenkins noticed that his colleagues were paying close attention. 'I can reveal that Agent Tanaka has recently matched a DNA link between the famous pirate Jack Rackham of 1720 and today's John Rackham, his descendant three hundred years later.'

'That's a peachy analysis! So pirate DNA is now proven and we have a fascinating new entry in the criminal hall of fame.' The comment came from the senior Director who had approved Miss Tanaka's *Operation Gallows Ear*. 'If history is repeating itself out there in Grace Bay do we have proof of Rackham's involvement?'

Jenkins shook his head. 'Not as yet. Last night a reggae concert starring the singer Sarahanna was successfully promoted by John Rackham. However there's no proof he attended the concert and his whereabouts remain unknown. The Turks and Caicos police had prior knowledge of the concert because Rackham gave them special passes to the event. One of their officers even cautioned Rackham for allowing his dog to molest the pink flamingos in West Caicos.'

The senior Director blinked. 'Pink flamingos! How did we get from flamingos to a boarding party of Royal Marines? This could become farcical.'

'Captain Barnet's marines will soon have answers,' Jenkins continued. 'He has a motive because Barnet's personal history is also intriguing. According to Tanaka's report, it was a Captain Barnet who purchased the ear necklace Lot 322 at the New Jersey auction. Because he bought it online Miss Tanaka managed to obtain DNA from the necklace before it was despatched to the Captain's home in Plymouth. But hear this. It was a Captain Barnet in 1720 who captured Rackham and his two female accomplices. He then transported the entire crew to jail in Jamaica where both women were spared the gallows when they were found to be pregnant. Now, three hundred years later, Rackham has two women as company while he travels with skilled personnel in aviation and digital skullduggery.'

The senior Director listened in amazement. 'With all this conjecture we must avoid the inevitable media interest. They might say we've lost all credibility if we cite so much coincidence. After Captain Barnet reports, we should meet again before updating State in Washington.'

One hour later, Captain Barnet did report. His marines had successfully boarded both vessels to offer assistance. A four man team had abseiled down in uncontested descent and set about releasing crew and officers, many of whom were found taped and bound. The yacht's helicopter crew had been discovered at dawn similarly bound and gagged on Providenciales while other crew members had been trapped in their quarters by overrides to the digital locks on each deck. The ship's engine was operational but the boarding marines had found evidence of vandalism in a gallery on the third deck. Many vacant spaces on the walls showed the spectred outlines where previously artworks had existed.

The marines had also rendered first aid to Dr. Roblado, the yacht's owner, who had been vomiting copiously. This was not due to loss of property which he refused to identify, but thanks to a foul-smelling fruit taped inside his mouth. Dr. Felix believed he knew the identity of the marauders and insisted that he would negotiate with them directly for the return of his property.

How the Department of State and the Head of Mission for the Columbian Government would process all this news was not something the FBI directors in Miami bothered to consider. For them, the game had moved on. With two agents active in the field, what should they now investigate? The answer was logical.

'Let's see what Tanaka and Bradley say. Somebody's crawling around the Caribbean with someone else's property. Let's focus on that single fact.' The Director of Operations made his decision and Jenkins keyed his direct dial for Miss Tanaka.

'Hi. Miss Tanaka. We believe a sizeable haul of priceless artworks was removed by persons unknown from the *Amazon Lady* overnight. Details are not available but if there's anything to achieve by apprehending suspects, you are authorised to proceed.'

In the background Jenkins could hear the sound of an aircraft engine as Bradley and Miss Tanaka gave their response. Then he closed his cellphone to address his colleagues. 'They will extend their search and head for West Caicos.'

The Director raised his hands in exasperation. 'Whatever next? Are they hunting pink flamingos or pirates? Which is it?'

51

John Rackham – Time to Go!

THE SUN HAS been up for two hours and we've spent the hours loading the jet here on West Caicos. Each item that we liberated from Dr. Felix has now been carefully encased in waterproof bubble wrap before being placed in our baggage hold.

Now our jet is ready for start-up. Helms has prepared a flight plan that will take us towards the huge interior of South America. When our spoils are safely concealed we will then commence negotiations about the future of each item. In some cases insurers may offer seven figure rewards for their safe return. Others may prefer to bid for the art on a discreet auction site. In any event we'll be donating one item anonymously to a charity favoured by Sarahanna. She's a superb influencer and this gesture will undoubtedly cheer her fans.

To be frank, we expect to make at least $15-20 million from redistribution of the artworks. Maybe more. Spread the goods, I say. Let others see these previously lost, but recovered, masterpieces.

So much for the commercial component. Annie will act as key negotiator and many disposals will be processed on the dark web with input from our not-so-crazy Ukrainian. Chad has surprised us with his devious abilities in the digital world. Now he's standing in the jet's hatch holding a simple radio.

'They have reclaimed *Amazon Lady* and police launch! The raid is big news, very big news!'

Annie and Mary join Chad and listen to his radio. 'Then we must get airborne,' says Annie.

'Yeah. Soon as possible,' I reply. 'Is everything on board?'

You'll recall that a wide stretch of camouflage netting conceals the jet's fuselage. Helms knows how to hide a large lump of aluminium with wings and he's done a fine job. I can barely see the aircraft until I'm nose up against it. I'm ready to follow Annie and Mary up the steps into the cabin when I learn that Swann and the blessed dog are missing.

'Where the hell are they? Where are Swann and Kludo?'

Annie frowns. 'She was outside a moment ago.'

Stepping back into the open air, I see no sign of Swann nearby. I'm about to wolf whistle when I hear the sound of an approaching engine. The soft purr of a light aircraft engine is unmistakeable and I duck back into the jet's cabin.

'There's an incoming aircraft. It's unlikely to land but get ready to start up. I'll find Swann.'

Outside again, the sound of an aircraft is increasing and looking across the scrub cover, I see it flying at low altitude, several hundred feet above the airstrip, coming straight towards our hiding place here at the end. It's a pale blue Cessna, a high wing 4 seater. I duck back inside the cabin to watch the aircraft's approach as it flies over the blocks of concrete at the centre point. Helicopters may land easily but fixed wing machines will need a full runway.

'Did they see us?' Annie is at my shoulder while the Cessna skims above our canopy, climbing again to circle.

I shrug. 'Ready Helms?'

'Ready when you are, boss.' Helms shouts back. Chad in the No.2 seat is on his laptop to keep informed of fast changing events.

'That's a Cessna.' I shout. 'And it's going round for another look. They may have seen us so we need to go now!'

'So where the hell is Swann?' Mary's at the door now, all fired up and angsty. 'We can't leave her, for God's sake!'

'We may have to.' Annie's voice has a hard edge to it. 'JR get out there and find her! Helms must start up. When Swann hears the engines, she'll come running.'

'We'll lose everything if we stay but how can we go without her?' asks Mary.

I duck back outside, down the steps onto the rocky ground of West Caicos. They're both right. And we don't have much choice in the matter. One runway between us and freedom.

'Swann!' I yell. 'Get back here right now!'

I look between the bushes and below the jet's undercarriage. I can hear the whine of the starter and seconds later one engine ignites. The same procedure will shortly light up its twin. Helms is a master at short take-offs but he's been flying most of the night, running the air bridge to *Amazon Lady's* floating treasures. If we stay here we'll lose all Helms has worked for.

Then it occurs to me the Cessna might be carrying Columbian amigos of Dr. Felix. He may have his own network in play, seeking us to deliver merciless vengeance! Either way the choice is stark. We must leave immediately. Looking up I see the Cessna lift a wing as it turns again towards the runway. They're coming round for another look. No doubt about it.

I retreat for cover under the camouflage. The wide sweep of the flecked netting spreads and lifts as the airflow gallops to the engines and their exhaust. Helms has assured me he can drive straight from this so-called hanger. He has camouflaged aircraft in Iraq and Afghanistan over the years but one snag, he admits, is to avoid sucking netting into the engines. That's another great thought to add to my problems.

The Cessna flies directly overhead on its second pass maintaining a low circuit altitude. On the first pass they will have seen the dragons' teeth. On the second pass maybe they were confirming any suspicions and doubtless photographing our base here in the scrub at the end of the runway. No. 2 engine is now lit and the shrilling roar of both jets grows by the second.

Then a black shadow races from the scrub. The dog. The dog!

Kludo runs to me. Then Swann appears, following behind.

'On board now!' I yell above the din of the jets.

Kludo flies up the steps and I push Swann's backside into the cabin. I follow and pull the stepladder, clamping home the hatch door as the jet lurches forward, riding over scrub to the tarmac.

The girls are in their seats and Kludo jumps up beside Swann. Annie and Mary are ready but this isn't over yet. I squat behind Helms in the cockpit as the hard tarmac comes to meet our nose wheel. The thud is repeated as each wheel hits the tarmac then Helms accelerates to the threshold. Looking to my left through the windshield, I see the Cessna turning again.

Helms has also been watching. 'He knows we're here and may keep circling till back-up arrives. Chad reports that a naval chopper has dropped marines on the *Amazon Lady.* They'll find landing on West Caicos a much easier and more compelling option.'

'Then we go immediately,' I decide.

'Royal Marines or Columbians, they'll all be after us,' says Helms. 'I'll hit full power then go low level to the south.'

There's much to be said about men who know war. Some are shattered by the experience. Others come out like tempered steel, strong and indestructible, just as our man Helms.

Helms pumps the jets to full power. The Embraer lunges forward with engines howling in a massive surge which almost knocks me off my feet. I grip their seat backs as Helms goes for take-off. Behind my shoulder in the cabin, I see that my three girls and the dog all strapped in, anxious and watchful as our speed builds rapidly. Ahead through the windscreen, I see the dragon's teeth racing towards us, rearing up like rocks in surf along a reef.

Helms is going for broke. 'I can't remember. Which is the solid one?' he shouts.

'Hell, I don't know.'

'Neither do I.' Then, holding the course straight down the centreline he heads towards the largest of the dragon teeth, Helms flicks back his head and smiles. 'Only jokin' mate.'

52

Duel on the runway

IN THE CONFINED cabin of the Cessna, Miss Tanaka had seen all she needed. Clearly some activity, probably criminal in nature, was in progress and, as FBI officers, they were obliged to investigate.

'Can you land this Cessna on half a runway?' Miss Tanaka asked the pilot via her headset.

'You have seen those blocks across the centre line. Which half do you prefer? The pilot asked. 'This side or the other? We might land in one piece, but getting airborne could be a different matter.'

Miss Tanaka looked over her shoulder. Bradley was busy with his camera, checking the recorded images from the first run along the runway. The concrete teeth across the runway appeared aggressive and defiant. Then after completing the low level run Agent Tanaka had seen a dog running in the scrub. It looked up as they flew over. She had of course recognised Kludo.

'Swann's down there.' Miss Tanaka shouted. 'I've just seen her dog. We should land to check the situation.'

Was this a suggestion or an order? Bradley was not immediately inspired by the proposal. Confronting armed and cornered pirates had not been on his menu that day when he left home, Now he very much wanted to return in one piece. 'Landing here is next to impossible. The runway's too short.'

'Our pilot believes he can land.' Miss Tanaka radiated determination. 'We're going round again for a closer look.'

'Did you see that camouflage netting at the end?' Bradley asked, reversing his camera so Miss Tanaka could see the image clearly displaying the profile of an aircraft, partially hidden below the speckled web of overhead netting. 'You see that? Somebody with that kind of toy will not be inviting playmates. Do you have any weapons to hand?'

'No such luck. How about you?'

Bradley shook his head. Carrying weapons was a serious offence in the Turks & Caicos. His Smith & Wesson at home was suitably hidden, but here on unofficial duties, the only weapon he carried was the camera. 'Better to patrol overhead until reinforcements arrive, that's my advice.'

Miss Tanaka took his point, but surely the immediate task was to prevent any aircraft removing art treasures that might disappear forever. 'We must land and negotiate. They won't stand a chance when the marines arrive, so maybe we can save everyone a heap of trouble?'

Her suggestion made sense. Bradley said. 'I'll tell Miami we're having a second look before deciding.'

So the Cessna was going around again for a second fly past. The pilot kept the runway on his left side to provide an unrestricted view of his landing options. Both halves of the runway appeared to be just within limits for an ultra short landing, but only just. On this pass signs of dog or humans were not evident, but at the far end they noted that the camou-flaged netting was moving.

Looking down onto the undulating material, Bradley saw the netting lift and rise like piled leaves moving in the wind. Now he saw human activity at the nose of an aircraft. Before he could bring his camera to bear, the view was broken when the Cessna turned downwind to fly the full length of the airfield. Like Miss Tanaka, Bradley felt certain that villainy was in play. FBI officers had a duty to investigate and arrest if possible.

While the Cessna flew the crosswind leg. Bradley keyed his cell phone, which remained in range of the radio masts on distant Providenciales.

'We are 95% certain there's an unidentified jet on the strip at West Caicos currently acting suspiciously.' Bradley spelt out the game plan. 'We intend to land and check on it.'

At Miami HQ, the FBI officers gave their approval. 'A good opportu-nity,' Jenkins told Bradley. 'Be advised that a Royal Navy chopper with marines is scheduled to arrive in fifteen minutes.'

'I copy that, but now I see an aircraft on the runway threshold and I confirm it's the jet used by the Rackhams. We're turning onto finals. Out.'

Bradley and Miss Tanaka could see the sleek Brazilian jet moving to the far end of the same runway they were now approaching. In their Cessna the pilot set 40 degrees of flap and clapped his hand to the throttle as he set up a short landing on the first half of the runway. The nose of the aircraft dipped aggressively pointing almost straight at the ground. She could see the concrete dragon teeth on the runway as she grabbed the facia panel seconds before the Cessna flared and hit the tarmac, rolling fast towards the toothy barrier on the strip. The pilot killed the engine and applied full brakes, hauling back the stick simultaneously.

Bradley and Tanaka knew they were down, but not safely. The jet was in full take-off mode, accelerating down the runway directly towards them. They could see the haze of exhaust rising behind the speeding silver fuse-lage as it stormed along the runway on the far side of the concrete pyramids.

'Jesus!' yelled the pilot. 'They'll never make it.'

'There'll be a crash!' Miss Tanaka heard herself shouting.

The Cessna was still rolling, reducing speed from 65 knots to 15 knots in ten seconds. Meanwhile the profile of the oncoming jet was enlarging every moment. The potential for an imminent fireball occurred to Bradley as a high speed collision with the dragon's teeth was the inevitable future for the accelerating jet.

The Cessna's pilot took avoiding action. He swung his aircraft off the tarmac into the low-lying scrub, coming to an abrupt halt when the propellor punched into a bush. Recoiling from the shock Miss Tanaka's hands flew to her mouth as the jet thundered through the dragon's teeth. Straight through, and shattering the blocks into fragments of crazy whirling cardboard in its slipstream.

A single block remained intact on the side of the runway. Leaning his back against the concrete block Miss Tanaka could see an old black man. A shudder ran down Miss Tanaka's spine. Swann had mentioned the old man. So he had been there all the time. How very, very odd.

Miss Tanaka unclipped her harness and pushed open the passenger door. Bradley jumped down behind her. Together they stood breathless as the Rackham jet reached the end of the runway where it rotated on blazing exhausts to climb up into the morning sky.

She took out her cell phone. 'Mr. Jenkins, sir. This is Agent Tanaka with an update.' She watched as the dust settled around the shattered dragon's teeth. The jet's pilot had been supremely skilful in avoiding the concrete tooth. But where was the old black man with silvered hair? Only then did she realise he had vanished. She felt a second frisson ripple down her back as she studied the slew of minced cardboard. No sign of the old man anywhere!

'Are you there, Agent Tanaka? What's your update?'

Miss Tanaka drew breath. 'The Rackhams have departed by jet to the south east, most probably taking whatever they lifted from the *Amazon Lady*. You may advise the Royal Navy that their marines will not be needed.'

THE END

ABOUT THE AUTHOR

Today's world of AI, international squabbling and jobs of sorry boredom have inspired the author to inject some fun into the pages of this novel.

George Almond, a serial adventurer, was first drawn to this story by a long-haired Polynesian girl who was terrified by ghosts. Later when visiting the Turks and Caicos he came across a Canadian accountant who also experienced spooky moments on the very same island where the pirate Calico Jack Rackham made his base in 1700.

Almond is busy on further writing projects, having published *Even Higher Than Everest* on Amazon some years ago. That book, he says, holds a special place on his hard-drive's heart, because it too is based on historic truths. Now he is compiling a book on all his many adventures *Take The Top Card.*

Read on, my friends. Just enjoy life while we can!

Sept 2025

ALSO BY GEORGE ALMOND

Even Higher Than Everest
978-1-78222-946-9

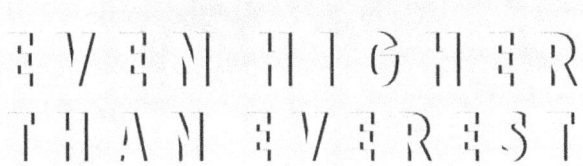

www.ingramcontent.com/pod-product-compliance
Lightning Source LLC
Chambersburg PA
CBHW070111030726
47506CB00002B/692